D0858575

ADVANCE PRAISE FOR
THE LAST CONQUISTADOR

"*The Last Conquistador* is a rare thing: a gripping thriller married to a mystery that has perplexed archaeologists for centuries—the existence of an Inca city that disappeared some 400 years ago. Elias has written a fast moving novel about a modern day Peru that can't escape its past."

—David Freeman, author of *A Hollywood Education* and *It's All True*

"To the great 'Lost World' tradition of history-fantasy literature created by H. Rider Haggard, continuing through Edgar Rice Burroughs and Jules Verne, and flourishing with Michael Crichton and James Preston, comes Michael Elias's rollickingly entertaining *The Last Conquistador*. To his gritty portrayal of contemporary Peru, brilliantly researched recreations of Incan Peru in its royal heyday, with all its ancient pomp and human sacrifice, plus a hot-blooded romance between a Hispanic FBI agent and his long-lost archaeologist lover, Elias brings a veteran screenwriter's gift for cinematic immediacy to this stunningly imaginative high adventure. The confidence behind its riveting blend of fast-paced modern thriller and time-traveling Lost City setting updates the genre and leaves us panting for a sequel."

—Peter Nabokov, author of *Where the Lightning Strikes: The Lives of American Indian Sacred Places*

WITHDRAWN FROM THE RODMAN PUBLIC LIBRARY

WITHDRAWN
FROM THE RODMAN PUBLIC LIBRARY

THE LAST CONQUISTADOR

THE LAST CONQUISTADOR

MICHAEL ELIAS

OPEN ROAD

INTEGRATED MEDIA

NEW YORK

RODMAN PUBLIC LIBRARY

38212006055427
Main Adult Fiction
Elias M
Elias, Michael
The last conquistador

All rights reserved, including without limitation the right to reproduce this book or any portion thereof in any form or by any means, whether electronic or mechanical, now known or hereinafter invented, without the express written permission of the publisher.

This is a work of fiction. Names, characters, places, events, and incidents either are the product of the author's imagination or are used fictitiously. Any resemblance to actual persons, living or dead, businesses, companies, events, or locales is entirely coincidental.

Copyright © 2013 by Michael Elias

Cover design by Mauricio Díaz

ISBN 978-1-4804-0003-0

Published in 2013 by Open Road Integrated Media
345 Hudson Street
New York, NY 10014
www.openroadmedia.com

RODMAN PUBLIC LIBRARY

For Bo Rogers

THE LAST
CONQUISTADOR

"*I did not come to change their religion. I came to take their gold.*"

—FRANCISCO PIZARRO,
Conqueror of the Inca (ca. 1476–1541)

"*I know that some day, by force or deceit, they will make you worship what they worship. When that time comes, when you can no longer resist, do it in front of them, but on the other hand do not forget our ceremonies. And if they tell you to break your silences, and force you to do so, reveal only what you have to and keep the rest hidden, close to your hearts.*"

—MANCO INCA,
Emperor of the Inca (1516–1544)

CHAPTER 1

NEVADO SALCANTAY, PERU

Nina Ramirez sat up. Blinding yellow light streamed through the thin fabric of her tent. The sleeping bag was twisted under her back, and her rib cage ached. Even after ten years of sleeping in it, she still hadn't found a way to get through a night comfortably. She pulled the iPod plugs out of her ears and listened to the world outside. It was quiet. No wind, thunder, or pellets of hail pinging off the roof of her tent. The weather had finally broken. For the last three days and nights, she and her graduate students from the Cuzco University Department of Archaeology had huddled in their tents on a plateau of Nevado Salcantay, the highest mountain in the Cordilla Vilcambamba. Gale force winds whipped blinding snow gusts across their camp; it was brutally cold and the air at twelve thousand feet was painfully thin. Digging was impossible under these conditions and wandering outside dangerous. Nina stepped out of her tent and greeted the Indian porters wrapped in their thick alpaca wool ponchos. They were already busy lighting fires and heating water for tea. The tethered llamas could also sense the change in temperature. They rose jerkily to their feet, shook out their coats, and began sniffing the ground, hoping for the odd weed that might grow at this altitude. *We're all together. Animals and humans looking for treasure buried beneath the snow.*

Nina squinted at the jagged snowcapped mountains surrounding the plateau. Behind the mountains, to the northeast, thin funnels of black smoke from the Amazon fires cut lines in the ice blue sky. The feeling came over her again that they were not the only ones on this peak. She scanned the site. Her team and the equipment were all in place; the footprints were theirs. The crumbled stones of the ancient buildings strewn over the area were the only reminders of any previous human activity. Perhaps the spirits of the five-hundred-year-old Inca mummies they were trying to unearth were whispering to her, angry at being disturbed. Nina shook off the irrational. She didn't believe in spirits; she was a scientist.

Nina took a whistle out of her pocket and blew a sharp blast. One by one, the students emerged from their tents and gathered in front of her. They had survived the worst of the mountain, and she was proud of them. She had confined her selections to her graduate students. After a seminar, she simply asked if anyone would like to volunteer for an archaeological dig that would involve a strenuous trek and freezing temperatures. The location itself would be revealed only when they were on their way. They would have to surrender their cell phones, as no contact with the outside world would be allowed once they were at the site. The four men and two women all accepted immediately. Since Edgar was also a film student, he would be the team videographer. Luis and Teresa were expert campers and worked part-time as tour guides for North American trekking companies. Cecilia and Roberto had been on expeditions with Nina before, and both were meticulous in their excavation techniques. And Julio, the youngest and brightest, was her favorite—probably because his dark Indian features reminded Nina of her father.

They had left Cuzco a week ago in a battered Cuzco University bus followed by an equally battered Mitsubishi FM557 flatbed with wood slats.

From Cuzco they drove north to Ollantaytomba, a small village famous for its ruins of an Inca fortress. There, the group hired local Indians as porters and drivers. Six llamas were led onto the truck. They would carry the equipment to the digging site: tents, food, stoves, digging tools, brushes, canvas bags, empty wood boxes, tarps, and plastic bubble wrap. The students were excited to be on a real expedition, out of the classrooms and museum basements where they spent long hours cataloging sherds of pottery, skeletal remnants, beads, and minutia of other archaeologists. The speed with which the expedition had been mounted alerted them that this was important.

The first night, the group made camp in a gentle meadow under the shadow of the mountain. The llamas grazed peacefully, and the porters busied themselves setting out the evening meal. Nina assembled her students.

"Because of global warming—put your hand down, Edgar, I know I'm supposed to say climate change—the ice packs at high altitudes are melting. All you have to do is look at the top of the mountain in front of you—where there used to be ice and snow there are now exposed rocks. This is bad for the planet and good for archaeologists. We are discovering more and more and more Inca sites. But there aren't enough of us available to excavate and preserve them. We're not doing a good job of protecting them from looters."

Nina knew that the looters were often the discoverers themselves. Peasant farmers clearing land in the jungle or a rancher searching for a lost calf might stumble across an Inca burial site. Underneath those crumbled stones, in sealed tombs, lay skeletons adorned with gold artifacts, buried with valuable pottery, or wearing miraculously preserved woven fabrics. These treasures presented an irresistible temptation to someone who could feed his family for a year for what a trader of Inca relics would pay. The majority of looters were professionals who followed archaeologists to sites and robbed the tombs at night. Or, worse, they returned with bulldozers and dynamite to uncover, and destroy in the process, the remaining artifacts. There was no shortage of traders willing to buy the country's cultural heritage and sell it to collectors and acquisitive museum curators.

"This time it's different," she said. "A few weeks ago, a technician on the Royal Dutch Shell trawler SS *Groote Beer*, anchored off the coast of Ecuador, was examining images sent from a satellite searching for oil deposits in the Peruvian Andes. This satellite took infrared pictures to determine earth temperatures as an indication of underground oil deposits. There was something strange about the configuration of boulders scattered near the summit of a mountain that attracted his attention. He enlarged the image. It wasn't just the size of the boulders but the regularity of their shapes. The technician was curious, so he sent a digital image of the boulders to an anthropologist friend at Leyden University in Holland. The anthropologist recognized the objects as . . ."

"Inca building blocks!"

"Thank you, Teresa. So the Leyden guy e-mailed the pictures to a colleague—Tomas Voigt in the University of Bonn's South American archaeology department—who had a big unreturned crush on me back when you were all babies . . ."

"It's called he was into you."

"Shut up, Edgar. Anyway, Voigt sent them to me and what did I see? Julio?"

"The ruins of an Inca site, which at twelve thousand feet might be a platform and temple for human sacrifice. Awesome."

"Why is that?"

"Because the Incas preferred to sacrifice on the mountaintops. No one knows why for sure."

"Not true," said Teresa. "There is the theory that they killed their victims at the highest possible altitudes to shorten their journey to the gods. And the Incas considered mountains holy places."

"But still," said Cecilia, "the physical effort needed to get to that height, hauling the huge stones, and then constructing the temple, living quarters, and sacrificial platform, it had to be an almost inhuman task."

"And it wasn't easy for us, either."

Nina interrupted. "Okay, okay. I persuaded the Army commander in Cuzco to send a squad of soldiers by helicopter to secure the sight until an archaeological expedition could be mounted. That's us. In any event, we can say this time the Internet beat tomb looters to the site. Everybody ready?"

Edgar raised his digging trowel and said, "We who are about to become famous salute you!"

Nina smiled. "Then get to work."

Within an hour, the teams had taped off a half dozen promising sites. Digging began. The Indian porters worked alongside the students, carefully scraping away thin layers of frozen topsoil, then probed the ground beneath with long needles. Nina walked from group to group, offering suggestions on digging techniques, making sure no one rushed. The work had to be meticulous and slow. Delicate treasure lay underneath the soil and it must be removed with the touch of a surgeon.

The morning passed. The high altitude was debilitating. Nina made sure the students took frequent breaks. They drank mugs of bitter cocoa-leaf tea from thermoses. There was a short lunch break of peanut butter sandwiches and potato salad, latrine visits, and back to digging. Nina wandered over to the jangle of rocks and boulders that must have been the sacrificial platform. She traced the faint outlines of a foundation that could have been a temple. She knew there were architectural mysteries to be solved in future expeditions, but her main concern was what might be under the ground. She prodded, poked, photographed, and made notes of her observations in her moleskin diary. There was something she didn't notice at first. She moved closer to the remains of the temple and saw a thick piece of wood sticking out between two large stones. It was a support beam for the structure that had been crushed by the weight of the stone. She took off her glove and ran her hand over the wood. It was freshly hewn. She wondered how it got in there. As she examined it more closely, she heard Julio's yell.

"Dr. Ramirez! We found one!"

Julio and his partner, Teresa, stood up in a shallow pit, waving their arms.

Nina pocketed her book and ran, her camera bouncing on her chest. She reached the dig site where Julio and Teresa waited. Stepping to the edge of the pit, she could see the outlines of a mound, the size of a burlap sack. It was underneath a layer of dirt, but she knew what it was—the mummified corpse of a sacrificed Inca child.

Everyone crowded around the pit. Nina told herself to stay calm, even as she knew they were on the verge of an amazing discovery. She just needed to get people to do the tasks they had rehearsed.

"Roberto, lay out the tarp and get a freezer chest."

She turned to the porters. "Can we get some hot water, please? We'll need it to melt the ice around it. Who's recording this?"

Edgar held up his video camera. "I'm on it."

While they waited, Nina asked Julio, "Can you tell me why you decided to dig here?"

"Like I said, the Incas sacrificed at the highest possible altitude so that the journey to the gods would be quick. I think this is the highest spot on the ridge. He pointed to the rocks. "And closest to the ruins of the sacrificial platform."

"Anything else?"

Julio hesitated, unsure, then said, "What the hell. I felt it."

Something's talking to him, too. "Very good. The digging force is strong in you, young Skywalker."

"Teresa confirmed it," Julio added, indicating his partner.

"Well, you two found it, now go ahead and bring it up."

Julio and Teresa returned to the pit. Edgar squeezed past Nina and began videotaping. His camera light illuminated the two students as they brushed away the dirt covering the half-buried mound at the bottom of the pit. Julio and Teresa worked meticulously to free the mummy from its frozen coffin. Gradually, as they scraped handfuls of dirt away from the mound, the earth began to yield other spoils: small clay pots that once held grains, a silver water jug, glass beads that rolled free from their decomposed string, seashells, and little gold figurines of llamas, snakes, and turtles that would accompany the victim of the sacrifice on its journey to the gods.

They passed each artifact to Cecilia, who placed them on a wooden tray. And from there, Nina imagined, they would eventually make their way to a final resting place—on a bed of green velvet under bulletproof glass in the National Museum. Once again, as her father liked to say about archaeologists, they were disturbing the universe and undoing the past.

Nina remembered the first time she had dug her trowel into a mound of dirt and heard the dull clang of metal hitting metal.

She scooped the dirt away with her fingers, gradually revealing a perfectly preserved gold Inca mask of Inti, the sun god. She pried away the pebbles embedded in its casing, then brushed away the dirt, never looking up, never making a sound, holding her breath as the image of the god began to emerge into a golden clarity.

"Why so glum, Nina?" he said. "You've just made a fantastic find."

"I'm sorry, Professor. I'm so excited I'm at a loss for words."

But a feeling of guilt, an uneasiness came over her. She was undoing the past.

The mound was still embedded in the frozen dirt.

"Just rock it back and forth gently—like a loose tooth." Nina looked over her shoulder. "Where's the hot water?"

"Coming now."

"Good. Now go easy. We don't want the shroud damaged."

One of the porters arrived with a plastic bucket of steaming water. He handed it to Nina.

She lowered the bucket to Julio, who spilled out a steady stream around the edges of the mound, melting the ice that glued it to the floor. As he poured the water, Teresa continued to tease the bundle back and forth. She stopped and looked up at Nina.

"It's coming free."

"Go on," said Nina, "get it out."

Teresa hesitated.

"It won't bite. It's dead."

Julio and Teresa put their hands around the mummy and lifted it to Nina.

It felt light in her arms, the dead body. A child with no weight, drained of fluids, muscles shriveled. *I'm thinking about what it could be even before I open it.* She could be carrying a bag of dust and bones. *Slow down.* She lowered the bundle onto the blue tarp. A freezer chest and an open medical kit were on the edge. Nina put on a gauze mask and latex gloves. "Edgar, are you recording this?" she asked.

He gave her a thumbs-up and moved closer.

Nina rubbed her hands over the bundle, quickly feeling for knots. She turned it on its side, selected a metal probe from the medical kit and untied each of the three fiber knots in the wrapping. Then she rolled the bundle back to its prone position. Cecilia stood by the medical kit and handed Nina a pair of large tweezers. She began to draw back the folds of the shroud. *Go slowly. Inch by inch. There. There. Oh, my God.* It was the five-hundred-year-old corpse of an Inca girl. She was curled in a fetal position, wrapped in a multicolored shawl. Her skeletal fingers clutched a gold llama figurine as if it were her favorite doll. The skin was taut over her bones, stretched and shiny, the color of mahogany. Her teeth and mouth were painted red.

"She's beautiful," Teresa said.

Beautiful? The Inca girl's skull had been bashed in and the black stains on the shawl were dried blood. She studied the girl's face and tried to find some emotion in it. There was none. She had been drugged before the sacrifice. Had it calmed her? *This is what a body looks like when the soul abandons it.*

"Julio, give me a hand, I want her in the freezer box right away."

She rewrapped the fragile body. Julio placed it in the freezer box and shut the cover. From one icy tomb to another. She turned back to the grave. Two of the porters were already shoveling the earth back into the hole. *We're like criminals, covering up the evidence of our theft.*

The students returned to their work.

The second discovery happened as Nina was checking her watch and about to announce that they would stop work for the day and resume in the morning, Cecilia's voice rang through the site. "Dr. Ramirez! Dr. Ramirez! We found another one!" Cecilia and Luis were jumping up and down, waving their arms like excited children.

"Everyone, we found another one!"

One mummy was extraordinary. Two at the same site was phenomenal, and it would confirm they had also discovered an Inca sacrificial site. There might be no end to the treasures that lay buried on this mountain peak. The mountain was revealing its secrets.

Students parted for her. Nina knelt at the edge of the shallow pit. The dirt here was thinner, and she could see portions of cloth showing.

"The topsoil was a different color," said Luis. "It was clear there was something buried underneath."

"And it was fairly easy to dig through the topsoil on this one, Professor," Cecilia added.

Nina nodded. "Cecilia, go down and see if we need some water to melt any ice away."

Then she lowered herself into the pit. "I need some light."

Edgar moved forward with his video camera and aimed its light at the mound.

"We don't need water. It's not even frozen," said Cecilia as she started to dig the dirt away from the sides of the mound with a small trowel.

"Use a brush, too," Nina said.

Cecilia alternated scooping and brushing as she moved the dirt away. In a few minutes, she had cleared enough to reveal another bundle.

"It's coming loose. Help me, Luis."

Luis climbed down into the pit. Together, they rocked it back and forth until it came free in their hands. They lifted the mummy and passed it up to Julio and Teresa.

"Careful. Same procedure. Put it on the tarp and get another ice chest. Edgar?"

Edgar recorded the proceedings on his video camera. Like the first, this mummy was wrapped in woven cloth and bound by fiber cords with knots. Gold figurines of animals were embedded in the cords. Nina felt the knots. They were moist and slippery. She didn't want to cut them. She reminded herself to be patient and work slowly. She needed to roll the knots in her fingers like dough, loosen them, then look for the ends of the cord and try to untie it. She felt the knot soften.

"Professor?"

"In a minute, Cecilia, I'm coming close on the first knot. There."

One more knot and she would be able to part the cloth. Her fingers were hurting. She closed her eyes and felt the knot. It was loose, as if someone didn't bother to tie it tightly and it opened easily.

"Edgar?"

"I'm here."

She pulled apart the mummy's wrap.

It was a boy this time, curled in the fetal position. A searing band of dried blood encircled his neck. There was a black gaping indention on his skull. A swab of red paint streaked across his mouth and teeth.

"Oh, Jesus!" shouted Edgar. "Somebody take the camera, I'm going to be sick."

"Professor?" Julio said. "Your hands. Look at your hands."

Nina looked down. Her fingers were covered in blood. The mummy was bleeding.

The boy was dead, but his death was so recent that his blood had not dried. Nina realized she was looking at a victim of the present, not the past. A few hours ago, she felt she was not alone, that someone was watching her. Now she wondered if it was someone who had witnessed this death. Or caused it.

CHAPTER 2

SALTILLO, COAHUILA, MEXICO

It was not the best neighborhood in town. Especially for a drunk American tourist staggering down the sidewalk, his arms around the waists of two overweight strippers. Breasts bursting out of tight dresses, tanned legs that were like arrows pointing up to delights unparalleled. They wore shoulder bags, too much makeup, and looked like the last memory of someone who was about to get rolled. If this tourist stood up straight, he would come in at six-two and 180 pounds. He wore a bent straw fedora, knock-off Ray-Bans, a cheap tropical shirt, Bermuda shorts, and a waist pouch with a Budweiser logo on it—an ugly American. The citizens of Saltillo forced off the sidewalk by this rudeness knew that no good would come from, or to, the man.

The tourist and his two female friends lurched into an alley. A few doors down, two uniformed soldiers leaned against a wall, a door between them. One nudged the other, taking note of the trio who weaved toward them.

The tourist winked at the soldiers, lowered his hand, and squeezed the tall woman's buttocks. She wiggled lasciviously and gave a yelp. One of the soldiers giggled, the other shook his head in disgust. The trio stopped in front of the soldiers.

The soldiers shifted slightly. The tourist embraced the shorter woman and gave her a sloppy kiss. He placed his hand on her dress and pushed it down so the soldiers could see her naked breasts.

Full breasts, pink nipples, and the distraction Adam Palma needed. A moment to reach into the woman's purse and take out the Colt Python .357 with a silencer.

It was easy. The soldiers reached for their guns, but it was too late. Adam fired two shots into their hearts with point-blank precision. They fell to the ground. The taller woman opened the door, the shorter one pulled up her dress, and together they dragged the soldiers into the building. Adam followed, picked up one of the dead soldiers, and slung him over his shoulder. He signaled to the women, and they climbed the stairs. The body was light, and he barely felt its weight. Dead weight. Adam counted two floors, then went down the corridor to the last door on the left.

He stood the dead soldier in front of the door and positioned his head to face the peephole. The women moved to the side of the soldier as he banged twice on the door.

"*¿Quién?*"

A grunt in no language was Adam's response.

There was a moment of silence, then the peephole opened and closed, locks turned to clicking sounds, and the door was opened. An armed man stood there, a pistol at his side. He started to raise his weapon, but Adam shoved the dead soldier forward. As the armed man staggered backward, Adam and the women burst inside. In one fluid motion, he shot the armed man and veered off down a hallway, the women behind him. The architecture of the apartment was in his memory as if he had lived there all his life. He knew there was another hallway, and as he entered he glimpsed an armed soldier rushing by. He ignored him and heard the thuds of the women's shots as he entered the short hallway. The tall woman nodded, and together they continued down the hallway to another door. Quietly, he felt the strength of it—flimsy, unlocked. He nodded to the women. They were ready. He took a breath, relaxed, and prepared to die as he leaned back and kicked the door open.

It was another lousy room with a television and couch for the guards and a chair and piss pot for the man with his hands tied behind his back, a strip of duct tape over his mouth, and a sleep mask taped over his eyes. His right hand was wrapped in a crude blood-soaked bandage where one of his fingers had been chopped off and mailed to his family.

The man raised his head jerkily. The soldier had his Beretta pressed against his temple. Adam understood the message, it was always the same: "Shoot me, I'll shoot the hostage."

He nodded and tossed his gun high in the air. The soldier let his eyes follow the arc of the gun. It was enough time for the tall woman standing behind Adam, her gun already raised, to shoot the soldier in the chest and blow him away from the man in the chair. Another soldier rushed in through the open door holding a gun. All weapons swept toward him. The soldier grasped the situation: He was alone and trapped. He lowered his gun and smiled.

Adam shot him in the forehead.

The women stepped forward. The short one tore the tape off the hostage's eyes and mouth. The other cut his ropes. He fell forward, weak from the loss of blood. Adam could see he was in shock and in no condition to manage the stairs. Adam pulled him to his feet. This one was heavy. He glanced at the women—he could read their expressions: *We need to get out of here now.* The women were strong and they hoisted the man on Adam's back. They made their way down the stairs, the short one holding her gun if anyone came up, the tall one behind Adam, ready if anyone came down.

Outside, a taxi was waiting, its doors open. Adam and the women maneuvered the man into the backseat.

The taxi sped down the alley. The man, dazed, mumbled to Adam, "Oh my God, thank you." Then he began to sob. One of the women leaned over and put her arms around him. Adam sank back into the seat, removed his hat and sunglasses. He rubbed his eyes.

He felt soul weary, tired beyond tired. The tall woman leaned over the front seat.

"Did you have to kill the last one?"

Adam touched his face. Something on his cheek. He pulled it off and looked at it. It was a piece of a dead soldier's flesh. *God have pity on both of us.*

"Stop the car."

The driver hesitated.

"Stop the fucking car."

The taxi pulled over. Adam stumbled out. The sun beat down, searing his eyes. Waves of nausea buffeted him. The ground shifted and swayed under his feet. Adam tore off his shirt and wiped his face. He clutched the roof of the taxi, gulping air—a drowning man hanging on for dear life.

"No more."

The bile in his throat tasted of blood and venom. Adam balled up his shirt and tossed it into the street. One of the women called from the taxi, "Adam?"

"No more."

CHAPTER 3

NEVADO SALCANTAY, PERU

Nina assembled the students and porters. "Our obligation now is to bring both corpses back to Cuzco, deliver the mummy to the university, and turn the other one over to the police."

"Party over?" quipped Edgar.

"It looks that way."

"Isn't it ironic, Professor," Cecilia said, "that we have two bodies of children—one is an important archaeological discovery, and the other is a murder. And they were killed the same way, five hundred years apart. What's the difference?"

Nina didn't want to discuss the morality of ancient sacrifice now, but Cecilia deserved an answer.

"Without excusing the practice, it was an integral part of an ancient society's religious beliefs."

"Cecilia, ritual sacrifice is common to lots of societies," added Luis.

"Goats and birds, asshole, not children."

"Really? What about Abraham and Issac, our ancient neighbors to the north, the Mayans, the Aztecs, the human bones under

Stonehenge, and of course Jesus who was sacrificed, albeit for our sins. Sacrificed."

Nina held up her hands for silence. "Not now."

She looked at Gonzalo, the head porter and said, "I want us off the mountain as soon as possible. Can we leave today?"

"I don't think that will be a problem, Professor. We have to fill in the digs and do some housekeeping, but we can get a good start. We'll have a full moon and we can travel at night, if necessary."

"One more thing about the second corpse," said Nina, "whatever it is, we have still made an important archaeological discovery, and you all should be proud. The second corpse seems to be an imitation of an Inca sacrifice, right down to the wrapping, trinkets, and the grisly manner of death, but it's a police matter, not an archaeological or even an anthropological one. It's simply child murder. Are we agreed?"

The students nodded.

"Good, now let's get off this mountain."

Nothing could be left behind. Every bit of garbage had to be hauled out, every hole filled in. Nina had no intention of leaving any clues for the tomb looters who would follow.

She packed the bodies of the children herself. They were wrapped separately in a plastic sheets, covered with ice, then another layer of plastic, then more ice. They were then wrapped in canvas and each one was strapped to the backs of two strong porters. On the descent, one porter walked backward facing the porter carrying the mummy, and another close behind, both ready to catch the man in the event he lost balance and slipped with his precious load. Nina went first, behind her the Indian porters, then the students struggling with the weight of their own equipment.

Behind a large rock, a boy watched them making their way down the mountain. His name was Quiso. He was no more than twelve years old, with brown skin and black eyes. He was so cold that his lips were almost blue. The woolen cap, poncho, and the soft leather boots he wore over his rough leggings were no match for the mountain temperature. From his hiding place, the long line of people looked like a thin black *gusano*, a worm. No, not a *gusano*, a *machacuay*, a snake deadlier than the black-and-yellow viper, whose bite could kill the jaguar, or the toad with the tiny horns that lived in the wet folds of the banana bunch. This *machacuay* was also a thief; it robbed holy sites. This *machacuay* was made of strange-looking men and women weaving unsteadily through the windswept snow. This *machacuay* unburied the dead and condemned them to an eternity of wandering, kidnapped from their souls.

Quiso shivered as the moving line of men and women passed him. He wondered where they were going and what they were going to do with their robberies. They faced a difficult and painful descent down the mountain, slipping and skidding on the icy trail. He knew a better way, an easy way, but it was secret and not to be shared with these thieves. As the last Indian porter disappeared into the snowy mist, Quiso uttered a silent prayer to the gods and the ghosts of his warrior ancestors to give him courage. He vaulted over an embedded boulder and started his own descent down the mountain. Following them was easy. Burdened by the weight of their equipment and the icy path, the people moved slowly. The boy kept a parallel course behind them and stayed out of their sight. When they stopped to make camp, he found a secluded crevice between two boulders and wrapped his serape around himself. In time, he was warm enough not to be envious of the fires they made. Later when they had gone into their tents, he stole into the camp and scooped some uneaten potatoes out of the warm coals of the cooking fires.

Quiso searched for the box containing his brother's body but realized it must be in the tent of the older woman. This was not the first time he had seen these men and women. They were the children of the Spanish, who had fought his people and drove them into the jungle many generations ago. Quiso had seen their silver birds scar the sky with long tails of smoke. He and Manco spied on the Spanish men piling bags of cocoa leaves on a metal carriage. When the carriage was filled, it made a frightening roar and lurched forward and disappeared on a path out of the jungle.

It was early morning when the line of people reached a village at the base of the mountain. They loaded all their equipment into two of the same kinds of carriages. Quiso was not afraid. He felt that he could face anything, experience anything. The soul of his brother was guiding him, strengthening him.

He waited until dark, then climbed on the flat bed of the carriage and crawled under a rough covering. He would follow the body of his brother to wherever the Spanish took him. And then when they weren't looking, he would carry him back to the mountain peak and put him back in the earth so his soul could find him. His father told him you measured your life life by counting your good memories.

Quiso remembered the time when he and Manco had been casting for fish in the Orinoco. Quiso slipped off a rock and was swept downstream. He struggled to stay afloat, but he was trapped in the powerful current. When he saw Manco, yelling from the riverbank, and their dog, Yurak, running ahead and barking, Quiso managed to roll over on his back so he could float downstream feet-first, using his legs to kick off the rocks. He drifted into a shallow pool. He waited for Manco. Yurak jumped into the water, took hold of his tunic sleeve, and tried to pull him onto the shore. And then Manco caught up with them, panting and out of breath. His worried look disappeared and they both laughed at Quiso's wet ride.

Quiso knew that was a counting memory because it was still alive in him and he could even feel Yurak's strong jaws tugging on his sleeve. And this ride in the roaring carriage would be one, too. It was carrying him and his brother faster than the current of the Orinoco. For a moment, he felt sad. This time, Manco would never be able to catch up with him.

CHAPTER 4

BOGOTÁ, COLOMBIA

The simplicity of the hotel room was pleasing to Adam—white-washed walls, a painted wooden dresser next to the bed, a thick blue water glass, a lamp, and a bright Indian rug on the floor. The bed was covered with an Andean wool bedspread in bold colors. It would do for the cold night to come. No Internet jack, no television, no fax, a heavy black telephone with a dial—no distractions. From the one window, if Adam found the correct angle, he could catch a truncated view of endless red-tiled Bogotá rooftops.

He spilled his briefcase out on the bed: phone, a pint of local cognac, the Colt Python .357, a slim toilet kit, a passport, and a glossy real estate flyer.

The cognac's peeling label read "Conquistador XXX." He unscrewed the tin cap and wondered how many more Xs it would take to merit a cork. The liquor in his mouth burned. He sloshed it around allowing the heat to erase another ache, the one that went with the memories of blood and the smell of cordite. Adam swallowed. The alcohol reached his stomach. He counted to five, and his hands stopped shaking.

He tapped a number into his phone and glanced down at the

real estate flyer; color photos of a house in Santa Fe: "three Bdrs, two Bas, designer kitchen, and set in a grove of piñon trees." In another photo, two saddled horses were tied to a hitching rail awaiting their riders. An interior shot showed a white-plastered living room with a rounded fireplace and a picture window with a view of the San Cristobal Mountains. His call connected, Adam tossed the flyer aside.

"Daddy?"

"Hey, Bunny."

"Hey. Everything go okay?"

"Mission accomplished."

"Want to Skype?"

"I can't. No computer."

Another wave of despair came over him, emptying his energy like a burst dam. Adam considered the cognac. Instead, he took a deep breath.

"I'm in Bogotá."

"Will you send me a postcard?"

"Tonight. For your stamps or bad taste collection?"

"You decide." There was a brief silence.

"Have you heard from the movers?"

"Day after tomorrow. Right on schedule."

Adam heard the sound of a dog barking.

"I think Roxy misses you."

"I miss her, too. Tell her I'll be home before the furniture gets there."

There was another silence. A moment passed, "Promise?"

"Bunny?"

"I know. No promises."

"I love you. That's a promise."

"Love you, too. Bye."

"Bye, Bunny,"

On his way to disconnecting, he heard: "Daddy?"

"I'm still here."

"I'm having weird dreams."

"Weird or scary?"

"I think both. Are you near Peru?"

"Bogotá. It's in Colombia."

"I know where Colombia is. I'm dreaming about Peru. Was I ever there?"

"No. But I was. In the Peace Corps."

"Can you inherit dreams?"

"I don't know. Want to tell me about it?"

"In my dream, I'm flying. And I'm wearing a white dress. And there's blood on it. See? That's weird and scary. How long can you live without a heart?"

"Why?"

"In the dream . . . I don't have one."

"You know what they say . . ."

And together, because they had it rehearsed, they said, "In your dreams."

She laughed.

"Why did we move, Daddy?"

"We wanted a change of scenery, remember? And Roxy wanted to chase rabbits."

"Right. Well, she seems happy."

He wanted to ask her if she was, too, but it was a question that was forbidden for now. His daughter knew that and, because she was kind, she said, "I'm good." Which was as close to happy that she could come.

"Bye, Bunny."

Adam held the phone up as his daughter disconnected the call. The image of a twelve-year-old girl holding a bullmastiff faded from the screen. Adam flipped the phone shut, opened his toilet kit, and tipped out the last two pills in a bottle. One more swig of the cognac to chase them down. He picked up the Python and went into the bathroom. He took off his clothes and found a space on the top of the stall for the pistol. Turned on the water, sat down on the floor, and let the water pour over him. *This is what I do.* He had saved a life, but at the same time, he'd lost a part of his own.

CHAPTER 5

LIMA, PERU

It was a tense contest with all the excitement and suspense of a World Series seventh game. Two out, bases loaded, bottom of the ninth, score 4–3, and a full count. The pitcher wound up and threw a fastball. The batter took a mighty swing and missed. The Yankees leaped for joy and Jimmy Del Vecchio headed for the dugout in misery. The players were nine-year-old boys and girls wearing Yankee and Dodger uniforms. In the bleachers, mothers and fathers climbed down to meet the players.

One of them, Gail Del Vecchio, navigated the steps to the field. She was just over thirty, and had not taken her eyes off her son, Jimmy, since he ran out of the dugout pounding his first baseman's glove. Now he walked to her, gloom on his face.

"I shoulda hit it."

"You had a double and a triple and drove in all the runs."

"Yeah, but not when it counted."

He had a point. Leave him alone. When all else fails, try ice cream.

"¿Helado?"

"I'm okay."

"You went two for three. You take that to the majors, you'll be earning ten million dollars a year."

"Really?"

"But the pitching's harder."

Jimmy nodded.

"Okay. *Helado.* Chocolate."

They headed toward the colorful ice cream carts. The baseball field sat in the middle of the Parque Centrale in Lima, Peru. It was a concession to the North American children and their fathers who played in leagues sponsored by various multinational corporations. The rest of the park was being used by Lima men in bright uniforms playing football. At the fringes of the playing fields were the white food carts that sold *papas rellenas*, fried mashed-potato balls; *sopa de camotes*, a sweet potato soup; *anticuchos*, barbecued beef hearts on skewers; and *helado*, ice cream. Poor children hawked Chiclets and stole shy glances at the Little Leaguers in their professional uniforms.

Ice cream cones in hand, Gail and Jimmy walked to their car. He waited patiently as his mother searched her shoulder bag for the car keys. It was just something she always did. When he grew up and had his own car, he would attach his keys to a loop on his pants. That way, he would never have to look for them. It was such a waste of time. He saw a flash of light from the shadows of the eucalyptus trees bordering the parking lot. Now his mother was emptying her whole purse on the hood of the car. "They have to be here," she said as she sorted through a hairbrush, a wallet, a scarf, sunglasses, reading glasses, a makeup pouch, a coin purse, and a copy of *Newsweek*.

There it was again. Like a big flashlight.

"I found them."

Jimmy glanced quickly at his mother as she put everything back in the purse. He heard the click of the key and knew she was about to open the door for him.

"Jimmy, let's go."

"In a minute, Mom."

He wondered if he really said the words or just thought them. He didn't hear the sound of his voice, but he didn't care. The flashing light washed over his body with a silver glow, and he wanted to touch it. But he had to get to it first. The sounds of the world— honking traffic, chirping birds, laughing children—dwindled and faded to a low hum as he got closer. His mother's voice was now a distant echo. A moment later, those sounds and his mother's scream were drowned out by a motorcycle engine. It came fast out of the trees, headlight flashing.

Gail saw the two men on the BMW R1100. They wore black leather jackets, black helmets with dark visors. The bike drove straight at Jimmy. *Oh, Jesusmary!* It was going to hit him!

She ran toward her son. "Move, Jimmy! Jump! You fucking bastards are going to run over my kid!"

The motorcycle swerved just enough for the passenger to grab Jimmy by the waist and sling him onto the bike between himself and the driver.

Gail's hands reached out for her son, but she was clawing air.

A few yards away, the peasant women looked away. This was none of their business.

On the pavement where Jimmy stood, one of the riders had dropped a round mirror the size of a silver dollar. It shone brightly in the black of a burned tire track. Its mirror circle was encased in seashells.

By the time Gail stopped screaming, the sound of the motorcycle's engine had melted into the steady growl of a Lima afternoon.

CHAPTER 6

PERUVIAN HIGHLANDS

In the dim light of the bus, Nina looked back at the sleeping students. She was exhausted and she longed for sleep, but it wouldn't come. There were too many questions regarding the corpses they were carrying back to Cuzco. She would perform a more detailed unwrapping and forensic analysis of the Inca mummy and other experts would be called in: a fabric specialist to scrutinize the wool, a jewelry expert from the Museo Oro del Perú in Lima for the trinkets, and a Lima University chemist to tell her the exact age of the mummy. The girl would be named, and possibly made the subject of a *National Geographic* cover story with an episode of NOVA to follow. Nina and her students would have a moment of fame. The Cuzco University provost would be pleased and organize a faculty dinner to honor her.

But this was all so fucked. What about the second corpse? Nina was transporting a murder victim in a freezer box away from the scene of the crime. Had the child been killed somewhere else and carried to the top of the mountain? And by whom? It would be a police matter, and they would surely want the body examined. But what would they find? An imitation of a five-hundred-year-old

Inca rite? She knew many Inca religious practices survived into the present—and even worked their way into the Catholicism of the Spanish. Saint's days had melded into the sacred rituals of the Inca calendar, and sometimes it wasn't clear whose religion had co-opted whose. Religious rituals in inaccessible mountain villages were performed by Indians who worshipped both Jesus and Pachamama, the mother of the earth. They prayed to saints and took communion with wine but also drank *chicha* in honor of Inti, the sun god. They celebrated the equinoxes with dance and prayer, speaking Quechua, but she had never heard of any ritual that included the *capacocha*, child sacrifice. There were occasional rumors of religious killings in modern Peru. A shaman near Lake Titicaca was suspected of murders that some locals claimed were acts of ritual sacrifice. A decapitated body was found on Cerro Santa Barbara, its head a few feet away, its face scraped off. The news was all over the TV, but nothing came of it. It was a murder, a particularly gruesome one, but it was still murder and nothing more.

She took out her phone and glanced at the image of herself and her father standing in front of Dulce, their llama. The sweet face of the beast was indifferent to the weight of the camping equipment strapped on its back. She tried dialing a number, but there was no reception in the deep mountain canyons. She got up and walked down the aisle past the sleeping students to the driver.

"Señor Delgado, will you stop the bus at the next gas station, please? I need to use a pay phone."

"Certainly, Professor. I think there's one about a half-hour away."

Nina returned to her seat and bunched up her parka for a pillow. She closed her eyes and leaned back in her seat. Sleep would finally come. And, with it, the dream that was a continuation of the picture on her phone.

She was in the jungle with her father. He was walking ahead of her, and she was following. She could smell his cologne, it was the scent of limes, and his lumbering torso divided by a thick leather belt that carried his machete, canteen, map case, and flashlight. "Follow me closely, Nina."

"*Yes, Papa.*" *His face was a replica of a Mezoluican stone mono-lith with bronze skin and thick black hair. His marriage to her mother was the reversal of the colonial practice—he was the Indian; she was the Spaniard. Nina inherited his skin color and hair, but she had her mother's delicate nose and lean body. Her brother, Arturo, had his father's trunk, square jaw, and slightly flattened nose.*

Her father's route in the jungle was familiar. She knew exactly how it would be: They would arrive at a clearing with an open view to the Amazon jungle below. The Amazon River would snake through the green carpet of trees. And, if they looked up, they would see a trio of con-dors riding the air streams. It wasn't a dream or a memory of a dream. It was a memory of a real event that had worked its way into her dreams. She had accompanied her father on this expedition; he had held out his hand to her and said, "Come, Nina, the city is just ahead."

And that was where the memory ended—but what city? She once asked her mother if her father had ever talked about a city in the jungle. Her mother laughed. "Your father was a marvelous man, but he also lived in two places: one was real and the other imagined."

Nina knew her father had instilled in her the love of the past and the accomplishments of the Inca. He always said, "Everything we discover, everything we dig up we are rescuing from the tomb looter. Isn't it better that our discoveries end up in a museum in Lima where many people can see the beautiful art that the civilization had produced? Or would you like it on the wall of a rich collector? This is our heritage, the proof that we are descendants of a proud, powerful, and creative civilization. The Indians we see today, poverty-stricken, laboring in the mountains and begging in the streets of Lima, are the descendants of that proud race, and they should be inspired by these artifacts to reconnect with that heritage."

She knew her father was right. She had seen sites where the looters had been too hurried to dig manually so they had set off dynamite to loosen the soil. They collected what survived the explosion what didn't was left as garbage. That was what she was protecting.

The bus driver was tapping her shoulder.

"The gas station, Professor. We're here."

She walked out into the cold morning air. She got change from the attendant and dialed a number. A man's voice came on the line.

"Nina?"

"Jorge, I want you to meet me at the institute with the team. We need to do an autopsy."

"A mummy?"

"Yes."

"Oh my God. Is it in ice? Have you wrapped it carefully?"

"Jorge, please."

"I'm sorry. I'm talking to you like a first-year student."

"Just have everything ready."

Nina hung up the phone and searched for more coins. She dialed another number. She told herself she was doing what she was supposed to do: call the police.

"Detective Sergio Varela, please."

There was a pause as the operator calculated how the detective would react to a call this early in the morning.

"It's Nina Ramirez. Please connect me to his home. He'll want to speak to me."

She pictured Sergio in bed rolling away from his wife, Anita, to take the call. No, she didn't want to picture that. Anita, who he would never leave, and Nina, who he would always love. So he said. Sergio, her brother's best friend, football teammate, drinking buddy—and her occasional lover. Arturo introduced them when she was a graduate archaeology student. She liked Sergio, but they had the bad timing to meet just as she was ending a disastrous love affair with an American Peace Corps volunteer.

Later she had asked herself why she didn't go to America with Adam. Everything was politics then, and politics viewed it as a capitulation to a North American. She would be another Yankee conquest. A prize. She imagined Adam asking his friends to guess what he had brought back from Peru. An Indian maiden. She was hardly a maiden. They made love on the first date in the back of his van because they knew it would be silly to postpone the inevitable. He said he would come back for her, and he did, but in between she let others help her come to her senses. Those stupid senses. Time went on, and Sergio met Anita and married her. That was the past and it was done. The present was that she was calling her occasional lover, a policeman, to tell him she was bringing the corpse of a murdered child to Cuzco.

"Sergio, it's Nina. I'm on my way back from a dig. I'm calling from . . ." She leaned out of the phone booth. "It's a gas station. There's a café and it doesn't have a name. We're near Ollantaytambo. I need you to meet me at the institute. Yes, it is. Very. You won't be wasting your time."

Nina stepped out of the phone box just as the expedition's truck roared past. In the bus, the driver started his engine. "Ready, Professor?"

She hadn't told him about the mummies.

CHAPTER 7

PANAMA CANAL ZONE

The Hawker 700 jet swept low over the Panama Canal, finally catching a flight path and landing on the tarmac of Tocumán International Airport. The sharp Panamanian sun bounced off the aluminum skin of the plane. The aircraft taxied to a trio of parked vehicles: an ambulance, a black Lincoln Town car, and a US Army Humvee. A woman in her sixties and her adult children stood next to the Lincoln. The plane's hatch opened, and Adam climbed down.

He walked over to the woman and her children.

"I'm Adam Palma. I'm with the FBI."

"How is my husband?"

"He's hurt, but he'll be okay."

The oldest of the children wearing a suit that was too hot for Panama held out his hand.

"Are you the one we thank?"

"I'm part of the team."

Before anyone could thank Adam, or the rest of the FBI hostage rescue group for South America, Walter Roberts, CFO of Ford Motors SA, emerged from the Hawker with a nurse holding his arm.

Adam continued toward the terminal. A man in a Lacoste shirt and khakis stepped out of the Humvee.

"Special Agent Palma?"

Adam kept walking. The man caught up with him.

"A minute. I'm Dobbs. From the embassy."

Adam stopped. He pointed at the Lincoln following the ambulance across the tarmac. "Dobbs, that was my last one."

Behind them, a fuel truck pulled up next to the Hawker and a worker in coveralls began to unwind a fuel hose from the tanker.

"I have to ask you to get back on the plane, sir."

"No way."

"Orders.

"I don't obey orders. I quit."

"Give me a break, Palma. I'm just the messenger."

"Bullshit. You're enjoying this."

"Believe me . . ."

"It'd take an act of Congress. You're in my way."

Dobbs slipped in front of Adam, blocking his path.

"I got one. Passed by both houses."

He was big, Dobbs. Notre Dame football defensive back. Adam realized he was facing a solid door.

"Right now, I'm crazy. I might just try something."

"Okay," Dobbs said. "I lied about Congress."

Adam opened his briefcase. There were two sample swatches of colored cloth.

"Which one do you like?"

"Huh?"

"Come on, Dobbs, which one do you like?"

"The . . . I don't know."

"Pick one, goddamnit!"

"Okay, the yellow."

"Me, too. It's for the living room curtains. My daughter and I are meeting the moving van in a couple of days. We'll show them where the furniture goes, put up my autographed pictures of the presidents, get my daughter enrolled in school, and start planting tomatoes."

Dobbs thought for a moment

"Okay, we'll take care of the move."

"You think we're in a negotiation."

"Well . . ."

"What about my daughter? You going to take care of her?"

"We can have a nice female agent stay with her."

"What about the curtains? I have to be there for that."

"Sir?"

"Tell the CEO of whatever company it is to pay the ransom." Adam slipped past Dobbs and headed for the terminal.

Dobbs called out, "It's not a CEO. It's an embassy secretary. They took her boy. Ten years old."

Adam stopped.

Dobbs went on, "No kidnap insurance, no deep pockets, no rich relatives, she's just a Grade Six State Department employee. Maybe she's lucky—there's also no ransom demand."

"Freaks and pedophiles don't ask for ransoms."

"It was two guys on a motorcycle."

"Where did this happen?"

"Lima. It's in Peru."

"I know where fucking Lima is."

Adam noticed the change in Dobbs's face. He had pushed the last button.

"Sorry, Dobbs. It's all loaded for me. You just stepped on my past."

Dobbs softened. "I know. But, if it helps, upstairs, they promise to leave you alone in this. You don't have anyone to report to."

"It helps."

CHAPTER 8

OLLANTAYTAMBO, PERU

The expedition arrived in the village as the sun rose over the eastern mountain peaks. The drivers led the llamas off the trucks, and they clambered across the cobblestones of the plaza and headed for their pastures. Nina signed release forms for the tents, stoves, cooking pots, and utensils that were unloaded and neatly stacked on pallets to be stored for the next expedition. As she counted out the *nuevos soles* for Gonzalo and his porters, he said, "You can prorate the amount if you like, Professor. We're short a few days."

"That's kind of you, Gonzalo, but you and your men earned full fees. I'll keep you informed."

She turned back to the plaza where Indian women were unpacking their handiwork for the first busload of tourists on their way to Machu Picchu. She realized she needed coffee. She walked over to a café where some of the students were sitting outside and asked the waiter to bring her a double espresso. She sat down next to Roberto and Edgar.

"I'll need your tapes, Edgar. Before we get to Cuzco."

"I understand. We wouldn't want them showing up on TV Mundo."

Nina hated sarcasm—it was fool's humor. She simply said, "No, we wouldn't, Edgar."

The discovery of the second corpse was a dark cloud hanging over the expedition. It would only get resolved when they arrived in Cuzco. Nina noticed that some of the students were talking on their phones. She hoped their conversations were not about the murdered child. If there were reporters and TV trucks when they arrived at the lab, it would mean that someone had tipped them off.

As the students boarded the bus, the driver lurched out holding an Indian boy by the collar.

"We have a stowaway, Professor. I found him in the back, under some blankets."

This wasn't what she needed now, she thought. Another impoverished Indian boy trying to get to Cuzco to find a job. What tales had he heard about riches in the cities that would cause him to abandon his friends and family? But what future was he facing in staying in his village and living out a backbreaking life as a peasant farmer? Either way, he was simply a Quechan boy who needed a ride and there were plenty of seats.

"Let him go," Nina told the bus driver.

She expected the boy to run when the driver released him. Instead, he stared at her defiantly. Nina smiled and said, *"Buenos días, amigo."*

The boy didn't respond. There was something about him that troubled Nina. Starting with his clothes. His serape was finely woven and the pattern was unfamiliar. It was red and black, and the diamond weave was tight and precise. He wore leggings and soft leather boots instead of the ubiquitous Nike knock-off sneakers. Who the hell was he and where did he come from? She tried again.

"Can I help you?"

He had an intelligent and alert face, but there was no indication that he had understood anything Nina said. Was he deaf?

Nina spoke clearly, making sure the boy could see her lips forming the words. "Can I help you?"

No response. Of course. He was Quechua—one of the largest groups of indigenous peoples in Peru. They were the descendents of the Inca and still spoke the ancient language. Nina spoke to him in Quechua.

"What is it you want, little one?"

The boy's eyes lit up. "I want to go on this," he said, indicating the bus.

"We are going to Cuzco," said Nina. "Do you want to go there?"

"Cuzco?"

"Qosqo," Nina responded, using the Quecha name for the city. The boy nodded.

"Will you tell me where you come from?" asked Nina. "Where is your village?"

The boy shook his head.

"Your name?"

"Quiso."

"Do you have family in Qosqo?"

"My brother."

"Alright, go ahead."

The bus driver moved aside, and the boy jumped aboard. He slid into an empty seat, pulled his serape around him, and put his face to the window.

The driver shrugged.

As the bus pulled out of the village onto the highway Nina glanced at the boy. There *was* something mysterious about him. It wasn't that he spoke Quechua, many people did. The problem was that he didn't seem to understand any Spanish. Could he have lived a completely isolated life in a mountain village? It was possible, but unlikely. She closed her eyes and replayed the unwrapping of the little boy on the mountain. She would worry about the dead one; the living could figure out their own problems.

Two hours later, the bus crossed a bridge into the outskirts of Cuzco. The poor part of the city began to reveal itself—dusty shacks of the poor, topped with tin roofs, sprawled on a labyrinth of unnamed rutted mud alleys crisscrossed overhead by pirated electrical wires. Women wearing bowler hats and long colorful skirts passed on their way to the city, where they had jobs as maids, cleaning women, or labored in small weaving factories. The lucky ones. The less fortunate staked out locations near tourist attractions, museums, and sidewalks outside hotels where they tried to sell trinkets, key rings, and cheap leather goods. Closer to the city center, shopkeepers unlocked metal shutters, workers lined up at bus stops, and taxi drivers filled their tanks at gas stations. In the distance, the spires of *la catedral*, Cuzco's largest church, soared into the clear sky. Built by the Spanish conquistadors after the defeat of the Incas, it rested on the foundations of Wiracocha, the great palace of the Incas. Cuzco, once the capitol of the Inca Empire was also a testimony to the resilience of Inca architecture. Despite the Spanish attempts to erase all traces of native civilization, the miles of interlocking stone-paved streets and three-foot-thick earthquake-proof walls were too daunting to dismantle. Their engineers marveled at the intricacies of the Inca stonework. It was said that the giant stones were so tightly fitted to one another that it was impossible to slide a knife blade in between them. The Spanish built their churches and palaces on the foundations of the very buildings they had sworn to destroy.

Nina looked back at Quiso. His face was pressed to the window, and, Nina knew, whatever he was seeing, he was seeing for the first time. She was correct.

The city was larger, noisier, and more complicated than anything Quiso could have imagined. He saw carriages moving, but nothing was pulling them. They coughed up black smoke and made noises that he had never heard before. What he felt was not fear, but the frustration that he lacked words to name the things he was seeing. He had so many questions: What were the people carrying in the sacks on their backs? What were the big pictures on stilts rising out of the ground with images of food and smiling half-naked women holding thin white sticks with smoke coming out of the end and the scribbles under them? There were large carriages with seats like the one he was in, carriages with animals in them, shiny carriages with two or three people, and most baffling of all, the little ones with no roofs and one or two people sitting on them wearing hard shiny helmets, scurrying around the big carriages like ants over the carcass of a bird. There were metal trees with ropes connecting one another sprouting from the roofs. And he had never seen so many different colors of people: light-skinned ones who must be Spanish, ones who were very dark, almost black, like some of the jungle people, and others who resembled men and women and children in his tribe. All the things he saw made him feel like his head would burst. He tried to store them in his memory so that he would be able to accurately recount them to his own people. But as he remembered the events that led him to this place, he realized he might never see them again.

All around him, the Spanish were sleeping in their seats, uninterested in the amazing things outside the window. Some of them had strings coming out of their ears. He wondered how he would live with such people. But there was the woman who spoke his language and allowed him to travel with them to Qosco. If she spoke his language, there might be others—people who would help him find a way to get back the stolen body of his brother. Had Manco made the journey to the gods before his body was taken out of the earth? How would his soul find his body on his return? Why did the Spanish treasure the bodies of the dead? Was it for the gold that was buried with them? Was it for the fabric woven so skillfully by the maidens? If so, why didn't they just take the gold and fabric and leave the bodies in the sacred mountains to be reunited with their souls that were hurled across the sky to the different constellations—the condor, the serpent, and the monkey—and finally to the house of Inti, the sun god? Quiso shuddered as he imagined his own soul newly returned from the gods, wandering aimlessly over the rocks of Salcantay searching for his body, crying out for the loss of its earthly home.

Quiso was with the Spanish, trapped in a roaring yellow thing that smelled like the black liquid that bubbled out of pools in the jungle floor. He was deeper in their world than ever. He knew people who had seen the Spanish up close. They spied on them as they walked the ancient trails or rode in fat yellow boats on wild mountain rivers. The people who had seen the Spanish talked about their colorless clothes, their carriages that spun so fast along the painted roads, and their silver birds that sometimes flew over the jungle.

It was forbidden to make contact with them. Everyone knew they were constantly searching for the Inca. His mother told him the Spanish lust for gold was so strong that they would never give up hunting their people so they could imprison and torture them to make them reveal the location of their treasure. But no one had ever spoken to the Spanish, or rode in their carriages as Quiso was doing now.

CHAPTER 9

CUZCO, PERU

Sergio Varela hated mornings in general and Cuzco's early morning traffic in particular. It was dense—the air was thick with noxious fumes from old and inefficient vehicles that clogged the narrow streets. He was a night person, always had been. As a child, he hated to go to bed. He kept a flashlight under his pillow for secret comic book reading, then an iPod for music. And now, as a detective on the Cuzco police force, he preferred night shifts. Early dinner with Anita and the kids, then the eight p.m. to four a.m. shift, home at five, occasional sleepy sex with Anita, kiss the kids good-bye on their way to school, and back to blissful sleep. And there was one other benefit of working late hours: Nina Ramirez. Nina, who got him out of his warm bed and wouldn't tell him why, just a hurried command to meet her at the university. A secret? Whatever it was, it wasn't their only one. Sometimes when things were really quiet in the city and crime was on a hiatus, he would drop in on her for a drink, a long chat and—if she was so inclined, and he never pushed—a short walk to the bedroom. The relationship was uncomplicated with no emotional strings attached. Just good friends. Until, and his cop's mind went over the scenarios, until they were found out, until she met someone, until he realized he was actually was in love with her—or vice versa—and since he was locked in to Anita, they would have to part.

Sergio drove his police Toyota into the gated courtyard of the forensic laboratory of Cuzco University and parked. Nina was waiting with her students. The sight of her always gave him a bump in the heart. There she was, just down from a week of camping and digging on a freezing mountain, unwashed, dressed in a parka and jeans, and she still looked hot. Better than her students. He wondered how that was possible.

"Hi, Nina. What am I doing here?"

"There's a problem with one of the mummies we excavated."

"What's the problem?"

Nina glanced at the students. They looked uncomfortable.

"Technically, or should I say, in anthropological terms, it is not a mummy."

"Then what the hell is it, Nina?"

Nina paused, choosing her words carefully. "It's a murdered child. Wrapped up like a mummy. Two of my students found it."

Sergio cocked his head. "Say that again."

"It's not a mummy, Sergio. It's a murdered child."

"You found a dead child on expedition," said Sergio, "and you brought it here? Where was the child found?"

"On Nevado Salcantay."

"Why didn't you leave it and call the local police?"

Nina explained. "It's an archaeological dig. If we had left it, it would be gone—the tomb thieves would have it."

He took out his pad and a pen, signaling the beginning of an interrogation. "Who found it?"

Nina touched his arm. "Sergio, it's important that we get the mummy unpacked as soon as possible."

Sergio nodded. "I want to see the corpse of the child now. You can deal with the mummy later."

"All right," said Nina. "Let's get both bodies in the lab."

Quiso watched the students carry the boxes out of the truck and on to the beds with wheels. Inside one of those boxes was his brother. What were the Spaniards going to do with him now? Through the barred window, he saw a white room with more beds and tables with trays of shiny silver knives and saws. His mind could not comprehend what would happen in that room. These people had already dug up Manco's body and put it in a bag and then a wooden box. What would they do now? Chop it up and feed it to their dogs? Quiso would save his brother. He fell in with the Spanish boys and girls entering the building.

Nina blocked his path. She didn't want this to become a case of giving someone a ride that turned into a rescue. There wasn't time for this boy. She spoke gently in Quechua. "I'm sorry, you can't come inside, son."

He didn't move.

"You're in Qosqo now. Is someone meeting you? Do you have a place to go? Do you need some money?"

Money was the universal technique of getting rid of someone without guilt. You don't ask, I offer, you take it and go away, and we all get to feel better. She reached in her shoulder bag.

The boy stepped back. His motion caused his poncho to open. He pulled the fabric together but she saw it—tied to his belt was a tangle of multicolored strings that were knotted at uneven intervals. It was a quipu—the only known pre-Columbian writing system in South America. The colored strings and knots of the quipu were the closest thing the Incas had to a written language. The distances between the knots could be read and transmitted information: One color might tell the size of the potato harvest in Tiahuanaco, another the catch of fishermen in Huanchaco, or the stores of grain and corn in the warehouses in Quito, or how many bolts of cloth were produced in Huánuco Pampa—all this would be stored on the quipu and sent to Inca administrators in Cuzco.

Almost casually, Nina said, "I see you are wearing a quipu."

The boy didn't answer.

"It is very pretty. Would you show it to me?"

He hesitated for a moment, made sure he knew where the entrance to the building was, then ran out of the courtyard.

Nina watched him go. He disappeared around the corner. Had she commited a major screw up, she wondered. Did she just allow let a boy wearing a quipu that could be the Rosetta Stone of the Andes, something that would unlock every secret of Inca culture and society, get away? Then she smiled. Fake quipus were available in every tourist shop—along with pan flutes, and Inca pottery—all made in China.

Once he was out of the compound and satisfied that he wasn't being followed, Quiso paused and pressed himself against a wall. He wanted to watch the activity in the street and figure out what to do next. The carriages no longer frightened him. He had seen enough of them on the way to Qosqo. He could see that the Spanish ruled this city. They had acquired weapons, transportation, and wore strange clothes. But if he looked carefully, he could see traces of his people. He pressed his spine against the ancient stone wall. Its intricate pattern of inlaid stone was familiar to him. He turned and ran his hands over the boulders that were placed on top of one another in irregular designs. He had studied the drawings of the stones and their patterns and lines and knew they told stories. Standing back, he could see the line that represented Lake Collasuyu out of which the god Tiki Viracocha emerged carrying the first humans. Another line showed how Tiki Viracocha created the sun, and then the moon and the stars to give light to the world. His father said the Spanish believed the Inca had no written language, and yet here it was staring at them on every building. Quiso rubbed his hands over the stones. Touching them calmed him. No matter what the Spanish built or tore down—Qosqo was still the sacred city. He remembered the prayer his mother taught him: "We are still here, and we will always be here. Inti loves the Inca people, and he will not desert us." And as he looked at the people rushing by him, Quiso realized he could see the Inca people. They wore the clothes of the Spanish, they talked the language of the conquistadors, but he could see in their faces that they were Inca.

He felt a sharp pain in his ribs. A man in gray clothes was holding a black baton, poised to jab him again.

"Move your ass, little boy. There is no begging here."

Quiso knew the man was speaking the language of the Spanish and the words were unknown to him, but the meaning of the pain in his side was clear. Quiso was young, but he had been taught survival techniques and combat. He practiced every day with his friends. He could defend against spears and swords and take down an opponent no matter what his size. The man holding the baton was thin and tired looking, and Quiso suspected he was weak and only picked on children. The man jabbed the baton again, but Quiso sidestepped it and trapped it under his right armpit, jammed his left hand sharply into the man's wrist, and twisted his own body. The man released the baton, and it fell to the ground.

The woman selling flowers had seen cops pushing kids around, sometimes even making them turn over a portion of their begging money. Merchants wanted them away from their storefronts, the tour guides considered them a nuisance, and the cops obliged by chasing them away. But she had never seen a peasant boy disarm a policeman. She dropped her flowers on the blanket and crossed the street. She was struck by the boy's dress. He was not wearing threadbare sneakers, or one of those disgusting black T-shirts with a skull. He was not from the slums of Cuzco. She wondered if he was one of the ones the old men talked about. It could be true. She hurried across the street waving off cars and motorbikes with her cane.

The policeman bent down and retrieved his baton. "Oh, we have a little fighter here."

"Señor."

She was steady on her cane—she looked the policeman in the eye and spoke gently, but firmly, as if speaking to one of her children.

"Is there a problem, officer?"

She knew the policeman would have liked to grab her by her neck and send her on her way, but across the street a small crowd of people was watching. There would be cell phones or video cameras recording the confrontation. She spoke quietly, confidentially to the cop.

"I hear there are many people who want to join the municipal police force. I think the mayor and police chief would not look kindly on an incident."

"This boy is begging on the street, señora, which, as you know, is against the laws of the city of Cuzco."

"Naturally, but you can see that this boy is from the country and doesn't know about our laws. I was watching him from across the street and I didn't see him hold out his hand to anyone."

She turned and glanced at the crowd across the street. Two students were holding up phones and recording them.

"Tell him that if I see him begging again, I will arrest him," said the cop as he holstered his baton and walked away.

The boy stared at her, unblinking. His features were pure Indian, a flawless cocoa skin, black eyes, and hair cut straight across his forehead. The weave of his fabrics was intricate, and the colors of the strands composing the cloth were brighter and more sharply defined than she had ever seen. It was clear they were handmade and not fabrics from any store or local factory. But who was doing such work? Those techniques had all but died out. This child must have emerged from the Sierra highlands where some villages still spoke Quechua, where the fields were still fed by aqueducts constructed by the Inca six hundred years ago.

She knew that wherever he was from, he must be hungry. The woman reached in her bag and took out a wedge of corn bread.

"Take it, my son."

Quiso broke the bread in half. He put one piece in his sack and ate the other. The woman motioned him over to a simple stone basin carved into the wall. A single copper pipe emitted a steady but faint stream of water. Quiso washed his hands, his face, and then lowered his mouth under the pipe and drank.

"How do you speak my language, lady?"

"There are many people who still speak it. Even some Spanish. Where have you come from?"

"From the mountains. I followed the body of my brother who was taken from the sacred Nevado Salcantay by the people inside that building. What do they want with him? Do you know?"

"Was there gold on his body?"

"Yes."

"The Spanish are not satisfied with the gold and silver they dig up from our ancestors. Now they defile the bodies of our dead and rob them of the gifts they carry to the gods."

"I have seen this with my own eyes, lady."

"Where did you get your clothes?" she asked. "What is the name of your village?"

The boy felt tired. The woman was asking too many questions.

"Thank you for the food, lady." He pulled his serape around his shoulders.

"You are not safe here. Come with me. I can take you to people who can help you."

Quiso didn't answer. The woman waited, and then realized there would be none.

"Be careful, my son. If you need me you will always find me in the plaza. On the steps of the Spanish temple."

Quiso nodded and glanced at the sun. He calculated that night would come soon. Then he would do what he had to.

CHAPTER 10

CUZCO, PERU

Nina asked the students to wait in the lobby while she went into the morgue with Sergio. Jorge followed, carrying the ice chest. He opened the chest and placed the bundle on a steel table. Nina put on rubber gloves and a white lab coat. She looked at Sergio.

"This won't be pretty."

"Nina, it's not my first."

For Nina, the arena of forensic postmortems and autopsies were fascinating. It was how the dead gave up information: how they died, when they were stabbed, what caliber gun shot them. In the morgue, medicine was an intellectual puzzle. It was amazing to her how much information a dead person carried about their death.

Nina untied the loose twine that held the cover and pulled it back. She looked at the corpse. She felt a profound sadness come over her. Was it the death of a child or the fact that his murder mocked the civilization she had spent her life studying?

The boy was curled in the same fetal position as the Inca mummy girl. His mouth was covered with red paint. There was a bloody indentation in his skull and a slash across the left side of his chest where someone had reached in and cut out his heart. But unlike his sister of five hundred years ago, the flesh of his cheeks was full and his skin hung loose over his white teeth.

"What's that on his mouth?" asked Sergio.

"Probably a mixture of dye and the *ayahuasca*—a hallucinogen that is used to calm the victim. Or . . ."

"Or what?"

"Or it's just red paint. I'm sorry, Sergio. This is a police matter." She covered the corpse with a sheet. "Dr. Molina should do a complete forensic autopsy, not me."

Sergio nodded.

"If there's nothing else, I want to examine the mummy." The politically correct dead child.

The Inca girl lay on a steel table, covered by a thick sheet of blue plastic. The room smelled of formaldehyde and lemon-scented disinfectant. Nina asked the students to come in from the lobby and to stand against the wall, a few feet from the tables, but made sure they had a clear view. Jorge assembled the instruments for the procedure—scalpels, surgical scissors, and pincers. A video camera stood on a high tripod ready to capture the unwrapping of the mummy. Jorge looked at Nina.

"A minute, please." Nina turned to her students. "We have wrenched the body of this girl from the earth to help us in our understanding of the Inca world—that is what we do as archaeologists. As we proceed, I just want to remind us that we must be respectful to her and her family for the acts we will perform."

Nina said to Jorge. "I'm ready to begin."

Jorge switched on the video camera and aimed it at the girl. On the mountain, Nina only allowed herself a brief glimpse of the mummy; she was aware of the potential damage that heat, sunlight, and exposure to the air could do. If the ice melted too quickly, the water would damage tissue.

"You did a good job in preserving this little girl," Nina said to her students. "There were many things that could have gone wrong. But she's in excellent condition. She looks about twelve years old, as a sacrificial victim, she must be a virgin. The cause of death is a combination of a blow to the head and the removal of her heart. Perhaps she didn't know that her mouth would be painted with the *ayahuasca* so that she wouldn't fear or feel the hammer that would crush her skull and the obsidian blade that would sever her carotid artery. But surely she knew that her family would be rewarded. In this life they would be given extra food, textiles, and animals. In the next they would reside with her in the palace of the gods for eternity."

CHAPTER 11

AIRPLANE TO LIMA

Adam settled into a leather seat. The only other passenger on the plane was a trim, studious man in a white shirt and tie, his suit jacket neatly folded on an empty seat next to him, a bottle of water on his tray, and a laptop booted up. He could have been anything from an undersecretary in the State Department to a fertilizer specialist in the Department of Agriculture. He didn't look up when Adam walked past him, signaling that neither of them should have any interest in the other after take-off. That was fine with Adam. He couldn't talk about his work anyway. Adam glimpsed at his computer screen. The man was playing SimCity. Adam considered telling him he used to play it with his daughter. It would open a conversation but also unleash a flood of memories of their life in Maui. They had lived in Lynn's cottage on the edge of the last pineapple field in Kaanapali. He commuted from his job as a US attorney in Honolulu on weekends, while Lynn was doing law out of the house, writing briefs and wills for single practitioner lawyers on the island. Katie was in third grade, and the Hawaiian sun was bleaching her hair to gold and tanning her skin to brown. They were water rats—weekends were spent on the beach swimming and snorkeling.

Katie had good friends, and she moved easily between the native and *haole* worlds.

"*Today she asked me what 'sovereignty' meant.*" Lynn said.

"*As in Hawaiian sovereignty?*"

"*None other.*"

"*Do you care if we give Honolulu back to the Hawaiians?*"

"*They can have everything but the Hilton.*"

"*They don't want it.*"

"*All the rest? It wasn't ours to begin with.*"

"*That's what she said.*"

SimCity. Katie had loved constructing a virtual city, one that was different from the Maui island architecture, where there were no skyscrapers, broad avenues, palaces, industrial zones, monuments, or massive government buildings.

"*Daddy, I'm building a theater where there will be concerts and plays.*"

"*And ballet?*"

"*Of course. And Cirque du Soleil and Britney Spears.*"

And then out of nowhere: "*When can I scuba?*"

"*That's a ways off. You will have to be content with snorkeling. Want to take Grandpa's boat and go to Molokai and look for sea turtles tomorrow?*"

"*Picnic and everything?*"

"*Everything.*"

Swimming behind Lynn and Katie, perfectly focused through the prism of his face mask, suspended in the space that is water, following mother and daughter, each a version of the other, gliding over the coral reef, their shadows scattering schools of butterfly and needlefish, he couldn't conjure a better memory and he was grateful for it as the sea turned blood-red and he was back in the room where it all ended.

Adam shook his head to erase that image as he had learned to do so he could return to other people's troubles, which after all, was his job.

He opened the manila envelope Dobbs had given him. There

were faxes, emails, and police reports of the kidnapping. One was from the Lima Police Department and another from SOP, a branch of the Peruvian military that shared responsibility for kidnappings with the police unless they were considered political. In the past, this had proven problematic, as members of the SOP were often involved in kidnappings themselves. There was also a report from the State Department officer in Lima with copies to the FBI.

The reports were essentially the same: A ten-year-old, male US citizen had been abducted by two men on motorcycle from the parking lot of the Parque Centrale in Lima. There were no witnesses except for the mother, Gail Del Vecchio, also a US citizen, and she could not provide any details other than the men were wearing black-tinted motorcycle helmets, and the motorcycle itself had thin tires and, at one point, executed what she knew to be a "wheelie." That would indicate a dirt bike, or a stripped down machine that could be anything from a Harley to a Suzuki. The police reports stressed that since there was no ransom demand from the abductors, they could not determine the purpose of the kidnapping.

There were photos of the crime scene, the skid mark of the motorcycle tire, and a snapshot of Jimmy in his Little League uniform. Adam could see that the boy wasn't sure if he should pose as a serious no-nonsense baseball player or just express what he felt—thrilled and proud to be in his official Little League uniform. Satellite photos of the park at the time of the abduction were provided, but trees and shadows made them useless. The boy's father, Sergeant James Del Vecchio Sr., was killed in Afghanistan, which ruled out any kind of custody or domestic situation. The mother asked that both sets of grandparents not be notified until there was more definitive news. A State Department HR evaluation gave Mrs. Del Vecchio excellent grades and noted that she was studying Spanish literature and advanced conversation at the university three nights a week. Her housemaid, Adela Valdez, was fully vetted by the embassy. There was a letter of recommendation to the State Department from Representative Harold Martin of Pennsylvania, who had employed Mrs. Del

Vecchio in his Harrisburg congressional office. He said that she was an outstanding worker and a change of environment might help her son get through the loss of his father.

Adam shifted his gaze from the crime notes to the window. Below, the brown ribbon of the Amazon River carved its way through the green jungle on its way to the Atlantic. Dotting the jungle were black cones of smoke rising into the air, the markers of Amazon fires.

"Impressive, isn't it?" The voice belonged to the other passenger.

Adam nodded and said, "It's a lot of jungle."

The man continued, "I meant the fires. You know there are thousands of them burning right now. Besides destroying the rain-forest's ecosystem and killing wildlife, they're releasing millions of tons of carbon and carbon monoxide into the atmosphere, and huge amounts of particles and nitrogen oxides. Add that to the fires burning now in Malaysia, Siberia, Australia, and New Mexico, the whole world is in fairly deep shit." He laughed. "When I speak to Andean governments, I leave out the part about deep shit. But if you go to Cuzco, you'll feel it." The man returned to his computer. Conversation over.

Another picture: Jimmy standing next to his mother. She had her arm around him—their heads were cocked sideways to each other with big smiles. The boy was comfortable in her embrace, and Adam figured she was trying not to squeeze too hard even though he was all she had. Ten years old. What were these people after? The anger rose in him, and he felt the familiar burning pain in his right hand. It started in his wrist and moved quickly to the end of his fingers. A doctor said it was a mild case of carpal tunnel syndrome. He didn't tell the doctor how the path was connected from his anger to the memory. If he had, the doctor would have sent him to an FBI psychiatrist for post-traumatic stress counseling. So he allowed the memory to come back as a pain, and shared it with the gun that was in his hand when he shot the man who held a knife to his wife's throat.

CHAPTER 12

LIMA, PERU

Adam told the embassy not to send a car to the airport. He preferred to take a random taxi because it was unpredictable and safer. He walked past uniformed chauffeurs holding name cards of disembarking passengers out to the curb crowded with tourist buses, vans, and private cars. A twenty-*neuvo-sol* bill to a dispatcher got him a shiny red-and-white Lima taxi. Adam tossed his bag in the backseat.

"English okay?"

"Yes, sir."

"I'd like to stop at the Sheraton, drop off my bag, and we can go on."

The driver nodded, punched the meter, and melded into the stream of airport traffic. Adam stared at the huge billboards lining the highway to Lima advertising cars, trucks, TVs, kitchen appliances, and vacation condos—none of which the people who lived in the slums behind the billboards could afford. He had passed through Lima years ago on his way to Cuzco as a young Peace Corps volunteer. None of it looked familiar, just the people, still hardworking, lined up at crowded bus stops waiting for transportation into the city. The driver drove silently. Adam glanced at the dashboard. Along with the rosary hanging from the mirror there was a statue of the Virgin Mary, a red-and-white flag of the FPF, Peru's national football team, and a posed picture of three adolescent boys in white shirts and wide smiles. Two of them looked alike, the third, the youngest, had blinding braces.

"Twins?"

"Yes, sir. Double trouble," he laughed, "and double fun."

"I'm Adam."

"Geraldo. Traffic sucks this time of day."

"Traffic sucks everywhere. And your English is good because . . ."

"Five years in LA. I liked it, but one day my youngest doesn't want to go to school anymore. He doesn't even want to leave the house. He finally admits that he's been invited to join a gang, and while he's making up his mind, my wife packs everything and tells me I can stay alone in LA or come back to Lima where it's safe."

Safe? Adam had a different take on it. Safe was where shit didn't happen to you while you were there. And that could be anywhere.

The driver edged his car under the portico of the Sheraton.

Adam found a room clerk at the long desk. "Please don't take it up to the room; just put it in a locker until I return." He handed the clerk his credit card and waited while he swiped it. Geraldo was leaning against his car talking into a cell phone. He saw Adam, flipped the phone shut, and held the door open for him.

"The US Embassy on Avenida Encalada."

"Sure thing. You have kids, señor?"

"A girl."

"My wife, she wants a girl. But what if it's twins again?"

"You will be up to your ass in debt and probably have the time of your life."

Geraldo laughed and found a lane to the highway that took them south out of the city.

The US Embassy in Lima was constructed at the edge of a suburban neighborhood ten miles from Lima's city center. Its location was inconvenient for anyone doing government business or a Peruvian national attempting to get a US visa, but, more importantly, it was also immune from mass demonstrations. Adam knew it was built in a time when security trumped design. The architect tried to give it some aesthetic value by attaching a modernist facade of oblong vents that would disguise the concrete understructure, but the effect was a big rectangle with holes.

The embassy was monitored by cameras and watchtowers built into the surface of the mountains behind the steel fence. Beyond the perimeter fence was a series of guard stations and concrete barriers to deter car bombs. Marines patrolled the grounds constantly. Two Peruvian army trucks filled with soldiers were parked on the sidewalk across the street.

Adam lowered his window and handed his ID to the Marine guard. "I have to ask you to step out of the car, sir."

Adam got out, and another Marine beckoned him to step away from the taxi. "Are you under any duress, sir?"

"I'm fine, corporal. Let me pay the driver and walk the rest of the way."

Adam handed Geraldo an American fifty and told him to keep the change.

"Thanks, *amigo*. I can wait if you like."

Adam thought for a second. "Better not. I may get a lift back."

Adam had less trouble making it through the next guard gate. One more display of his ID to the Marines at the door and he was buzzed into the embassy building. He gave his name and FBI ID to the receptionist. While she was checking everything twice, he noticed that the walls were covered with paintings. The place looked like a museum. There was an alternating mixture of Peruvian and American art in corresponding genres. Pre-Colombian pottery next to Navaho pottery, Spanish primitivism next to Southwestern Colonial Spanish, late Peruvian regional next to California plein air, and bold adventures in abstraction borrowed from the Museo de Arte Contemporáneo in Arequipa, along with reproductions of Jasper Johns, Willem de Kooning, and Andy Warhol. A nineteenth-century Peruvian painting of a Spanish conquistador stopped him for a moment. The face of the Spanish warrior was cherubic—tinted pink cheeks, full lips, and an expression of indifference as he sat straight in his saddle while his horse reared back on two legs. Adam remembered the rule for equestrian poses. One hoof raised meant the subject was wounded in battle, two meant he died in battle, and all four hooves on the ground meant he died in bed. The angels hovering over his head were about to escort this warrior through the gates of heaven, accompanied by trumpet blasts and pings of golden harps. Not bad for a guy who probably began his military career an impoverished *campesino* in Cadiz.

"Special Agent Palma?"

An efficient-looking young woman in her twenties wearing a business suit and white blouse was holding a small walkie-talkie. She held out her hand. "I'm Elizabeth Griffin. I'm to take you to your meeting."

"Lead the way."

Elizabeth kept up of a steady stream of small talk perfectly timed to take them across the foyer to an elevator. Adam got a weather report, admitted that his flight was comfortable, and said that this wasn't his first time in Lima.

"Just a minute."

He stopped in front of a framed drawing of a woman in swirling water with a comic book caption: "I don't care! I'd rather sink— than call Brad for help!"

"First time I've ever seen Roy Lichtenstein on an embassy wall."

"First time I've met an FBI agent who knows who he is."

"I majored in art at Quantico."

She laughed.

"Who's in charge?"

"Linda Casey, Ambassador Casey's wife. She was a senior curator at the Dallas Museum of Art."

"Too bad not many people get to see all this."

Elizabeth smiled. "Well, we do, and it's one of the perks of this posting. If you like, after your meeting I'd be happy to show you the rest of the collection."

Another time, in another country, and he would have accepted and later discussed art, government service, the wine they were drinking, and whether Mick Jagger would outlive them both, but he just wanted this job to be over.

"Thanks." And he added apologetically, "I'm all business."

She nodded and pressed the elevator button. They rose past the two floors in silence.

A Marine guard at the door to the ambassador's office suite made one more inspection of Adam's pass. Inside the suite, the decor suddenly turned from stark white and frosted glass to dark wood paneling. It was obvious to Adam that the ambassador had no affection for his wife's taste in contemporary art, and probably ordered his staff to make his offices resemble the white-shoe Wall Street firm where he used to be a senior partner. Antique English hunting prints and a signed photograph of the president glowed in the subdued light of floor lamps.

Adam recognized Jimmy's mother immediately. She was just thirty, but because she hadn't slept for twenty hours and her son had been snatched out of her arms, she seemed a lot older. She had a sweet roundish face, full lips, and a button nose. The ambassador offered his hand to Adam and began the introductions.

"I'm Dick Casey, and this is Gail Del Vecchio." He added, "Special Agent Palma is with the FBI."

Adam went right to her and saw her expression change. He had seen it before—it was hope. It happened when someone new entered the mix, the person she was waiting for. The one who would cut through everything and get her son back. Adam read her thoughts, and they saddened him because all he could guarantee was that he would try as hard as he could to find her son. Her look said *you're different. You know what it feels like when you have the hole in your heart and the pain in your gut that will make you drop everything but breathing. If you will find my little boy and return him to my loving embrace, God give me another chance, I will never ever make the mistake of letting him out of my sight even for a second.*

Adam also knew, as the days went by and her child wasn't found, he would join the ranks of inefficient cops, indifferent bureaucrats, and hectoring journalists who didn't care and didn't try hard enough. And he would be despised along with the rest of them. But for now, he said the words she wanted to hear, "Mrs. Del Vecchio, I will do everything I can to get your son back. Everything."

Two Peruvian military policemen of fairly high rank and a man with a yellow legal pad entered the room.

Mrs. Del Vecchio ignored the men and said to Adam, "I turned my back for one second. Looking for my damned car keys. I ran after him. Fast as I could, I swear to God. I can't believe it." Her eyes were red-rimmed but dry, and she was strong. "The motorcycle was faster. You have kids?"

"A daughter."

"Then you can imagine. Or can you? Ever lose her in a crowd? Or a mall?"

"You didn't lose your son, Mrs. Del Vecchio. He was taken away from you. You never had a chance."

It was bring-your-daughter-to-work day. Mom headed up the pro bono department at a law firm and Dad worked for the FBI.

"Bunny, you can spend the day with me at the J. Edgar Hoover building or Mom can take you to Bernard, Wolfe, and Thomas. At Daddy's office, you can visit a firing range, a computer center, a fingerprint lab, and a rogue's gallery, which means you can see pictures of the ten most wanted . . . and at Mom's law firm you can see, what?"

"Lawyers working," his wife said.

"That doesn't sound very exciting, does it?"

"But I'm interested in seeing what it's like to be a lawyer. If I'm a

lawyer, I can stop people from polluting the atmosphere, I can defend innocent people, and I can prevent cruelty to children."

"Then, after you become a lawyer, you can join the FBI and arrest people for Mommy to defend."

"Very funny."

"I'm just jealous," he said to his wife on what was to be the last day of her life.

Gail said, "No, I never had a chance."

Mrs. Del Vecchio if we had the time, and your son was in the next room watching television so he couldn't hear us, I would tell you about having a chance.

There was a guy I found online who had a taste for travel to a country in Southeast Asia where children came cheap and he was seeking a new traveling companion to hold the camera while he starred in his own home movie. His name was Atreus, aka Joseph Keefer, and he lived in cyberspace. I found him in a chatroom where you had to know someone to get in. So I did. My contact was a convicted felon awaiting sentencing in a Seattle prison. In exchange for a password, he got a shorter jail term. Atreus and I danced around for six months or so, exchanged emails, and since I understood every one of Atreus's euphemisms for obscenities to be performed on girls under ten, Atreus was pleased to find a kindred soul. I played hard to get and extremely paranoid, and so did Atreus, but we finally satisfied each other that neither of us was an undercover cop, and therefore agreed to meet for cappuccinos at the Starbucks in the Suvarnabhumi Airport in Bangkok. Atreus turned out to be in his mid-thirties, a wrestling coach and a Latin and Greek instructor at a fancy prep school in the Midwest.

This modern Atreus fellow was damaged goods and proud of it. There was a "get to know each other" phase during some wholesome Thailand tourism. We visited a couple of refugee camps on the Cambodian border where childhood was short and precarious. We were pals now, and with the cooperation of an undercover Thai policeman, we arranged a casting session with some desperate mothers and their daughters. I set up the camera in the hotel room, and recorded Atreus's bargaining with a tearful mother just before the cops broke in and arrested him. Following a

*short trial, Mr. Keefer found himself in a Bangkok prison where he could
contemplate his fate following his extradition to the United States.*

*And what does he have to do with you, Mrs. Del Vecchio? Turns out
Atreus/Keefer never forgot a face, and he remembered mine. So when
he finally was released from San Quentin, scarred and beaten royally as
is the case with child offenders in prison, he found the way to find me.
And on that day when you bring your daughter to work, he followed my
wife and daughter from the law offices of Bernard, Wolfe, and Thomas to
the ladies' room on the ground floor. I was waiting outside eating a hot
dog from Merman's cart when I saw people running from the building
screaming that there was a man inside with a gun. . . .*

"You look around and your child is gone," Mrs. Del Vecchio was
saying. "And there's that panic and there's that thing in your heart
and you think it's stopped. . . ."

"I didn't have time."

"What?"

"I'm sorry. I was thinking about a similar situation."

"Then you see him and it all goes away and you swear you'll
never let him out of your sight. Isn't that what it's like?"

*Exactly right, Mrs. D. I pushed my way into the women's bathroom.
There he was, my pal from Bangkok, Mister Atreus. His nose was pushed
to one side, and there were fewer teeth in his mouth, but I recognized
him, and he looked glad to see me. My wife lay on the floor in a puddle
of blood from the bullet that had severed her carotid artery. Atreus had a
handful of my daughter's hair in his fist. He was jamming the pistol he
had just used to shoot my wife into the side of Katie's head. She was ten at
the time. He opened his mouth to begin what he probably figured would
be one of those witty conversations you see in movies. I wasn't interested
in what he had to say, so when he opened his mouth a little more, I put
two rounds in it, which exploded on impact and blew the back of his
head into the wall. And now it's not about me not wanting to leave my
daughter alone for a minute. It's about a twelve-year-old girl who won't
use a public bathroom and takes our well-trained and dangerous bullmastiff, Roxy, with her when she goes into her own.*

"Yes, Mrs. Del Vecchio," Adam said out loud. "I understand. I do."

Adam wasn't sure she heard him. She was somewhere else. He wondered if she was in the past, wondering how it happened, in the future, playing out the good news and then the bad, or in the present when she continued, "And then I wonder. How could anyone live with that feeling all the time? How can I?"

"I'll find him. I'm good at finding people."

For the first time since her son had been taken away, the possibility of his return was real. The ambassador coughed a few times and got everyone's attention.

"I know the Peruvian police will want to brief Special Agent Palma, and we shouldn't keep Mrs. Del Vecchio any longer."

Which was a cue for Elizabeth Griffin to say with kindness, "Would you like to stay with me at my apartment, Mrs. Del Vecchio?"

"I'd rather stay in my own place. Maybe somebody will call."

"I think that is a good idea," Adam said as he handed her his card. "Any time. You can call me any time." She smiled weakly. "And I will call you so that you will know everything I do."

As Elizabeth escorted Gail to the door, it opened and a man entered. "Sorry I'm late." He looked at the Peruvian cops, waved, and strode to Adam. "I'm Richard Perrin. I'm in the CIA and I play well with others."

Adam smiled and shook his hand as Elizabeth and Gail exited. The Peruvian cops were back into doing man things: one stretched and rearranged his balls, and the other lit a big cigar.

Richard said, "Two men on a motorcycle?"

The Peruvian cigar smoker answered, "We believe there was a car or a van waiting. It's possible they made a mistake—they took the wrong child. There were three other foreign children in the park, children of ambassadors. And the son of a Coca-Cola executive."

Richard nodded. "That makes sense."

Adam said, "Only if there is a ransom demand. If there isn't, then they got the right kid."

"Then it could be political. Right now, we have an active APRA, FREDEMO is quiet, and MRTA is making some noise. Who do you like?"

"Who do I like?" Adam remembered the last major terrorist action—the 1997 Japanese embassy hostage crisis. Fourteen MRTA members occupied the Japanese ambassador's residence in Lima in December 1996, holding seventy-two hostages for more than four months. Finally, armed forces stormed the residence in April 1997, rescuing all but one of the remaining hostages and killing all of MRTA militants. "I don't like any of them," said Adam. "It also doesn't sound political. Two days. You haven't heard from anybody, right? No demands, no threats."

"Nothing."

"Any access to high-level documents? What did Mrs. Del Vecchio read in the course of her work?"

"She was assigned to the vice consul in charge of trade relations. The vice consul assists US companies in promoting trade and commerce in Peru. If you want to sell Chicago frozen pizza here, he'll tell you who to talk to. She's his secretary."

Adam looked at the Peruvian cops. They had gotten over their interest in being in the ambassador's suite, and they were bored. In terms of crime that was occurring in their city, the abduction of a ten-year-old boy was not high on their list of priorities.

Adam knew that what kept them there in the ambassador's office was a directive from a superior officer who had received a similar directive from someone close to a cabinet minister who was close to the president. On the other hand, what really concerned them was the presence of an American cop on their turf. If he solved the case, they would look bad, and if he didn't, he would just cause trouble along the way. Adam knew he wasn't going to make any friends and that the best they could do for him was let him tag along with a couple of detectives assigned to the case. If there was a ransom demand, they would want him to stay out of the way as they set up an exchange of money for the boy. There was also the possibility that the kidnappers were members of the police.

"And what about the boy? Any weird adults in his life? Teacher, soccer coach, neighborhood priest? Anybody want this kid for his good looks?" asked Adam.

"Not as far as we can see."

"So, no demands for money, prisoner trades, manifestos to be printed, and no child molesters."

"Well, what's next? What are you going to do?" asked the ambassador.

"Right now, we have to wait for the kidnappers to get in touch with her or contact the embassy," said Richard. "But they will. The reason they haven't is because they're making it up as they go along or they realize that they may have taken the wrong child. That's good because they will probably just let him go and he'll be home soon."

"And if they call her?" asked the ambassador.

"You call me and I'll deal with them," said Adam.

"You are aware of our official policy," said the ambassador. "We don't negotiate with terrorists."

"I do. I'll negotiate with anybody."

CHAPTER 13

AMAZON BASIN, IQUITOS, PERU

U nder the late afternoon sun, a Sikorsky UH-60 helicopter dropped out of the sky and settled down on a rough clearing in the Amazon jungle near the Colombian border. The heavy rotors blew a whirlwind of dirt into a grove of coconut palms that shaded a group of one-story buildings. The helicopter was painted jungle camouflage green. It was armed with four 70 mm rockets and two M134 miniguns on each side of the fuselage. Other than the two snarling bullmastiffs painted on its boom tails, there was nothing else to identify it. There was no International Civil Aviation Organization number. This twelve-million-dollar machine wasn't registered with any country's airline, aviation agency, or private individual. If it had ever landed at any airport, there was no record of its appearance. Its pilots never filed a flight plan or communicated with any air traffic controllers. Technically, it didn't exist. Its pilot, Reuven Weiskopf, received training at Andrews Air Force base in an exchange program with the Israeli Air Force. Upon completion of his training, he resigned his commission and went to work for Haliburton, ferrying contractors and US administrators to and from the Green Zone in Baghdad. He mastered evasion techniques, low-altitude flying, night runs, and became familiar with every defensive and offensive weapon on the company's helicopter. When he had gathered enough experience, he flew the machine to the deck of an oil tanker in the gulf, where it was spray-wrapped and lowered into an empty storage hold. When the ship docked at the port in Paita in northern Peru, it was unwrapped and flown by Reuven to a heavily guarded *estancias* where the helicopter's owner, Olivero Contrero, resided.

Olivero Contrero was a dog breeder, stamp collector, cattle rancher, and chief executive of the second largest drug cartel in Peru. He was forty-seven years old, and he kept houses in Colombia, Brazil, and Chile, all stocked with food, servants, and diplomatic passports. Today, on this visit to one of his cocaine labs in the middle of the Peruvian Amazon to meet with his Colombian counterpart, he was also a babysitter. His wife, Jessica, was in the middle of planning the wedding of their eldest daughter. She insisted on a quiet house—no video games, no yelling around the pool, and no drum practice, so she ordered Olivero to take their fourteen-year-old son for the day. "Get him out of my hair, or I will lose it." The threat was serious, and her husband quickly agreed. Olivero, though normally not a reflective man, often wondered at his capitulation to the wishes of his American-born wife. She had made it clear when he proposed to her that any notions he had of machismo in marriage would not be tolerated. He was deeply in love, had an MBA from Wharton, and vowed to reserve his toughness for dealing with business associates or threats within his own organization. Discreet and non-flamboyant, his reputation among his peers was secure. He was feared and respected. But, why, as he had asked himself many times before, did he so easily give in to this woman half his size? Perhaps because she was smart, gave him an honest opinion of everything he asked, knew his business, and was unfazed by the violence that surrounded it. "Olivero, my grandfather was in the Louis Lepke mob, he dumped more people in Kiamesha Lake than they will ever find. He took on the Italians *and* the Irish, and he was buried in Queens Beth Israel Cemetery with a loaded .38 revolver in his casket."

Ronaldo, their son, was a boy of extraordinary beauty. He had the best of each parent's features—his father's height and broad shoulders, black hair, and green eyes, his mother's sharply defined cheekbones, thin nose, and flawless complexion. There was almost a feminine beauty to his face. Had he let his hair grow any longer, been smaller and less muscular, or displayed any fear, he would have been bully bait.

Olivero had different levels of security, but the ones closest to him were former Israeli soldiers—they were intelligent, calm, and had no criminal connections, which made them less vulnerable to threats. They were well trained in firearms and hand-to-hand combat, but they were also judicious, with none of the sadistic qualities of many of the mercenaries on the market—men who had honed their skills in government death squads or genocidal campaigns. No Serbs, Chileans, or South Africans need apply.

Olivero needed protection, but he wanted efficiency—he didn't need an army. The Israelis also had no ambitions to take over his operation. Samson Scharff had given himself a vacation trekking and hiking through South America when he was discharged from the IDF. He was a student of Shotokan karate, and his plan was to travel around South America, then go to Los Angeles and train with Sensei Hidetaka Nishiyama. His present job—driving Ronaldo to and from school and taking him to karate class—was easy. Although, no one in his right mind would consider kidnapping Olivero Contrero's son, Samson drove a plain blue Toyota Camry that was customized for ultimate protection. It was armor-plated, with bulletproof glass, and coded voice commands.

The helicopter hovered a few feet above the ground. Samson jumped out, holding a 9 mm Uzi. In the cockpit, Reuven was poised for a swift liftoff if there was a problem. A man in tan fatigues came out of one of the buildings and walked toward Samson. They shook hands and exchanged a few words.

Samson turned back to the helicopter and gave a hand signal to Reuven. The helicopter lowered to the ground, and Reuven killed the engines.

Ronaldo and his father climbed down from the helicopter. The boy was carrying a ball. Olivero strode across the clearing and entered a wooden building with a thatched roof. Watching them go, Samson wondered about the state of Olivero's mind. Every entrance to a building could mask a potential assassin. Was it something you got over or did your heart skip a beat every time you crossed the threshold of a restaurant with your wife, entered a football stadium, pulled up to your son's school, or started your car. Were you fatalistic or just extremely cautious? Samson waited until Olivero and the man entered the building.

"Hey, you want to kick the ball? Or work on *tekki sandan?*"

Play football or practice *kata*, the formal exercise in which he faced imaginary opponents. It was the basis of all his karate training. Ronaldo glanced at the sun brushing the tops of the palm trees. In another half hour it would be dark.

"The ball now, the *kata* later. Okay?"

"Sure. Anything you say." Samson leaned the Uzi against the helicopter strut. Ronaldo tossed the black-and-white ball in the air and bounced it off his forehead. Samson stopped it with his chest and let it slide down his torso to his foot.

"Not bad, dude. Can you do that on the move?"

"Try me."

Samson dribbled the ball away from the helicopter to a clear patch of ground. At the same time, Ronaldo ran to a parallel position sixty feet away. Samson nodded and dribbled the ball downfield, then kicked the ball to Ronaldo who passed it back to Samson who eluded an invisible defender and deftly rolled it past an imaginary goalkeeper. Samson fell to his knees shouting, *"Viva Peru! Viva Peru!"*

"Okay, Ronaldo, a long one this time." Samson waited until the boy trotted to the other end of the landing strip.

"Ready?" Samson backed away from the ball so he could gather speed for a big kick.

"One minute."

Samson paused. Ronaldo's attention was somewhere else.

"Hey, dude, ball coming!"

But the boy was already walking toward the edge of the clearing and into the jungle.

Ronaldo felt the ground give beneath his feet, but it wasn't like walking in mud. It was like taking steps on a giant sponge that sucked him down and raised him up. There was something at his back pushing him, too. Not wind, but it didn't matter. He was light and knew that if he got enough speed he would lift off the ground and fly. The light on his face was dancing on his eyes and jerking him forward. Someone was yelling his name, but the sound dissolved into the screams of the macaws and monkeys. Unimportant. Words, shrieks, names, and a command: Walk, come closer. Closer. Now. The light was warm. The light was off. Then a cloth closed over his nose and mouth. For a moment, he tasted something sweet, and then there was nothing.

It occurred to Samson that Ronaldo was playing with him. He liked to hide, knowing his Dad's bodyguards went crazy when he did. The kid was probably behind a tree and would jump out and try to scare him.

"Ronaldo! Ronaldo!" He counted to five. One, two, three, four, five.

Fuck that. He tore out his phone and pressed the special button that sent a text: *"Ronaldo problema!"*

He grabbed his Uzi and crashed into the jungle. "Ronaldo! Where are you? Ronaldo!"

Something made him stop and pulled his gaze down to the

jungle floor. A shaft of sunlight wormed its way through a gap in the trees and reflected on a small round mirror. It shone brightly against the brown mud of the path. A circular mirror encased in tiny seashells. Behind him, Samson heard the sounds of footsteps. He knew it would be Olivero and the others. He also knew he had lost Ronaldo on his watch, and for that there would be an explanation, but not an excuse.

CHAPTER 14

LIMA, PERU

Adam walked out of the meeting in the ambassador's office feeling uncomfortable. If the kidnappers did make a mistake and abducted the wrong child, they might as easily kill the boy instead of releasing him. It would be less risky than having a witness who could identify them. The Lima police were efficient. They had informers and contacts. And if this were a low-level criminal act, they would eventually get wind of it. But would it be in time to save the boy's life? If it was a political act, then there would have to be some sort of demand and Adam could step in. What if it were none of those? Most kidnappings of Americans were corporate employees whose companies would pay the ransoms. It was a cost of doing business in South America.

American corporations turned to insurance companies who then hired local middlemen to negotiate the release of their clients. Soon the middlemen were helping the kidnappers arrange the abductions and splitting the ransom money. A whole new industry was born. Eventually, the insurance companies got smarter, insisted on a higher level of security, and started bringing in their own negotiators. They also restricted the movements of employees and constructed secure gated communities for their families. It worked for private companies, but it wasn't practical to build secure housing for all embassy families, especially in "friendly" countries. Embassy officials moved around less, and if they did, they were well protected. Diplomatic kidnappings were rare and those of children almost unheard of. Why would anyone kidnap the son of an embassy secretary in the commercial department? It didn't fit any of the categories and it didn't make any sense. But he remembered a couple.

"It was Daddy," the boy had said. "Daddy came to the party in his uniform, and I went with him."

But Daddy was dead. His plane had gone down three months earlier over a patch of the Caribbean. When traces of the wreckage were found, it was determined that a gas leak caused the plane to drop into the ocean. After a month, there was no body unless you could interview a whole bunch of sharks.

Everyone said the kid was crazy, but Adam didn't think so.

He wasn't crazy. It turned out Daddy had a boat waiting after he ditched the plane. His ex-wife had inherited millions in insurance money, and the only way Daddy could get his hands on it was to kidnap his own son. So before they could send the kid for therapy and ADHD medications, Adam believed him. Finding Daddy had been easy.

And then there was the time Adam traced kidnappers to a Nevada ghost town and his jeep broke down and he had to borrow a horse and ride into a deserted western town. It was like being in a cowboy movie. The kidnappers decided against a shoot-out and listened to reason. They all walked out together.

Adam realized he was lost. Where the hell was the elevator? Who designed the building and how could he get the hell out of there?

He saw an exit sign above a door, entered a stairwell, and descended a floor, then tried to open the door, but it was locked. He descended two more floors, found himself on what he assumed was the ground floor, and easily pushed open the door. He was in a dimly lit hallway. The walls were tiled plain white and had framed black-and-white reproductions of vintage photographs on them—the Grand Canyon, the Golden Gate Bridge, Niagara Falls, Zion, Hoover Dam, and Monument Valley—the same photos repeated themselves over and over again, and the repetition of the pictures provided no reference points to his location. The corridor itself was just wide enough for a golf cart and curved so there was no long view. The only noise was the soft hum of air conditioning. He came to an intersection where the corridor split. No signs, no directions. Which way? He was in a tunnel under the building—a long one, longer than the length of the building itself. It must be an escape route for embassy personnel.

Adam figured there were concealed doors that would open in emergencies and seal the occupants in "safe rooms" with food, weapons, and communications until help arrived. And probably an exit that would emerge onto an empty lot a few blocks from the embassy where a helicopter would be waiting to fly people out of the city. Safe rooms were mandatory in all embassies, but this tunnel was immense. He flipped open his phone and hit a speed dial. No service. Adam glanced at the ceiling. There were sprinkler spigots at regular intervals and air-conditioning vents and, even though he couldn't see them, he knew there must be surveillance cameras.

Adam remembered the bored Marine guards he had observed staring at television images on the banks of TV monitors. Surely, they were observing him. He stopped and looked up.

"Can someone help me? I seem to be lost."

Feeling foolish, he continued walking, expecting a golf cart to come speeding to his rescue. He came to another intersection of the tunnel. There was a difference in the quality of the light coming thorough the passageway on his left. A possible exit. He entered the corridor; the angles sharpened from the curved roll of the walls to ninety-degree turns. A right, a left, another right, the corridors were shorter; he could negotiate them in ten steps. Adam stopped. He heard footsteps. Where? Behind him, ahead of him? He retraced his path, stopped and listened—nothing but the faint sound of the air from the overhead vents. He retraced his steps and heard them again. Someone was in the corridor with him. What the hell was this? He was trapped in the intestines of some mad architect's design under the US Embassy. And then, as he came around one more corner, he saw a figure seated behind a table under a dim overhead lamp. Male, female, Adam couldn't tell, but he could see blue and red, it must be a Marine in dress uniform.

"Hey." Adam approached the desk. "I think I'm lost. Can you . . ."

The figure stood up. It wasn't a Marine. It was a huge barechested man, wearing a gold mask covering his face—a jaguar. Flat nose, pointed ears, mouth open in a frozen growl. The red Adam saw was the cloak around the man's shoulders; blue was the streak of war paint across his chest.

I'm insane or I am in the last moments of a costume party, but this bastard is holding a knife in one hand and a stone club in the other and I know for sure that he is going to try to kill me.

He instinctively swiped his palm edge to parry the knife and at the same time thrust his fist toward the man's throat.

The man was faster. He leaped over Adam and landed behind him.

I must have imagined that, but he is behind me, so I need to spin and draw my gun in one motion. But the fucker knewws what was coming, he swung his war club and knocked the gun out of Adam's hand.

Adam stepped in closer to block the arm that swung the war club, and still was able to parry the knife thrust. *I survived the club and a knife attack and this bastard is thinking what to do next.* The man surveyed Adam at a harmless distance. Then, like the jaguar on his face, he arched his back and hissed, "Pizarro dies."

Pizarro's dead. But not me. He's going to come now. Drop low and spring up into his balls. The man circled him, but Adam moved with him, waiting for the attack. *Follow with the eyes, let the eyes lead the body. But I'm dizzy. I'm losing focus, the guy in an animal mask is real, and he's going to kill me. My gun. Get the gun. I can see it. I can inch to it, dive for it, blow this thing away, but I can't feel my legs. . . .*

Adam opened his eyes and was looking up at a young Marine. Red and blue. Red piping on his blue tunic.

"Are you alright, sir?"

He tried to get up. Nothing worked. He started to shake.

"You want me call a medic, sir?"

"No. I'm okay." He felt for his gun. It was in his shoulder holster. He was supposed to be dead, but instead he smelled the Marine's aftershave.

"How did I land on the floor?"

"I didn't see it, but I'd say you slipped, sir."

The young Marine offered his hand. Adam ignored it and got to his feet.

"What is this place?"

"We call it study hall." He pointed to a pile of books on the small table. "I'm working on my MA. You want to get out? The exit's right there." He pushed a button under the desk and a door behind him swung open.

Adam stepped outside. The door shut solidly behind him. There was no lock, no handle or markings—just a thick metal plate in the concrete wall of the embassy building. Across the street, Geraldo sat in his taxicab. He rolled down his window.

"Taxi, señor?"

Adam opened the door and slid into the backseat.

"What are you doing here?"

"Señor, every once in a while, some kind of man goes in the front and comes out the back. I figured you for one of those guys. Where to? The Sheraton?"

Adam reached in his pocket and pulled out his notebook. "Calle Lorenzo."

"No problem." He put the car in gear and pulled out onto the highway.

Adam leaned forward in his seat. He could still see the man in the jaguar mask in his mind. Where the hell did that come from? "Geraldo, is there someplace we can stop and I can get a drink?"

"It won't be fancy, but you can get whatever you want."

The truck stop was a combination supermarket, restaurant and bar. Magazines, DVDs, CDs, candy, toilet articles, local food products, and strands of lottery tickets hung from a wall like ribbons. Tough men and tougher-looking women sat at the bar and sipped cups of maté, or downed shots of thick black coffee—whatever it would take to get them through the next stage of their trip back to Buenos Aires to the east, or Santiago to the south, or Quito to the north. There was a cafeteria with a long steam table, offering the staples of Peruvian cuisine: beef hearts on skewers, potatoes of every color from yellow to purple, broiled guinea pig, stews, Chinese food, and pizza.

Geraldo wandered off to check out the magazines while Adam found a place at the bar and ordered a shot of vodka, a jolt to clear his head. Was he experiencing the world from the left part of his brain, the dream part? He could be living the dream part and dreaming the living part. He knew an ex-con who told him that when he was in San Quentin, he used to dream that he was living a normal life on the outside. The dreams were chronological—the events followed one another in a regular time line. Every night, he went to sleep in his cell and dreamed a day in his life outside of the prison. In the dream, he had a family, a good job, a commute, even a shrink. And then he would wake up in the reality of San Quentin. Then he started having nightmares in his "outside" life that he was in San Quentin. Was Adam that man, living in two worlds?

He signaled the bartender. *"Otro vodka, por favor."*

But he knew the blood was real, his daughter's despair was real, and there was the possibility that they were crossing over, intersecting into a Möbius belt of a twisted reality that rolled downhill into unreality and back into reality.

He knew he had seen too much, suffered too much, and killed

too much. All he wanted, he realized, was to finish this job, bring home a kidnapped child to his mother, and go back to New Mexico to be with his daughter. They would garden together and tend their horses, and she would regain her strength, finish high school, and go to college. He wanted her life to follow the path that was laid out for her before her mother was killed.

Geraldo joined Adam at the bar.

"*¿Puedo comprarle una bebida? ¿Uno vodka?*"

"*No, gracias.* You ready, Boss?"

"I'm ready."

"Back to the Sheraton?"

Adam handed him a piece of paper. "First, take me here. And I'm going into one of those doors."

Geraldo laughed. "Sure. How long?"

"Fifty minutes. Time is money, right?"

"Always."

CHAPTER 15

SACSAYHUAMÁN, CUZCO

The Incas designed their capital city of Cuzco in the shape of a crouching puma. Where the puma's head would be, they built Sacsayhuamán, a giant fortress on a hill overlooking the city. The interior was a labyrinth of passageways, scores of rooms with multiple entrances, secret passages—all intended to confound any invader who might breach its walls. Once inside, the enemy could be isolated and attacked. Wide stairways provided access to the upper ramparts with convenient access to weapons and food storage areas. It had access to underground springs, and its defenders could survive and outlast a prolonged siege. The walls were jagged, like the teeth of the puma, but this configuration of jutting triangles was also a sophisticated method of defensive construction. Pockets of attackers would be driven into the crevices where concentrated fire—arrows, rocks, and spears—could be hurled down on them. The Spanish tore as much of it down as they could, but enough of the interior walls and rooms remained for it to be a tourist attraction.

Inside, the Spanish had removed the tapestries that covered the walls, pulled up the woven rugs covering the floors, the wood frames of the windows, the gold candle holders that lit the corridors, the fish tanks, the potted plants, the jade and amethyst chairs, the tables inlaid with precious stones and seashells. They stripped the divans and sleeping pallets of alpaca and llama furs; from the armories the rows of spears, war hammers, short bows and quivers of arrows, helmets, and jeweled suits of armor. They had taken everything of value, comfort, and art. What the Spanish couldn't melt, unravel, or pry away, they burned. The only thing Pizarro's conquistadors, with their armored horses and blessings from the Virgin Mary and Jesus Christ, couldn't destroy were the stones that made up the fortress of Sacsayhuamán.

The fortress overlooked an expanse of grass where Cuzco school-children played football, sharing the space with grazing llamas and tour buses. Tour guides barked facts and figures in a cacophony of competing languages from handheld microphones and bullhorns. They explained the history, construction, and wonders of the sacred fortress of Sacsayhuamán, always adding: "If you can't remember Sacsayhuamán, then remember 'sexy woman.'"

A group of Parisian couples and their children on a seventeen-day tour of Peru encircled their guide. Their boutique travel company promised an exploration of the "fascinating and fragile ecosystem of the Machu Picchu Cloud Forest," which would, ironically, contribute to its fragility. They would be given oxygen masks in high altitudes, a visit to a local shaman for a fortune-telling session, a French-speaking archaeologist to discuss the ruins, and an anthropologist versed in Inca history and culture. Native porters were provided to pitch tents, carry camping equipment, and haul purified water.

None of this was of much interest to Gabrielle and Vincent, two of the French teenagers who had something in common: They were bored beyond belief. They had no interest in the gold jewelry in the Museo Nacional de Antropología, Arqueología, e Historia del Perú, were indifferent to the marvels of Inca stonework, and were having trouble keeping the Mayans, the Incas, and the Aztecs straight in their minds. Their iPod earplugs never left their ears, and they giggled and flirted through dinners at Lima restaurants. The idea of visiting Machu Picchu held some interest for them, but that was another week away. During their time in Lima, their parents forbade them to go out on their own into the city or sample clubs and discos. They did have an interest in cocaine and were aware that cocoa was grown in Peru. Huge canvas sacks of the leaves were common enough in street markets. And in most restaurants, there was a ceramic bowl of washed cocoa leaves and a pot of hot water for tea. The teenagers drank it, but it was bitter and they didn't feel anything. Finally, one of the younger guides took them aside and explained that in order to get high from the cocoa leaves, you had to add an alkaloid—lime or potash—while you chewed the leaf. He promised to get them some on the trek to Machu Picchu. This appealed to the teenagers. They pictured themselves telling their friends in Paris that not only had they been to Machu Picchu, but they had gotten high on the same cocoa leaf that the Incas used.

The guide continued into his microphone, *"La forteresse servi de base pour la grande rébellion Inca contre les Espagnols en 1536. Il pouvait accueillir cinq mille troupes."* The sound of his words echoed off the walls of the fortress and melded into the same speech simultaneously being spoken on this day in English, Japanese, Spanish, and Mandarin.

Gabrielle and Vincent slipped backward into the crowd until they were only a few feet from one of the many entrances to the fortress. As Vincent led Gabrielle into this defiant and physical monument of the Inca Empire, he felt something of that power. He also felt a warm feeling in his crotch as he imagined himself alone with Gabrielle, kissing her while his hands raced over her body in search of an opening in a shirt, a skirt, a thong, anywhere he could touch bare skin. Dusty streaks of light filtered through the openings in the walls, and the amplified voices of the tour guides grew dimmer as they walked deeper into the deserted fortress. Their sneakers shuffled over packed dry earth. Occasionally, a tuft of grass or weed sprouted out of a corner, its life shortened by a wandering llama. The teenagers moved swiftly through the labyrinth of rooms and tunnels playing a game of tag and tease. "Catch me," Gabrielle said, but she let him kiss her first. They were in a small chamber with a natural stone bench against a wall on the upper level of the fortress. Through a round opening in the roof, they could see the cloudless blue sky. Vincent leaned forward and kissed Gabrielle on the lips. There was something different about this time. No resistance, no teasing, she was as hungry for him as he was for her. He placed his hand on her breast, and she didn't move it away. He reached down and under her blouse, and she adjusted her body to give him room to explore. Vincent took her hand and slowly led it down to his penis. He felt it harden under his jeans. She was stroking it now, outlining its shape. Should he unzip his fly or let her do it, he wondered as they both heard the noise. It sounded like a baby's cry. She pulled back from him and they both realized the room had suddenly grown dark as if a cloud had passed over the open hole above them, and for the first time they realized how creepy and scary the stone chamber was.

"Nothing," he said.

He pulled her to him. Start over. Gabrielle froze.

"Listen. I heard it again."

"I didn't." He moved his hand over her breast, but she pushed it away.

"We should go."

"Another few minutes." He touched her shoulder then danced his fingers up the side of her neck. She relaxed and brought her lips to his.

"Oh, shit!"

"What?"

"Look."

A baby llama, a *cria*, had wandered into the chamber. It looked up curiously at the teenagers. Then it made the baby sound that they heard. Gabrielle laughed and reached out to pet the animal.

Vincent stood up.

"Shoo!"

"Oh, it's so cute."

No, it's not cute. It's a smell cousin of a camel that's standing between me and your hand on my cock.

He stood up. "Go! Get out!"

The llama ignored him. This was its territory, and there was food and shade to be found here. Vincent stole a glance at Gabrielle to see how forceful he could be with the intruder. But the llama was no longer on her mind. She was staring at something on the ground. A bright object, a round mirror surrounded by pieces of seashell. She picked it up, and looked in it. She saw her face, the hole in the roof above her, the sunlight streaming in.

"Look, Vincent. Look what I've found."

"Give me a minute." He raised his hand to the llama.

"Out! Get out." The beast didn't move.

"Seriously, Vincent, look at this."

Christ, now I have to admire some piece of cheap jewelry. His cock rubbed pleasurably painfully against his jeans. He would give one fast appreciative look at the mirror she held and then get the llama out of the room so he could get back to playing with Gabrielle's lovely tits.

"Beautiful."

"But look closely. Do you think it's old? Maybe it's valuable?"

"It's worth what you can buy it for outside from the old ladies. About half a Euro."

He nudged the llama with his knee. The animal barely moved. Gabrielle was still engrossed in the mirror so she did not see Vincent plant a sharp kick into the llama's flank. It leaped back. Vincent got up and herded the frightened animal out of the chamber. Behind him, if he had turned around, he would have seen Gabrielle bathed in a bright burst of sunlight coming through the hole in the roof. Like an angel about to alight to the heavens, she stood on tiptoe, her arms raised, reaching up to the source of the light. In the corridor, Vincent swatted the rump of the little llama and watched as it trotted away. He was proud of himself; he had tamed the beast. He returned to the chamber. It was empty.

CHAPTER 16

LIMA, PERU

In an office in the Miraflores district, Adam sat facing a man in a three-piece suit reclining in an Eames chair reading a letter. Finished, the man leaned forward and handed it to Adam.

"I don't know Dr. Gradstein personally, but I am aware of his reputation. You are fortunate to have him as a psychiatrist."

He had a slight European accent. German, Austrian, Czech. No revealing diplomas on the walls, just a few delicate pen and water-color landscapes.

"Yes, I am."

"How can I help you?"

"I may be in Lima for a while. As Dr. Gradstein says in his letter, it is important for me to 'stay in touch' as it were, with someone when I feel I need to hear a professional opinion."

"On what, may I ask?"

"Whether or not I am insane."

The man laughed. "That's easy. You are not insane. Five hundred *nuevos soles*, please. Cash, and I do take American Express." He folded his hands in his lap. "Now, how would you like to spend the remaining forty-seven minutes of your session?"

"The people I work for don't tolerate psychological weakness. Ambiguity, doubt, or skepticism is suspect and cause for dismissal. I think I'm in trouble and I need a qualified person to listen discreetly."

"I'm listening. And I am qualified."

"I've been experiencing hallucinations."

"Plural. Tell me about one."

"I'm in the basement of the American embassy and I am attacked by an Inca warrior wearing a jaguar mask who says I am Pizarro."

The doctor nodded. "I see. Well, then I will retract my initial diagnosis. You *may be* insane. Shall we start at the beginning?"

Psychiatrists always wanted to start at the beginning. Well, Adam would sing for his meds if he had to, and maybe this guy would have something useful to say.

"I'm in the hostage removal business," began Adam. "I grew up in cold North Dakota prairie country where my ambition was to get as far away as possible. My mother's Spanish, and my father comes from Dutch stock. Holland didn't need Peace Corps volunteers, but Cuzco did. When I finished my two years, I became a cop in Minneapolis and went to law school at night. Graduated, got a job in Honolulu as an assistant US attorney, met my wife, we had a girl. When she was ten years old, my wife was murdered in front of her, and I killed the murderer. It's been two years. Neither of us has recovered."

The doctor cocked his head to the side and closed his eyes, as if he was rehearsing what he would say next, so that it would come out precisely.

"Can you tell me more about the hallucination in the embassy?"

"I figure I fainted and saw the Marine coming to help me as an Inca warrior who was coming to kill me."

"And why Pizarro?"

"I'm in Lima, I'm half-Spanish, and my mother's family is from Extremadura, which turns out to be the birthplace of Francisco Pizarro."

"More, please."

"I lived and worked for a few years in Cuzco in the Peace Corps. I speak Spanish and some Quechua."

The doctor nodded and smiled, "I see. Maybe not so insane. Do you know Ambrose Bierce's story 'An Occurrence at Owl Creek Bridge'? A Confederate soldier is captured and sentenced to hang as a spy. The noose is placed around his neck, the trap is sprung, and as he falls, the rope breaks. He escapes, makes his way back to his home where his wife and child are waiting. As he rushes to embrace them, he feels a pain in his throat, and then a blinding light and he dies—the rope never broke. Perhaps you fainted, and as you fell to the floor, the entire drama of the fight with the Inca warrior played out. The more relevant question might be why did you faint?"

Adam shrugged. "Jet lag?"

"Perhaps. And since you are in possession of a forged letter from a distinguished American psychotherapist, I will give you my two-cents analysis. But for a lot more than two cents. You are suffering from post-traumatic stress disorder that makes you hypersensitive to feelings of guilt. This, in turn, leads you to seek refuge in an alternate universe, which in this case mirrors your present environment. As you said, you are in Lima, you may be related to Pizarro, and it is perfectly appropriate that an Inca warrior in a jaguar mask punishes you for your or Pizarro's sins." And then, somewhat enigmatically, Adam thought, the doctor added, "The war is never over."

"Can you translate that into a prescription?"

"I think propranolol would be appropriate."

They parted with a handshake.

Geraldo opened the taxi door for Adam. He slid into the back-seat.

"Thanks. A quick stop at a pharmacy and then the Sheraton."

"Everything okay?"

"Almost everything. There were a couple of issues with my mother, but we got those out of the way pretty quickly."

Geraldo looked up into the rearview mirror.

"I travel a lot. Some guys need hookers. I need to talk to shrinks."
Geraldo nodded and pulled out into the street.

Adam entered the hotel and snaked his way through a wall of tourists and stacks of suitcases in the lobby. He looked at the haggard faces waiting to check in or settle their bills. In the elevator on a small television monitor, Wolf Blitzer mouthed questions to a senator while below them stock prices flowed across the screen.

Adam found a cold Andean beer in his mini-bar, for which he would pay nine dollars the next day. He used it to wash down the pill. He cleared the desk of invitations to the exercise room, spa, and restaurants, and then opened the envelope and slipped out photos of Jimmy Del Vecchio along with a police report. There was also a picture of Jimmy's father in his Army uniform, the one that the Army sent to the hometown newspapers along with Sergeant James Del Vecchio Sr.'s obituary.

Gail Del Vecchio didn't have to ask her husband's forgiveness for her failure to protect their child. Adam also knew how she was doing the "ifs," as he called it. If only I had only seen the motorcycle coming . . . if only I had not let go of Jimmy's hand . . . if only we didn't stop for ice cream . . . if only I found my keys . . . if, if, if, if. When Jimmy resisted holding his mother's hand because he was a Yankee who had gone two for three, if only Gail had said, "I ironed your name on the back of your uniform and a number on the front. You can still hold my hand." Adam had said to his wife, "If only I had gotten here faster." She shook her head. "You protected her when I couldn't." She said those words because it was the right thing to do and then she died—the blood still pouring out of her white throat.

CHAPTER 17

SACSAYHUANÁN, CUZCO, PERU

The sun was disappearing behind the walls of the fortress. The tour buses were long gone, replaced by Cuzco police cars and a Peruvian army truck. Flashlights blinked from the fortress as police and soldiers clambered over the walls. The tour guide had set out folding chairs for the four parents, but they were still pacing helplessly. Periodically, the mothers embraced, sobbing in each other's arms while their husbands smoked nervously. A policeman leading a dog walked over to Sergio Varela.

"Anything?"

"Not really, sir. The dog followed a scent to a hole in the roof. If someone took her, it must have been there, and then to a road behind the fort where they likely had a car waiting."

"Alright, send Pablo to see if he can make a print of the tire tracks and tell the rest of the men to return to the station. We're done here."

The policeman nodded, and Sergio walked toward the parents of the missing girl. The husband was a big man in his forties, with a prosperous paunch. He kept looking over his shoulder as if his daughter might suddenly appear. His wife was younger, attractive, with a schoolgirl's straight blonde hair brushing her shoulders. She was tiny compared to her husband, but she beat him to Sergio and faced him.

"Well?" she asked.

Sergio ignored the woman's rudeness. A terrified parent got a free pass.

"I can only tell you that a kidnapping is a rare crime in Cuzco. And I will be frank: Our city is dependent on tourism. This is something the police, the entire city administration, and the federal authorities will take very seriously as it affects our very existence. I expect a ransom demand shortly from the kidnappers, and we will pay it. And then when your daughter is safe in your arms, we will pursue these despicable criminals to the ends of the earth."

The father asked, "How will they know where to contact us?"

"Your daughter will tell them. Stay at your hotel; keep your phones on. There will be plainclothes officers in the hotel watching over you. This should be over soon. I am so sorry." Sergio turned to go, then stopped.

"One last thing, señora." He took a plastic bag out of his pocket and held it up to Gabrielle's mother. Inside the bag was the shell-encrusted mirror. "Does this belong to your daughter?"

"No."

"Could it be something she bought recently?"

"I know every piece of jewelry she owns. It's not hers."

CHAPTER 18

LIMA, PERU

Adam stepped out of the hotel. For the last three hours, he had placed telephone calls from his room. He made promises he couldn't keep, lied to his case manager in Washington, persuaded a woman at the State Department to call her friend at the CIA, and impersonated two different people. Eventually, he got what he wanted: an appointment. He shrugged off the moneychangers clutching thick wads of *nuevos soles*, and looked around for his abductors or potential killers. On the sidewalk, pickpockets were sizing up passing tourists. Adam picked out the skinny teenage boy in the Alianza Lima football jersey leaning against a parked taxi listening to his iPod, the tired commuter in a threadbare suit buried in his newspaper waiting for a bus, and a married couple standing at a juice bar nursing their cans of Inca Kolas. Adam sent them all a smile and shook his head in a clear "don't even think about fucking with me" message. And, each of them in their own way understood and retreated back into their role of football fan, commuter, and husband and wife. Adam crossed the street and headed towards the Plaza de Mayor. He chose a narrow, moonlit street, where his shadow bounced along the towering walls built by the Inca. He walked slowly, keeping to the middle of the street.

The car was punctual. It came straight at him, braking to a halt and pinning Adam in its high beams. It was impossible to see the make of the car or its occupants. Adam spread out his arms and opened his palms so they were visible and empty—no weapon. The car doors opened and two men got out.

"Keep your hands up and face the wall."

Adam felt the man's hands on his body frisking him.

"Turn around."

The other man waved a portable sensor over his body searching for transmitters.

"Cell phone?"

"Left it home."

Both men wore shirts and ties under their sports jackets. One jacket had leather elbow patches. If it wasn't for the black ski masks covering their faces, they could be members of a university faculty. Adam realized that they probably were. They spoke a flat Spanish with no traces of a Lima accent. They could have been from any South American country. Lima was seeded with revolutionaries holding forged passports, crusading journalists, exiles on paramilitary hit lists, and those who had experienced "enhanced" interrogation techniques.

The man on his left handed him a sleep mask.

"Put it on."

He guided Adam into the backseat of the car. The two men got in on both sides of him. Adam smelled Old Spice on his left and sweet pipe tobacco on his right. "Keep your hands clasped in your lap."

"Like in church."

"Yes, like in church. You know, I haven't been to see the priest in a long time. Perhaps, it will be your death that I confess to."

Adam let it go. This wasn't easy for anybody. These guys talked tough, but he knew they were wondering if they were being followed, observed, marked, and their own death was minutes away. It was part of the job. The driver turned up the volume on the car stereo. A tough heavy metal band doused the car. Adam said, "Charlie Parra, right?"

"We're impressed, but no more talk."

The driver turned it louder to make sure. They drove for an hour, over smooth paved streets, bumpy rutted roads, and then back on pavement. Adam knew they could be back to the same street where he was picked up.

The car stopped, the music ended, Adam felt their hands on his arms as he was led out of the car. A door slammed behind him, and he heard one of the men say, "One flight of steps, the rail is on your right." Adam guided himself down the stairs.

Another set of hands gripped him and turned him around.

"You can sit."

He felt for the chair behind him and sat.

"You can take off the mask."

For a moment, the single desk lamp facing Adam was blinding. When his eyes adjusted, he could see people facing him, but the direct light shining into his eyes reduced them to silhouettes. The glow of their inhaled cigarettes gave brief illumination to their faces, but not enough for him to recognize anyone.

A new voice said, "What do you think we could get for you, Palma?"

"A ransom? I'm flattered but probably not much. I'm about to retire. The Bureau would save money on my pension."

"Then a simple bullet in the head."

"Bullets are never simple. I'm just here to talk."

"Then begin."

"An American child was kidnapped. His mother is a low-level State Department employee, and my government is now involved. There's been no communication, and no political or monetary demands have been made. Anybody want to take credit? Make a deal?"

A different voice came out of the dark. "We know your deals. You come back."

"Not this time. I only want the child."

At the same time, on the street above the basement, a half-ton Peruvian army truck and a squad of Lima police in two Humvees turned off their engines and coasted noiselessly into position. Army Special Forces in combat gear leaped out of the truck and took up positions around the square. Police K-9 units clambered out of the Humvees, the dogs muzzled so they couldn't bark. The few pedestrians on the street slipped away as fast as they could. In the modest apartment buildings surrounding the square, lights were extinguished, window shutters closed, and iron grates were lowered. Within moments, the area was deserted and silent.

In the basement, a figure rose out of the group and walked to Adam. He could see bright red lipstick through the opening in her ski mask. She adjusted the light aiming it away from his face, out of his eyes.

"We're revolutionaries."

She had a gentle voice. A mother, of course. She was whom he'd come to see. "We don't kidnap children. It's what criminals do. It's reprehensible."

"I agree and I'm happy to hear that," replied Adam. "I just want the boy back with his mother. I need you to help. It's in your interest."

"Our interest?"

"I can give you something for your . . . help."

A man in the rear of the group stood. He was in his forties, burly, wearing a cap and a leather jacket.

"What do you have to offer beside this silly threat from a government that is more afraid of us than we are of it?"

"I can give you the name of someone in this room who is working for Peruvian State Security."

"You have proof?"

Adam reached into his jacket pocket, took out a packet of papers, and handed them to the woman at the table. She laid them out on the table, and two men joined her in examining them. The woman turned to the group. "Jaime?" A young man in the group stood up and pushed his way toward the door, but he was immediately wrestled to the ground.

"Get him out of here."

"As I said, I only want the boy returned," said Adam.

In the basement room, the ceiling lights began to blink on and off.

There was no panic, but the faceless figures moved quickly toward different exits. The man in the black leather jacket approached Adam. At the same time he felt the barrel of a gun against the back of his neck.

"Put the gun down, Léon. We always suspected Jaime." Another man gestured to the blinking lights. "This is his work."

"What do we do with him?"

"I'll take him."

The man with the gun slipped away.

"My name is Victor," the other man said as he reached into his small backpack and took out a flashlight. "Follow me."

The tunnel was once part of an Inca water system that, like everything else in the city, had been corrupted, abused, or dismantled by the Spanish. The murky trickle of water at its base quenched the thirst of rats and nothing else. It was a labyrinth of interconnecting passages. Rotted beams barely supported crumbling walls where the Spanish had pried loose stones in a vain attempt to find treasure—the result of torturing an Inca priest until he told them where gold was buried. They didn't find any, two soldiers drowned, and the Inca priest died knowing that he had sent the Spaniards on a futile mission.

"Do the police know about these tunnels?" Adam asked.

"Of course," said Victor. "But they have lost too many men chasing us down here. They prefer to wait on the street for us to emerge."

"And how will it be different this time?"

"It may not be. It's better if we split up. You don't want to be around if they catch us both."

"I could make a case."

"It wouldn't work. I'd be shot trying to escape. And I wouldn't put it past them to shoot you, too. They don't like coming into the tunnels. Just keep going, and don't try to figure out where. The dogs make noise, but they can't smell much down here. You'll come out somewhere. Good luck. If I hear anything about your kidnappers, I'll get in touch with you."

He tossed the flashlight to Adam and disappeared into another tunnel. The barking of the dogs grew louder.

Adam had no idea where he was going. At one point, he sensed Victor ahead of him, but he didn't call out. The sound of tramping boots splashing through the puddles gave no clue to the location of the pursuing soldiers. He realized he could turn a corner and bump into them. Then he heard the shots. They were rapid fire—bursts from an M16. Adam kept moving, shining the flashlight to the ceiling at intervals looking for a ladder, a manhole cover—a way out.

To his right, he saw a tangle of thick wooden beams. Adam leaned into the web of four by fours and aimed his flashlight. There was a small door along the floor. He would have to squeeze through the tangle of beams; it would be like crawling through a giant's game of pick up sticks. A dull thud of an explosion resounded through the tunnels. The acrid aroma of the CS gas reached him almost immediately. In a minute or two, the chemical would react with moisture on his skin and in his eyes, causing a burning sensation, and he would be forced to close his eyes. He would be disoriented, dizzy, and gasping for air. He reached out and pushed at the door. To his surprise, it opened easily, and he fell into darkness. He was lying on a cold and dry stone floor. He swung the flashlight around him. He was in an empty room. A rat glanced at him and scurried out of the light. The rodent was a good sign; if it got in, there had to be a way out. He listened to the thudding of boots passing by. He was safe for the moment. He looked at the walls again. Where was the exit? He shifted his position. He was sitting on it—a narrow trapdoor. He lifted it and peered down. The room below was eerily lit with shafts of light coming through barred windows. Adam squeezed through the door and fell the remaining few feet to the floor. The walls were covered with painted images of animals, warriors, and Inca gods. There were piles of artifacts—Spanish and Inca. Conquistador helmets, rusted iron swords and lances, Inca war clubs, and a pile of dusty human bones. The room was part armory, museum, sarcophagus, and junk pile.

An open archway led to a stairwell. A light from above illuminated the stone steps. Adam switched off the light and began to climb the stairs. Suddenly, there was a noise—a clanging of bells. The clangs were random: a trio of beats, a pause, then another, then two, then one, then two more as if the bell ringer was distracted by something else. Another sound was added to the clanging—the neighing of a horse.

At the top of the stairs, Adam opened another door and entered an empty chamber. The air was cooler. He was getting close to an exit that would lead him outside. A few more feet and the tunnel led into another chamber. This one was furnished, but sparsely—a few wooden chairs around a long, heavy table. Red velvet drapes covered the walls. The sound of the bells grew louder, and the horse's neighing created a crazy counterpoint to the bells. Adam parted the drapes and found a door. He opened it. He was in the nave of a cavernous Catholic church. The only light was from the flickering candles on the altar and the faint illumination of the stained-glass windows of the church. Around him were statues of Spanish saints, martyred prelates of old, their faded and peeling paint aging them even further. Gated private chapels of the rich lined the walls.

On the altar, the sacramental objects were ready for the next mass. A gold chalice stood next to an arrangement of flowers; there was a silver ciborium for the host, and a holy water pot and sprinkler. There were no worshipers or clergy in sight. The church was empty. Above him, the ceiling towered into darkness. And then the noise—the clanging of bells and the slap of leather against leather. Thick carpet cushioned the stone floor. A scream; Adam froze. A bird flapped its wings furiously bouncing against the beams overhead trying to find an exit.

Adam followed the manic flight of the bird. It finally landed on the head of a life-size statue of a conquistador astride a very real-looking horse. Adam realized it was the result of a taxidermist's work. The conquistador was in full armor, and a large crucifix lay across his saddle. The sculptor placed statues of two Inca soldiers kneeling at the feet of the horse looking up in reverence at the Spanish warrior, who was now their acknowledged lord and master. The sign on the base of the statue read:

Francisco Pizarro ca. 1476–1541

Pizarro sat ramrod tall on a leather saddle facing straight ahead, indifferent to the Incas at his feet, as if he had more important business before him. Though fairly crude in execution, the artist had captured the essence of the conquistador—his monumental satisfaction in being Spanish, Christian, and a conqueror. Adam imagined an Inca soldier facing this huge and strange animal, hearing the clanging noise that had startled Adam multiplied on the plains of Cajamarca by two hundred, the sun reflected on the long, slender, and deadly spears aimed at his heart. No one in the Southern Hemisphere had ever seen anything like this. If he had been that Inca soldier, he knew he would have had to summon up a degree of extraordinary courage to not drop his stone war club and run like hell.

Adam reached out and touched a flap of the armor. It fell to the floor. Tin. The bird screeched, startling Adam as it flapped away. He blinked in a sudden glare. Light was now pouring through the stained-glass windows. Daylight? Had he been in the tunnels all night? He looked at his watch, it was a little before six. Where did he lose the time?

Adam rubbed his eyes, turned from the statue, and raced down the church aisle. He flung open the heavy wooden doors and stepped out onto the steps of the *la catedral*, Lima's oldest Catholic church. Despite the morning sun, he shivered as he crossed the street and entered a café. Painted on the walls were four menus with the flags of France, Germany, Great Britain, and China. Adam ordered bacon and eggs, orange juice, and coffee. As the waitress put the coffee mug in front of him, his phone buzzed. Adam listened for a moment, stood up, and placed some bills on the table. He had another appointment. He was a popular guy.

CHAPTER 19

CUZCO, PERU

Nina took the phone call in her van on the way to her mother's house. The face of the screen read "Dr. Molina, Pathologist."

"Lotte, I'm driving. Let me pull over." She tossed the phone in her lap and pulled into a McDonald's parking lot. "Are you calling about the autopsy?" she asked.

"Yes. Detective Varela asked me to do it. Nina, I don't know what to make of it."

"I warned you. It's sick."

"I agree. But before I call him, there's something I want to discuss with you. Something very strange about this boy—"

Nina interrupted. "He was murdered so it would look like an Inca sacrifice. That's strange enough."

"It's more complicated," said Lotte. "There were grains in his stomach. It was a recent meal. He died before he had a chance to digest them. I sent some samples to the botany department. It turns out they don't exist. Or, they don't anymore."

"Lotte, I'm not following you."

"The grains. They're extinct. And there's more. The boy has no medicine in his body. No antibiotics, no vaccinations, nothing over the counter. He never took an aspirin or had dental work."

"And the red paint on his mouth?"

"Some kind of hallucinogenic. Fucked up my rats."

"Ayahuasca?"

"Probably. I plan to do more tests."

"Thanks. Will you send me the autopsy report?"

"No problem."

Nina reached for the ignition and paused, realizing she was in no condition to drive. She wondered about the boy and what had happened to him. She had held fast to the notion that he was murdered in a demented imitation of an Inca sacrifice. Now she wasn't sure it was an imitation.

CHAPTER 20

LA ROSA NÁUTICA, LIMA

It was a cold winter morning in June as Adam's taxi pulled into the parking lot of La Rosa Náutica, supposedly the best seafood restaurant in Lima. It sat at the end of a pier that stretched a quarter of a mile out into the Pacific. Getting out of the taxi, Adam felt as if he were in a prison. The lot was surrounded by a high fence topped with coils of barbed wire, and there was a guard tower with two men behind .50 caliber machine guns keeping watch so people could enjoy their *ceviche* in safety.

It was off-season, so most of the amusement booths along the pier were closed. Adam liked the empty quiet as he walked on weathered wooden planks of the pier, the waves smacking against the pylons below. Gray seabirds were skydiving for fish, but business was bad all around. No fish, no customers. Adam walked past the closed up candy stall and the ring tosses, then stopped at a silent merry-go-round. The animals were suspended in time on their brass poles at different heights—all beautifully painted in bright colors. Llamas, horses, a swan, a goose, and a space car from the Jetsons. That would have been Katie's choice. Adam made a promise to himself to tell her about it when he got home. Home. What was a home for a child? A place to feel safe. The house in Taos had thick walls; a savvy live-in nanny, Maria; and Roxy, Katie's bullmastiff that weighed more than Katie did and knew in one sniff if you were a friend or not. Katie was safe. She just didn't have a mother. Adam saw the restaurant ahead. It was time to turn to business. La Rosa Náutica was popular with well-heeled tourists coming down from a trek through the Inca trail or a visit to Machu Picchu. All the tables had a view of the Pacific. He could see waiters and busboys inside, setting their tables in anticipation of a busy lunch.

Hanging on the entrance door was a *cerrado* sign. A maître d' opened the door for Adam and ushered him to a table in the empty restaurant. He snapped his fingers and a moment later, a waiter placed a pot of coffee and two cups on the table. The waiter poured a cup for Adam and moved away. Adam looked around for his guest—or his host.

Two men in business suits entered the restaurant and took seats at a nearby table. They glanced at Adam then pushed aside the table settings in front of them and each placed automatic pistols in place of the plates and silver. One by one, the waiters and busboys abandoned their work and drifted into the kitchen. Another two men in suits emerged from the kitchen. One went to the front door; the other kept his gaze on the kitchen. The man at the door spoke quietly into a cell phone.

Adam sipped his coffee. Five men, all armed, but so far none of them had frisked him. They knew who he was. He had an appointment.

The windows of the restaurant shook as a Cobra helicopter hovered a few feet above the dance floor outside the restaurant. Two snarling bulldogs were painted on its boom tails. A ladder was lowered out of the door and a man in combat fatigues carrying an M16 rifle leaped out. He surveyed the empty pier, then turned back to the helicopter door and waited. A moment later, a tall man in a leather flight jacket, ignoring the outstretched hand of the bodyguard, jumped to the floor of the pier. He ducked under the rotor blades, and the helicopter rose above the roof of the restaurant.

Under the flight jacket, the man wore a yellow Polo shirt, tan slacks, and mahogany loafers. To Adam, Olivero Cortero looked more like a prep school teacher than a major narco-trafficker. He walked to Adam's table, sat down, and, without a word, poured himself a cup of coffee. His face was tired, grieved. He fumbled for a pack of cigarettes, offered one to Adam.

"No thanks."

"I appreciate you coming."

"It was a free cup of coffee."

"Would you like something to eat?"

Adam shook his head. Cortero reached into his jacket and handed Adam a photograph of a teenage boy in a white karate *gi*, his fists raised in a fighting position.

"My son. He was kidnapped. I want you to find him."

"You know I work for the US government."

"When executives are kidnapped, you rescue them. You arrange ransoms for their release. You take revenge."

Adam shrugged. Not a yes, not a no.

"I'm sorry. American citizens only."

"Someone has kidnapped him. Who would do this to me?"

"An enemy. A fool."

"I will make any deal you want."

"I can't help you. My advice is to pay whatever they ask. I'm sure you will arrange the revenge."

Adam stood up. The bodyguards shifted their attention slightly.

"Thanks for the coffee."

"There hasn't been a ransom demand. It's twenty-four hours—no communication."

"None?"

Cortero took a black velvet bag out of his inside blazer pocket. He emptied it out on the table—a round mirror with a ring of seashells around it.

"This was found on the ground where he was taken."

Adam sat back down.

CHAPTER 21

LIMA, PERU

Mid-week, during school hours, the Little League Baseball diamond in Lima's Parque Central was empty. Adam squeezed through the metal gate and walked to the pitcher's mound. He picked up some dirt, rubbed it in his fingers, focused on the imaginary batter, and decided to see if he could throw an inside fastball. Put some fear into the batter. A voice called out from the bleachers.

"You play Little League when you were a kid, Special Agent Palma?"

Dobbs. He vaulted over the fence. Dobbs was in good shape, and he took a stance in the batter's box.

"We didn't have Little League. We had 'you bring the ball, I have a bat, and your history notebook is home plate.'"

"Yeah, small-town shit. Let's see what you got."

Adam smiled. He liked Dobbs. He went into a full windup and whipped the imaginary ball. Dobbs swung his imaginary bat.

"Christ, I never saw it." He walked out to the mound. "You were a federal prosecutor before you joined the FBI, correct?"

"I was a lot of things. I was in the Peace Corps, I drove a cab,

I was a failed painter, a cop, and even a father." And now an Inca warrior in a gold jaguar mask had just beat the shit out of him, and he was hearing voices. He could go to Washington and mention half of what he felt and feared to a Bureau shrink and he would get his pension on the way out the door, or he could stay here and find Nina and ask her one more time—or three more times—to come back to New Mexico with him. That idea was pretty crazy, but Dobbs didn't know her, and, oh, yes, he had promised a mother that he would find her little boy who was kidnapped.

"Did you hear what I said, sir?"

"Have you come to get me, again?"

"There has been another kidnapping. In Cuzco."

"I'm sorry to hear that. Tell me why this one is my business."

"Fourteen-year-old girl. Her father is French, but the mother's an American citizen. She was on a tour with her parents. Took her out of an Inca ruin outside the city called sac . . . sac . . . something."

"Sacsayhuamán. Think sexy woman."

"Thanks. We're pretty sure it's the same group. No ransom demands. What's going on?"

"Chaos, Dobbs. Chaos."

They walked back to Dobbs's car in silence.

CHAPTER 22

CUZCO, PERU

Cuzco airport was bustling with tourists. Adam dodged backpackers and Peruvian soldiers carrying M16 rifles. It hit him just as he emerged out of the terminal and on to the curb. He felt exhausted and his head was throbbing. The air. Now he remembered—Cuzco was 11,000 feet above sea level, the Matterhorn was only fifteen hundred feet higher. He knew it would be a few days before he became acclimated to the altitude. But the air itself smelled toxic and felt grainy in his mouth, like a fine sandstorm. He realized he was breathing ashes from the Amazon fires. The man on his flight to Lima was right. Around him, some people were wearing gauze masks over their mouths.

"Señor Palma?" He turned to his left, a trim man in pressed jeans and a collarless leather jacket was approaching, a smile on his face. "I'm Detective Sergio Varela. Welcome to Cuzco."

They shook hands as a police car pulled up. A uniformed cop flipped the trunk and took Adam's bag and tossed it in.

"You don't look well," said Sergio.

"I'm not used to the altitude."

"It takes a while. But I can give you something that will help."

"Cocoa tea?" Adam asked.

"Valium. It works faster."

They got in the car. As they pulled away, Sergio reached into the glove compartment and brought out a vial of pills. He passed them back to Adam.

"Some water?" asked Adam.

"Sorry," replied Sergio as he handed Adam a small plastic bottle of water.

"First time in Cuzco, Mr. Palma?"

Adam studied Sergio's face. The man was either a liar or dumb. He decided to go with the former.

"If you don't know how many times I've been here, you're not qualified to work with me."

Sergio laughed. "Very good. Twice. You were a volunteer here in the Peace Corps, and I believe you came back six months later to propose marriage to the medical student you left behind."

"The last bit is personal, and not in any dossier."

"I know Nina. She's a friend."

"I see. And do you know our history?"

Sergio shrugged. "Not much."

Adam wondered what "friend" meant in Cuzco. He'd better tread lightly.

"She does some forensic work for the department. Does she know you're here?"

Adam shook his head.

"I'm sure she will be pleased."

Pleased? Is she married? Children? Not a word in twelve years. Come on Sergio. Some news.

"She is still beautiful."

You read minds, Detective. Now business. Work.

"What can you tell me about this kidnapping?" Adam asked.

"The girl simply disappeared," replied Sergio. "She and a boyfriend slipped away from their tour group and went into the fortress. He left her alone in one of the chambers for a minute, and when he returned, she was gone. We searched the grounds with a canine unit, but there was no trace of her. Everyone insists she had no reason to run off. She was happy—no family problems. We're considering it a kidnapping. So far, there have been no ransom demands."

No demands, Adam thought. This makes three. The American boy in Lima, Olivero's kid in the jungle, and now the French girl. If the abductors didn't want anything for the children, then why did they want them at all?

Sergio and Adam continued to talk about other things. Police-work, wars—the one on drugs, the one on terror, and the changes to the city since he had left. Nothing profound, but it passed the time until they arrived at the fortress.

Sergio's driver took the car across the lawn right up to the fortress. There were still some policemen milling about, guarding the crime scene, but they were more interested in keeping warm and fighting off boredom. Adam's arrival was welcome. The men hoped it was a prelude to being sent home. Adam and Sergio followed one of the policemen inside. He led them through the narrow passage-ways to a small chamber where another officer was waiting.

"This was the last place the girl was seen."

In the room, Adam noted the opening in a wall just a few feet above the hard dirt floor.

"We assume there were two kidnappers," said Sergio.

"One follows her in the room," said Adam, "knocks her out, then with help from the second, lifts her up through the opening."

"Obviously."

Adam climbed up on a stone bench jutting out and peered out-side. There was a muddy track. Useless for tire markings.

"And a vehicle waiting," said Adam.

"Obviously."

"The kidnappers left something behind, correct?" asked Adam.

Sergio smiled and reached into his jacket pocket and produced a plastic bag. Inside was a shell-encrusted mirror.

"You've seen it before?

"It's the calling card they leave behind. I already have two."

"So we have a serial kidnapper?" asked Sergio.

"Obviously."

CHAPTER 23

CUZCO, PERU

Adam fought to stay awake on the drive back to Cuzco. Sergio took a couple of calls but spoke quietly, not wishing to disturb him. Adam wondered if he had met Sergio before but wasn't remembering him. He said he was a friend of Nina's. They were both cops, he had a kidnapping that seemed to be linked to Adam's, and they knew the same woman. Big deal. Cuzco was a small city; people knew each other. The question was, how well. And why was it a question? Ah, this was too much on top of the jet travel, a couple of Sergio's Valiums, a parent's grief as well as his own, all too much. He opened his window for a burst of cold air and immediately felt better. His phone buzzed in his pocket. A picture of his daughter appeared on the face.

"Hey, Bunny, how are you?"

"Daddy, I miss you. I watch happy families on the sitcoms and they suck, but I still want one."

"When did you start watching television?"

"My shrink said I should. She thinks it would put me in touch with normal people. I saw one where two guys are raising a boy. I can't figure out the reason why, but it's funny. I don't think they're gay, though."

"I'm in Cuzco."

"Didn't you used to live there?"

"I helped build a school."

"Are you chasing bad guys? Are you rescuing fair maidens? Are you slaying dragons and chasing alien creatures? Are you breaking all your promises to me? Fuck you, Daddy."

The phone went dead. He turned to Sergio.

"My daughter."

Later in his hotel room, he spoke to her for an hour. Her therapist said she was afraid of everything and everyone except her father, and when she needed to feel brave and tough, she took it out on him, and it was a good sign. And, then at some point, when her anger abated and she was feeling less afraid, he got around to the truth about what he was doing.

He told her that children were disappearing, and it was a mystery. He told her about the parents: Olivero, Gail, and now the French father and mother.

"I think that's the worst thing that can happen to a parent—losing your child." Katie said.

"Yes."

"But it's pretty bad to see your mother killed in front of you, which is why I'm fucked up."

"They say fucked up is temporary, Bunny."

"I've heard that."

There was a pause, a space, where he had learned not to jump into, or argue about what she was feeling. In a moment, she filled it.

"Daddy, do everything you can to return. What are the dogs like in Peru? I'm getting sleepy, but I want to hear more about the mirrors. Do you have one?"

"Why did the chicken cross the basketball court?"

"It must have something to do with fouls. I know. He heard the referee calling fowls."

"Smart kid."

He put the phone down and drew the curtains.

The phone rang.

"It's Varela. I'm at the bar."

The bartender was pouring a second Johnny Walker Red for Sergio and, to save him the trouble, Adam asked for the same on the rocks.

"You don't care for our famed Pisco sour?"

"Not much. To your health."

They drank and nodded for the bartender to refill their glasses.

"Do you know the novel *Sergeant Getulio*?"

Adam shook his head.

"It's about this badass cop. A sadistic, brutal bastard. His specialty was making a guy sit on a dresser, stuffing his balls in a drawer, shutting it and locking it, leaving him a knife, and then setting the house on fire. Badass."

"I get that part."

"Getulio is just a few weeks away from retirement and gets a last assignment to transport a prisoner to the capital city. It is dangerous. The prisoner is a guerilla. He's crafty. He has comrades who might try to rescue him. They have to walk, take buses, and finally a train. But somewhere along the way, Getulio realizes he's not delivering the prisoner. The prisoner is delivering him. Getulio's the one they're going to shoot when he gets to the capital. And what does he do? He completes the job."

"What are you telling me, Sergio? You have your balls in a drawer or you're a cop who doesn't give up."

"My balls are where I want them. But I'll find these kidnappers."

"Thanks for the drink. Lovely story."

He started to get up. But Adam realized he liked this guy, so he sat down again. The bartender refilled their glasses. Adam put some bills on the bar.

"On me, this time."

Eventually, they lost count of whose turn it was to pay for the next round, so Sergio asked for dice and they rolled for drinks. When they couldn't read the dots, the bartender called a police car for Sergio.

Adam and Sergio lurched out into the street and the breaking dawn. Sergio leaned against a telephone pole for support.

"You want to know about me and Nina, don't you?" asked Sergio.

"Your business," replied Adam. "Not mine."

"You know the word *lealtad*?"

"Loyalty. Like a Boy Scout."

"She is a woman of extraordinary loyalty—to her work, her coworkers, to her choices. She makes it and that's it. You, my friend, were a choice she made and unfortunately I arrived too late."

"Bullshit."

"Shall we duel for her?"

"Good idea."

Sergio reached behind his back and took out a small Beretta automatic.

"Shall we say twenty paces?"

"I left my gun upstairs in my room."

"You can borrow mine."

"Then you won't have one."

"Right."

"We'll do it without guns." He returned the Beretta to his belt and backed away from the pole. He turned his back to Adam and drew an imaginary pistol. "This belonged to my grandfather. Twenty paces."

Adam put his back against Sergio, who marched forward counting off the paces.

As he walked away, Adam turned and shot him in the back ten times.

When he reached twenty Sergio turned and raised his arm, aiming fingers at Adam.

"Sorry, dude, you're dead."

"I trusted you."

"Big mistake."

"Am I dying?"

"Yes."

Sergio collapsed on the sidewalk, clutching his chest.

"Tell me about you and Nina."

"She and I . . . she and I . . . I'm dead. You will never know. But you should call her."

Adam laughed and held out his hand. Sergio grabbed it and lurched to his feet.

"You okay with me being on this case?" asked Adam.

"Do I have a choice?" replied Sergio.

"No. But I'll defer to you."

"Yes. It's my country."

They shook hands, and Sergio got into the waiting police car.

"Get some sleep."

A wave of cold fresh air suddenly sobered Adam. He took out his phone and tapped a number.

Since it was someone he shouldn't call and it was five thirty in the morning, maybe he wasn't as sober as he thought. Before he could cancel, the call a voice came through.

"*Hola.*"

"It's Adam."

There was a pause, and if the connection was better he might have heard the sound of Nina drawing in her breath and holding it.

"After all this time," she said, "you assume that I am still living in the same place, without a man to look at me wondering who is calling me at five thirty in the morning, no one to tell 'Don't worry, darling, it's just an old boyfriend who hasn't called me in more than ten years. Don't worry, my sweet, I'll get rid of him. Probably here on a trek along the Inca trail and wants some sightseeing suggestions while he's in Cuzco.'"

"I made none of those assumptions. I'm just calling the only number I have."

"And it's early in the morning."

"I have no sense of time. In fact, six hours just disappeared."

"That's not my problem. I can't help you."

"You can. A pot of coffee."

"And where are you heading now?"

"A taxi stand."

"Are you going to tell the driver everything about us?"

"Except your name."

"Make sure you get out at the wrong house. I don't want him to know where I live."

"Is there a man?"

"No."

In the taxi, since he was still a little drunk, he did tell the driver everything.

"I was a Peace Corps volunteer."

"A worthy institution," said the driver.

"We built bridges between the peoples of the United States and the Andes," said Adam.

"Literally?"

"Not quite. I helped build a school and a medical clinic. It's where I fell in love."

"Am I taking you to see her?" asked the driver.

"I asked her to come to the United Sates with me, and she refused. And I refused to stay in Peru."

"So much for building bridges."

"We had our lives to live."

"And now?"

"I married. I had a child. My wife died."

"So you want her to love you again and take her back to where?" asked the cabbie.

"New Mexico."

"She will feel at home."

"Maybe."

"Go slowly with her."

"I will. Stop here. She doesn't want you to know where she lives."

Adam gave the driver a huge tip and waited until the car disappeared around the corner. The house was behind a thick wall, but the gate was left ajar. It was only a few steps to the open front door, and Adam didn't listen to the taxi driver's advice about going slowly. Nina stood a few stairs above him when she backed up to let the door swing open. Her robe separated, and they fell and fucked their way up to the first little landing where the floor was softer because of the rug. Her breasts were the same small size, and the nipples were pink, and her stomach still had that tiny roll an inch below her belly button, and she was embarrassed, but it was one of his favorite parts of her body. And he could smell the coffee as he came into her and stayed hard, and she came a few moments later as she said she would if he would just not move. Then they dragged themselves up the stairs, his pants at his ankles and her bathrobe trailing behind her. But they only made it to the next landing where, under the watchful gaze of the Blessed Virgin stashed in a wall alcove, his shoes tumbled down the stairs and his pants came off and she said "again" as she climbed on him, because he was still hard and satisfying and neither of them had made love with anyone like they were doing, no matter who they loved in the meantime, and they both knew it. And again he smelled the coffee, which is what they used to call medicine after making love in the morning.

Because it was a Sunday and neither had to be anywhere, they went into the bedroom and fell asleep next to each other. He woke up five hours later, alone, and there was music and movement in the kitchen.

"You cry in your sleep."

He shrugged.

"They are soft whimpers. Like a baby. And you talked, too."

"Did I give away any secrets?"

"Pizarro. You said, 'Pizarro.'"

"A distant relative."

"It's your guilty gringo conscience."

"I never met the man. The family connection is tenuous, at best."

"God doesn't split hairs. Pizarro destroyed a great civilization, murdered my people, and brought misery and death to an entire continent."

Nina grabbed Adam's hair and pulled him to her. "And you are a close second."

Somehow that seemed to be an invitation, and they made love again. This time, there was more love. He pressed his body to hers trying to imprint himself onto her and receive the same from her. He wanted to leave a mark, be dented, and have a living, breathing memory of Nina so that if he never saw her again, he would surely be able to close his eyes and feel her.

Later they stood side by side on her balcony terrace overlooking the city. The tiled roofs sprouted satellite dishes and pots of geraniums hung from windows. It was a quiet Sunday morning; people were in church.

"Where's our school?" asked Adam.

She took his hand and pointed out over the rooftops.

"Over there. It's doing well. You left something good behind."

"I suppose it's not all I . . ."

She cut him off. "What are you doing here?"

He would have liked to say that he had come to be in love with her again, to ask her again to come to America with him and introduce her to his daughter, Katie, and say, "This is Nina, and she will be living with us."

"I'm looking for children. One was kidnapped in Lima, another in Iquitos, and yesterday a teenage girl was taken from her parents here at Sacsayhuamán."

"Is this what you do now?"

"Yes."

"You find children."

"I find other people, too."

"And the rest of your life?"

"My wife was killed. I'm trying to raise my daughter who's twelve, and I swear this is my last job."

She nodded.

Adam said, "You?"

"I am a very busy archaeologist and professor. I have no personal life to speak of."

"Sergio?"

"Ah, Sergio. You have met."

"We are working together on this."

"Then you should know we see each other occasionally." Nina paused. "'See each other' means we sleep together."

Adam moved behind her and put his hands around her and reached under her bathrobe and caressed her breasts. He kissed her neck again and again, and he knew he could never get enough of her. She turned around and pushed away for distance.

"I don't think we love each other—I know I don't—and if Sergio does, he has never told me. But love isn't a requirement these days. Does that bother you?"

"Yes."

"Well, you aren't allowed to be bothered yet."

He told her the details of the kidnappings—that there were no ransom demands, which excluded criminals; no political demands, which excluded revolutionary groups; and how two of the abductions were by men on motorcycles, which somehow excluded random pedophiles. The other thing was that each time one of the children was taken, a jeweled mirror was left on the ground. He took one out of his pocket and handed it to her.

"This is what was left at the crime scenes. Do you know what it is?"

Nina let it sit in her palm, feeling its weight. She raised it to her face and caught her own reflection in the mirror. "It's Nazcan. From the south. The Nazcan were great astronomers. They placed these discs as markers on the earth to mirror the stars. It was a way of charting their movements. You see the reflection of the star in one part of the mirror; the next night, it's not there. Something moved—the earth, the star, a planet. Later on, there were more sophisticated methods, and the movements were recorded on a quipu, and these *espejos* became popular. My mother's generation used to carry them in their purses. They are trinkets now. But this is a good one."

CHAPTER 24

CUZCO, PERU

Quiso noticed that most of the citizens of Qosqo crossed the street at the corners. The ones who didn't risked a collision with carriages that neither slowed down nor made any attempt to avoid them. He was impressed by the bravery of the people who ran dodging and weaving from one side of the street to the other.

But the noisy carriages obeyed the man in the gray suit and cap who had chased him away yesterday. He wore white gloves and when he raised his fist, the vehicles stopped, and when he signaled them to proceed, they roared past him. At the intersection, Quiso waited with some others for the man to signal him and the others to cross. He lowered his eyes, walked by him unnoticed, and continued into the courtyard of the building where Manco's corpse was held.

The courtyard was empty. There were many openings in the building; the invisible walls, which the old lady called 'windows,' that did not allow you to pass through them. The door in the front had a chain through its handles and a large lock, so he knew it was useless to even try. He circled the building, peering into the ground-floor windows. The rooms were dark, but he could see tables covered with papers and strange devices. There weren't any beds, so they must be workshops of some kind. The old lady said the windows sometimes moved up and down. He tried one but he couldn't budge it. He tried the next, and the next, working his way along the wall. If he couldn't open one, he would find a rock and smash through it. The next one moved slightly. A thumb measure at most, but when he stuck his fingers in the opening and lifted, the window started to slide up. Slowly but surely, the opening expanded until it was large enough for him to squeeze inside. It was exhilarating and frightening at the same time. He was in the building where the Spanish stored their stolen bodies, Quiso prayed to Inti to give him the courage he needed to find his brother.

Nina pulled her car into the courtyard. She and Adam got out and walked to the front door of the morgue. Nina unlocked the door, and they walked into the reception room.

"It would be nice to have security, but we can't afford any. This way."

Adam followed her down a corridor and she unlocked another door. He smelled the pungent odors of a morgue: formaldehyde and pine soap.

"The light switch is over there. Would you mind?"

Adam hit a panel of switches and the overhead fluorescent bulbs sputtered to life. Morgues were the same the world over: shiny stainless steel tables, rows of tools—saws, probers, scalpels—ready to cut, pry, and saw open the body and reveal the causes of death: the knife entrances, the body blows, the bullet paths, the stopped hearts, the ruptured arteries, the organ failures—all done with no need for anesthesia. The pain had already been inflicted.

Nina opened the door of one of the refrigerated units on the wall and pulled out a drawer. Adam wheeled over one of the steel tables.

She lifted the wrapped bundle and placed it on the table and then pushed it back under the stronger lights.

She unzipped the body bag and revealed the dead boy. His smile was frozen in the red paint around his mouth, lipstick gone awry. Blood was coagulated around his chest where his heart had been torn out.

"Jesus. What am I looking at?" asked Adam.

"He's about ten or twelve. We unearthed him on a mountain, Salcantay. We were looking for Inca mummies on a burial site. We found two corpses. This is one. The other is an Inca girl. She was killed five hundred years ago."

Nina described in technical terms exactly how the boy had been killed. The hallucinogenic dulled his consciousness, then a quick blow with a stone hammer to the skull. She showed Adam where the boy's chest had been opened, the aorta severed, and the still-beating heart removed.

"The other child?"

"It was a perfectly preserved mummy—the victim of a five-hundred-year-old Inca sacrifice."

"And this one?"

"It was killed a few weeks ago. But done in exactly the same manner."

"So is there some sick Inca copycat killer?"

"I don't know. But they got it exactly right. And here's the craziest part—"

Adam interrupted, "Did anyone report this child missing?"

"No."

"Did the police check all the surrounding villages?"

"Yes, of course."

"Then no idea where he came from?"

"No."

"The crazy part?" asked Adam.

"A friend of mine did the autopsy," said Nina. "She said this boy had no traces of any medicines in his body. He never had an antibiotic, an aspirin, or cough medicine. No vaccinations, either. This is not impossible, but improbable."

"Doesn't sound crazy," said Adam. "I assume there are places in the highlands where there are no health services."

"He also had grains in his stomach that don't exist anymore," said Nina. "His body was wrapped in a way that would have ensured his preservation for another five hundred years. He was decorated with gold Inca trinkets. Real ones. He is, or was, an impossibly healthy Andean child. I could say he was Incan, but that is ridiculous—he didn't die five hundred years ago, but two weeks ago. Not to mention that he was carried to a mountain plateau twelve thousand feet high and buried in an Inca ceremonial site in exactly the same manner as the Inca mummy."

Quiso observed that the doors off the hallway all had windows. He peered in each one and could see that they were small, with only room for a chair, a table with books and papers, and a square box with a blank window. At last, he came to one that was larger and had shelves that contained boxes and crates. He tried the handle, but it was locked. He needed something to break the glass window. Then he saw the metal can standing against the wall of the hallway. He picked it up. There were smelly paper cups inside, but it had weight and would do. He lifted it and thrust it against the glass. It shattered, throwing shards of glass like a beehive exploding. He didn't feel anything, but when he touched his face, his fingers came away bloody. He reached through the open window, opened the door, and entered. There was a long table running down the center of the room and shelves on both sides all the way to the ceiling filled with pots and vessels, fabrics and feathered cloaks. Everything was familiar to him. He had seen objects like these before. He picked up a large cooking pot that was decorated with images of birds, warriors, and gods.

He held it in his hands, turning it, reading the story of the emperor Atuhualpa and his ascent to heaven after his death, accompanied by his servants, his llamas, his treasures, and his favorite wives.

Adam and Nina both heard the noise—a glass window shattering. Nina started for the door, but Adam held her back.

"I'll go. You wait here."

Nina shook her head and said, "It's my building."

Adam released her, and together they left the room. The noise of the breaking glass had come from the back of the building. Adam drew his gun but kept it hidden behind his back. He figured there was no point in surprising someone with an exposed weapon. Whoever was breaking into the building was probably a thief, and they were rarely armed.

The broken glass of the door was spread on the floor, and the door itself was open. The garbage can used to smash it lay on its side, spilling out refuse.

Nina came up to him. "Our storeroom."

Adam eased himself into the room. Steel shelves lined the walls filled with pottery, faded reed baskets, clubs, spears, and dried bones on trays. Everything was neatly labeled and tagged. A long table occupied the center of the room. On it was an old computer, baskets of labels, rolls of string and tape, and rolls of bubble wrap and brown paper.

Adam peered under the table. He returned his gun to its holster. "Tell him to come out," he said to Nina.

Nina bent down and looked under the table. A moment later, Quiso emerged, lips trembling. His eyes darted around the room looking for an exit, but Adam had already taken a position in front of the door. The boy was trapped.

"Where do you come from?" asked Nina.

Quiso remembered what he had sworn with his life, on the lives of the gods and his family; the oath that forbade him to ever reveal the answer to that question. What would he say to this woman who spoke his language? The big man who blocked the door wouldn't be as easy to escape as the man yesterday. The woman asked another question.

"What are you looking for in here?"

"I am looking for my brother."

"Why do you think your brother is in this building?" Nina asked.

"I know he is here. He came in the yellow wagon. He was taken from the mountain where he was buried."

"What is the name of the mountain?" asked Nina.

"*Sallqantay.*" said Quiso.

Nina turned to Adam and said, "He says he wants to see his brother. The boy they found on the mountain."

"Show him," said Adam.

"Come with us," said Nina. Quiso looked at the two Spanish people. Was this a trick? But the woman spoke his language, and the man wasn't angry that he had broken into the building. The elders had spoken about the treachery of the Spanish, how they had betrayed the Inca time and time again until the Inca rose up and fought to drive them out of the empire. These were old stories, and they told of a time long ago. Now Quiso was in their presence, in their city, in their building. He was fearful, but also curious. He doubted that they would return Manco to him. But once Quiso knew where Manco was hidden, he would have a better chance of finding a way to rescue him.

Quiso nodded to the Spanish woman and said that he would go with them. Adam and Nina shut the door behind him, and the three of them walked down the hall. The Spanish man was on his right, and Quiso knew that he was ready to grab him if he tried to escape.

Nina took out a ring of keys, unlocked the door, and they entered another room. Nina went to the wall and opened a shiny steel door. She nodded to Quiso to come closer as she pulled out a tray. A figure was wrapped in a blanket made of a material he had never seen.

"You will need to come closer," said Nina.

Quiso was not afraid. He had seen so much that was strange and evil in his short time among the Spanish that nothing could ever frighten him again.

He strode to the table. Nina unzipped the body bag and pulled back the bubble wrap that protected the body inside.

Quiso knew that his brother was dead. He had seen him die. That was a fact. He also had seen the Spanish take him out of the ground on the top of the mountain and bring him to this place in their truck.

Manco. His bronzed face was tranquil, unchanged since the moment the *ayahuasca* had been painted across his mouth. It had taken his fear and transformed it into euphoria, and then to a promised blaze of light so he didn't hear the stone hammer crack his skull or know that his body was dead. His soul could take flight and journey to the sun to see Inti. Quiso looked at the Spanish couple. They sensed something and moved away from him.

Quiso leaned in closer to Manco and whispered, "Speak to me, brother. The Spanish cannot hear."

"I don't want to be here," Manco said to his brother. "Take me to Sall-qantay and put me back in the sacred earth so my soul can find me when it returns from the gods. Will you do this for your brother, Quiso?"

"Yes," he whispered.

"If you do this I will come to you in your dreams and tell you the wonders of the gods and the palaces they live in and the amazing things I have seen. I will put visions in your dreams and let you ride the golden llama and sit astride the giant condor and you will see what I have seen. Do this. But hurry."

The Spanish woman was at Quiso's side.

"Is this your brother?"

"Yes. His name is Manco."

"And yours?"

"Quiso."

"My name is Nina, and the man over there is Adam. Where do you live, Quiso? Are you from the mountains?"

Quiso was silent.

"Do you know who killed your brother?"

"The priest," replied Quiso.

"What was the name of the priest?"

The Spanish man and woman were careless. They had left some knives on the table. It was easy for him, once she told him that he must wait to talk to someone else before they could let him go. Whatever their plans for him, he wasn't going to allow them to be in control of his freedom. He edged closer to the silver table against the wall and snatched two knives. They were thin and light, but he knew they were extremely sharp and would cause harm to anyone who came close. But they made no attempt to disarm him. They said things to each other that Quiso did not understand, but it was clear they were not going to try to prevent him from leaving. He turned and ran out of the room. In the hall, he found the open window and climbed out of the building into the courtyard.

He turned and saw the Spanish man and woman come out of the building. They were following him, but he was willing to take more chances than they were, and he dodged the noisy vehicles in the street, and soon he had left them behind. The image of Manco lying on the metal table drowned out the noise of the city and he heard his brother's voice. *"You were brave, my brother. Now you know where I am. Now you can rescue me."*

Quiso headed south toward the edge of the city closer to the foot of the mountains. The streets grew narrower and darker. Soon he was in a part of the city where the streets were unpaved, where there were tin-walled shacks and blue paper roofs that rustled in the wind. The children were poor and barefoot. He noticed some older people staring at him as he passed by, and once he thought he heard an old man call out to him in his own language, but he continued walking, wanting to put as much distance as he could between himself and the Spanish. He could see the peaks of the mountains rising over this city of shacks, but there was no straight line to get there. He had no way to navigate a straight line out, but as long as he could see the mountain peaks, he could make some progress. It was at a fountain where women were filling bottles with water that he noticed the man. He was not Spanish, he had a broad flat nose and black hair sticking out of his colored wool cap and, like Quiso, he wore a cloak over a rough blouse, leggings, and sandals. Out of the corner of his eye, he saw the man watch him as he bent under the faucet and drank the cold water. When he stood up the man was at his side.

He spoke Quiso's language even better than the Spanish woman. "You are not safe here, my son."

The man looked familiar. Had he met him once? Was he a citizen of his city who had also ended up in this strange place, lost like himself, with nowhere to go?

"I do not know you."

"No," said the man. "But I know who you are, and where you come from. I will take you to people who can help you find your way home."

"I won't leave without my brother."

"I understand. Come with me."

Quiso followed him through the streets and alleyways, deeper and deeper into the city of the poor, the jungle of shacks and huts. The sun was setting above them and there was less and less light. One or two of the huts had magical candles he had seen before in the streets of the other neighborhoods. These were small and flickered on and off and had no flame. The man seemed to know where he was going, and Quiso followed him obediently until he halted in front of a hut with a blue door.

An old man sat on a box at the side of the entrance. His white hair spilled out from his cap. He lifted his stick and barred their entrance. Quiso looked at his eyes and realized he was blind. The old man quickly stuck out his hand and pulled Quiso closer.

"Let me get a smell of you, my boy."

The blind man's fingers around Quiso's wrist were like a condor's claw. If he had wings, he could lift the boy into the air and fly away with him. He sniffed around Quiso's face, then grabbed his coat and smelled it, inhaling the scent as if it were perfume. He ran his fingers over Quiso's face as lightly as if they were brushed by the wind.

"Ah, my little Inca. You must come in and tell Titu how you came to Cuzco."

The blind man lowered his cane and motioned them inside. It felt like home. The walls were not the hardened clay and thatched roof of Quiso's house, but the wooden planks were solidly put together. Despite the flimsy appearance of the shack from the outside, it was strong and well constructed. The dirt floor was hard packed and covered by a thin layer of straw. Attached to the walls were intricate woven tapestries depicting hunting and harvesting scenes that were familiar to him. The room was lit by dozens of candles. A charcoal fire glowed in a corner where a woman was making quinoa cakes. She looked up at Quiso and smiled, offering him a plate.

"You must be hungry."

Quiso nodded and took the plate. His eyes adjusted to the dim light. There were two low platforms on the floor covered by animal hides and blankets. The woman whispered something to the old man.

The blind man said, "She says you are carrying a quipu."

"Yes."

"Will you come closer so I may read it?"

Quiso opened his serape. He felt the blind man's gnarled fingers come alive and nimbly dance up and down the series of knotted strings.

"I can't see the colors," said Titu, "but there is much here for me to understand. Why are you carrying this? Are you a messenger or did you take this from someone?"

"My father gave it to me when I left the city," said Quiso. "He said I would find someone who would understand its message."

The old man turned to the man who had found him. Quiso could see the sadness in Titu's face.

"It's happening again."

CHAPTER 25

CUZCO, PERU

At precisely 12:30 p.m., the doors of Saint Cecilia High School opened, allowing scores of teenage girls in white blouses and green plaid tartan skirts to burst into the bright sun.

Saturday was a half-day at this academy for the daughters of Cuzco's rich. Some students craned their necks searching for their parents in cars. Others sped off toward a bus stop, and a few, in pairs, headed home by foot. The rest dug out their cell phones, sent and received texts, made plans for the weekend, and got in a last few minutes of gossip before returning home for the family mid-day meal. In the street, like hungry lions circling a herd of antelope, male teenagers on motor scooters observed the girls and picked out their prey. Wedged in between a parked truck and a van, two motorcyclists on BMWs also watched the girls through the black visors of their helmets. One of the men nodded at the other as thirteen-year-old Elena Maldonado chatted with her friends on the steps of the school. Her black hair was parted in the middle and ringed with thick braids. Two white wires cascaded down from her ears into her iPhone. The motorcycles glided out into the street slowly. Their engines were muffled and hardly noticed in the traffic.

Elena faced the approaching motorcycles. One of the drivers held up a mirror, found the noon sun, and deflected the rays into her eyes. The girl rubbed her eyes as if to clear them of the intrusion. She shook her head, walked out into the street, and began to make her way calmly toward the waiting bikers. A car screeched on its brakes, narrowly missing her. She continued walking, transfixed on the light, ignoring the traffic around her. Elena sensed voices calling her name, and the shrill screams of teenage girls were muffled through her earphones. The motorcyclists gunned their engines and shot forward covering the fifty yards in seconds. They came to a screeching halt on each side of her. The rider on her left thrust a rag over her mouth; her knees weakened and she collapsed into the driver's outstretched arm. He lifted her limp body over the gas tank.

A school security guard appeared, holding his gun but not quite sure what to do with it. He pushed through the crowd of hysterical girls. But the motorcycles had disappeared around the corner. The guard holstered his gun and got on his phone.

The teenage boys had also seen the kidnapping. They kick-started their own motorbikes and scooters and roared off down the street after the motorcycles.

Adam and Nina were pulling into Cuzco police headquarters when six cops and Detective Varela dashed out of the building.

"We've got another kidnapping," said Sergio. "Come with me."

Adam and Nina followed him into his car. Sergio turned on his siren.

"A girl from Saint Cecilia's," he told them. "Two men on motorcycles just snatched her off the street as she was coming out of school."

"Where they are now?" asked Adam.

"They were last seen on Mercado."

The sounds of a helicopter engine roared above them.

"Isn't it kind of stupid for them to do this in broad daylight?" asked Nina.

"Not if they make it into the slums," said Sergio. "Or if they have a truck stashed somewhere that they can roll into or maybe an empty warehouse. But I think they miscalculated."

On the streets of Cuzco, the teenage boys were narrowing the distance between themselves and the two men on the motorcycles. Noon traffic and crowds of tourists and pedestrians all conspired to slow down the kidnappers' escape. The kidnappers ran a red light, followed by a phalanx of teenagers. A policeman in a white helmet blew his whistle and reached for his walkie-talkie.

His report was forwarded to Sergio in the police car.

"Have as many cars as available block the entrance to Mercado," Sergio radioed headquarters.

Calle Mercado was lined with small auto repair shops and dozens of small *fabricas*, divided by narrow alleys leading into the urban maze of shacks where the workers lived with their families.

"If they make it into the alleys, we could lose them." Sergio said to Adam and Nina.

Another voice came over the radio. "Chief, they're heading for the Plaza de Armas."

Sergio smiled. "That's a big mistake."

On Saturdays, the plaza was transformed into a gigantic flea market. Booths and stalls filled the plaza. Making matters worse, the vans and trucks of the sellers were parked throughout the area blocking exits. There were no clear passageways through the stalls.

Still the chase continued. People jumped out of the way of the motorcycles, but the kidnappers couldn't develop any speed or distance from the students as they drove through the narrow aisles overturning stands of merchandise. From the steps of the cathedral, tourists and worshipers watched the chaos below, some of them videotaping it with their cameras. Police sirens wailed in the distance.

In the police car, Adam leaned over and tapped Sergio on the shoulder. "We need to take the kidnappers alive."

"I gave those orders," said Sergio. "But if they are armed, I can't guarantee my men won't shoot."

Adam nodded. He knew the odds. The police in Cuzco weren't any different from cops anywhere else. If either of the kidnappers were armed and displayed a gun, the cops would use all the firepower they had.

Sergio's car entered the plaza from the Calle Triunfo and stopped as it faced the wall of stalls of the flea market. The plaza was enclosed on three sides by covered porticos with restaurants, cafés, and shops. The cathedral at the north end completed the square. There were only two entrances on either side of the cathedral. Sergio's cars and three police cars now blockaded each entrance. The motorcycles were trapped. But where were they? Adam and Nina got out of the car as more police cars pulled up behind them.

"From the cathedral steps," Adam said.

He and Sergio sprinted to the top and looked down on the square. Below them, the entire population of the flea market had contracted like a swarm of bees into a tighter circle. This left a track, an open passageway around the perimeter of the crowd where the students were pursuing the motorcycles on their smaller bikes and scooters. There was no escape. The kidnapped girl was still unconscious and splayed across the gas tank of the motorcycle. As the kidnappers reached the far end of the square, they abruptly skidded their bikes to a halt, tires smoking, and faced the pursuing students. The students slowed, circling the kidnappers. There were enough of them to make a chain around the two BMWs. The students began shouting insults and curses. The kidnappers watched the students, their reactions hidden behind their impenetrable black visors. They were trapped. The students continued to circle the kidnappers, taunting them, making obscene gestures.

Adam and Sergio raced down the steps of the cathedral, gathering up policemen in their wake. They made their way blindly through the flea market.

The students were a unit now, a superior force, outnumbering their adversaries. They could rescue their classmate, be heroes, and punish the kidnappers. In South America, kidnappers were rarely caught and almost never brought to justice; they bankrupted families, psychologically scarred their victims for life, and often, after being paid, simply killed them. They were despised. One of the students, Iván, a strapping six-footer, stopped his motorbike, dismounted, and faced the kidnappers. The other students stopped also. He took a few steps forward.

One of the students called out, "Teach them a lesson, Iván!"

"Show those bastards!"

Iván removed his helmet and swung it around a few times by the strap. This was his weapon of choice. The other students cheered him on.

One of the kidnappers reached into his saddlebag and pulled out a .44 automatic. Iván froze when he saw the gun. His face turned white, and a huge stain began to spread out in the front of his pants. The rider gestured for Iván to move. Iván turned and fled, flinging aside two students who weren't fast enough to get out of his way. Then the gunman moved in his seat and shifted the weapon to three other teenagers sitting on Vespas. He waved the gun from side to side indicating that he wanted them to move and create a space. The boys nodded, dismounted, and backed the Vespas away. There was now an opening in the circle.

The kidnappers revved their engines.

Adam burst through the crowd into the empty space the students had created. He stopped in front of the two riders. One of them still had the young female victim straddled across his bike, but he now held a gun to her head. Adam could see she was moving; whatever drug had knocked her out was wearing off. If she awoke and began to resist, she would be a real liability to the rider, and he would be forced to dump her or shoot her. The sounds of police sirens were getting louder. Options for the abductors were dwindling.

"There's no escape. You have to surrender!" shouted Sergio.

Adam couldn't see any reaction behind the driver's opaque mask. The kidnapper revved his engine.

Adam moved in front of the motorcycle, blocking its path. The engine screamed. A gloved hand released the brake and the BMW leaped forward.

At the same moment, a single round from a police marksman hit the rider in the back. Adam grabbed the girl and pulled her off the motorcycle. The BMW spun crazily and skidded to the ground, coming to a sliding halt on top of the dead driver.

The other kidnapper hesitated. Then he reached into his saddlebag and took out a handgun. A volley of bullets rained into him.

A policeman walked over to the fallen men and kicked their weapons away. Blood flowed out of their leather garments. The red rivulets streamed over the cobblestone floor of the plaza in a freakish map of the arteries from which they originated.

Sergio issued orders to his men. They moved the crowd back away from the bodies. Another policeman shut down the engines of the BMWs. A female officer took off her jacket and wrapped it around the young girl and lowered her to the ground. Another gave her a sip of bottled water. The girl nodded gratefully as she slipped in and out of consciousness. An ambulance siren blared in the distance. Sergio and Adam knelt down beside one of the dead kidnappers and removed the motorcycle helmet. The man was in his twenties, maybe younger. He had dark skin and crudely cut black hair. It was an unremarkable Indian face except for the fine lines of cat's whiskers tattooed under his nose that spread out across his cheeks. Sergio moved to the next man and removed his helmet. The man had the same cat's whiskers tattooed on his face.

Adam turned to Sergio and asked, "What is this?"

Sergio shrugged ignorance.

"The tattoos are Machiguenga," said Nina. "They are an Amazon tribe. It's rare to see them in a city. They stay in the jungle. What's left of them. Driving motorcycles and kidnapping children. It doesn't make any sense."

Sergio stood up. "I'll meet you back at the station, and we'll see what we have."

Adam took Nina by the arm. "A drink."

CHAPTER 26

CUZCO, PERU

The waiter placed glasses of beer and a plate of sunflower seeds on the table. The sun was setting and the shadows grew longer on the Plaza de Armas. Adam and Nina watched the tourists wandering into alternating patches of darkness and light.

"Tell me more about the Machiguenga."

"Do you want the history or the legend?"

"Is there a difference?"

"History is only someone's version of what happened. If you don't agree with it, you turn it into a legend. You and I have a history: We met, fell in love, and you left me."

"That's not quite accurate. I asked you come with me. You refused."

"That's your legend."

"The Machiguenga, please. My head is spinning."

"Okay. The history begins with the capture of the Inca emperor Atahualpa by the evil Pizarro."

"See if you can tell it objectively."

"You mean without insulting your family."

"It is only a rumor that I am a descendant of Señor Pizarro. The rumor by the way, was kept alive, by my aunt Clara, who, as everyone in the family knows, was quite mad."

"If we had a sample of Pizarro's DNA . . ."

"And I turned out to be a descendant? Would you like me less?"

"The murderer of my people, the destroyer of a great civilization." She squeezed his hand. "Yes, I would like you less, but there'd be enough left over to still love you."

"Good to know."

They were talking now like they used to. Where Nina never hid anything or held anything back. She remembered saying she was flattered by his marriage proposal but would accept it with only one condition—instead of her moving to New Mexico, Adam had to move to Cuzco. . . .

"Your relative and his soldiers," Nina continued, "defeated my Inca army with cannons, horses, rifles, and armor. He also faced an Inca army demoralized and weakened by civil war and smallpox. After, Atahualpa was captured—and once he was, the Inca soldiers gave up the fight."

"Like killing the queen bee."

"Exactly. But they didn't kill him, they offered to ransom him. Gold, of course. A modest amount, say just enough to fill the room he was being held in. Make that from floor to ceiling. The Inca agreed and returned with a few dozen llamas carrying the gold. Unfortunately, Pizarro wanted more. He told the Incas that if they wanted their emperor returned, they would have to bring another roomful of gold. The Incas left and began to assemble the second ransom, but Atahualpa managed to tell them not to trust the Spanish and not to deliver the second ransom."

"And once they realized the gold wasn't coming Pizarro killed him."

"Yes."

"So where is the second ransom?"

"That brings us back to the legend. In the last days of the war against the Spanish, two thousand Inca escaped into the jungle.

They built a city called Vilcabamba. And they brought the second ransom with them."

"The lost city of the Incas—that no one has been able to find."

"Actually, every time an Inca ruin is discovered, it becomes the lost city of the Incas. But there's never any gold."

"Is there any truth in all this?" Adam asked.

"We all agree that the Incas delivered the first ransom for Atahualpa and assembled a second one. We also know the Inca army retreated into the jungle after their defeat in Cuzco. Did they really take the second ransom with them? If not, then where is it? But the truth has been enough to motivate driven people into the Amazon jungles. Sir Walter Raleigh was one of them. The Victorian explorer P. H. Fawcett made four expeditions into the Amazon searching for the Lost City, and disappeared on the last one. Eighty years later, a modern team equipped with sophisticated survival equipment and communications followed Fawcett's route and just disappeared. It's better not to look."

She signaled the waiter for the check.

"But there is another lesser-known and interesting part of the myth."

Adam sighed impatiently.

"The Inca use Indian tribes to protect the city and the gold."

"You said 'use.'"

"Did I? Sorry. Used."

She picked up the bill. "On me." She smiled. Adam knew the look. He had kept it in his memory for a long time, and there were unsaid words that accompanied its slight variations. This one said *what are you going to do about me?*

"Will you have dinner with me tonight?"

"I'll cook. Come over around ten. I'm working late."

CHAPTER 27

CUZCO POLICE HEADQUARTERS

The Cuzco police station was in a nineteenth-century colonial building. Adam showed his identification to a guard and entered a lofty atrium with cascading staircases. Though things had quieted down since the violent days of the Shining Path, the security was still intense. Helmeted police patrolled the halls clad in bulletproof vests with MGP submachine guns.

"Adam."

He looked up. Sergio waved to him from the highest landing.

As Adam climbed the stairs, he went over his conversation with Nina. Were the kidnappers the same ones who had abducted the boy in Lima, the French girl out of Sacsayhuamán, and Olivero's son in the jungle? The one thing that linked them all was the round mirror. Nina's tale of the Machiguenga, a tribe never conquered by the Inca who served them as mercenaries was interesting, but what the hell did it have to do with kidnappings today?

He greeted Sergio, who was holding a door open.

"In here."

Sergio led Adam into a large room where two men were sitting at a table poring over papers and photographs.

"Allow me to introduce you to my two lead investigators, Gonzalo Remy and Roberto Glave."

Adam figured Gonzalo for his late fifties, near retirement, and there wasn't much that happened in Cuzco he didn't know about. Roberto was younger, maybe thirties, intense and studious. Adam knew the speech by heart, and he gave it to them in his best Spanish.

"I'm here because one of the kidnapped children is an American citizen. It's your case, and I'll do my best to stay out of your way. I'm allowed to offer assistance from the FBI in any way I can, but again, I recognize that this is your jurisdiction and I'm a guest."

He saw the hint of a smile in the older cop's face. Roberto said, "You did a good job in the plaza. If she had still been on the motorcycle when the firing began, she wouldn't be alive."

Adam turned to a large corkboard on the wall. On a large map of Peru, pictures of the three children were pinned to the locations from where they were taken; Lima, Iquitos, and Cuzco. It would be four if they hadn't stopped the one today.

Sergio took a sip of his coffee and made a sour face.

Gonzalo looked up. "The techniques are similar, correct?"

"More or less. The one thing in common to all of them is there have been no ransom demands."

"You know what that means," Gonzalo said. "They are probably dead."

CHAPTER 28

CUZCO, PERU

It was after midnight. The lab was deserted at this hour. Nina preferred it that way. Seated at her desk in her dark office, illuminated only by a desk lamp and the soft light of her computer, she reviewed autopsy reports and edited them into final documents to be forwarded to the Ministry of Health and Science. She didn't like to work at home. She dealt in death and its causes and she wanted to keep her home free from that science. She plugged her iPod into the computer, scrolled down her playlists, and clicked on her "work" file. There were no vocals, classic romantics, jazz, folk, or anything nostalgic or soothing in the file. She wanted music that matched the violence in her reports. The Shostakovich string quartets would do; the discordant and clashing chords, the harsh rhythms kept her on edge.

If the crash hadn't happened in the moment of silence between two movements, she wouldn't have heard it. The sound froze Nina in her chair. An earthquake, most likely. She glanced at the miniature Calder mobile on her desk. It wasn't moving. Perhaps it was Carlos, one of the lab technicians, who lived outside the city and occasionally spent the night on a cot in his office. She looked at the time: 2:30 a.m. The buses had stopped running at midnight and that would explain his presence. "Carlos?"

There was no response.

"Carlos?"

Nina got up out of her chair. She scanned the room for a weapon. On her desk was a model of an Inca war club in a Lucite case and a rusted kukri, the Ghurka curved knife she bought in Nepal. On the wall, there was a bola from a trip to Argentina, and a delicate wooden Oaxacan letter opener that couldn't cut scotch tape. They were just souvenirs—useless crap. A flashlight would do. When she got out to the corridor, she saw that the door to the autopsy room was open.

CHAPTER 29

CUZCO POLICE HEADQUARTERS

Adam could see that the cops working on the kidnappings were on their last legs, exhausted after hours of dead end phone calls, fighting the department's slow computers, and searching through the case files of other missing children. Looking for similarities, methods of operation. They searched the files for abductions, runaways, child abuse, anything, any crime to do with children in Cuzco. They went back ten years, then twenty. Periodically, they got up from their desks and stared at the wall with the photos and biographies of the victims, their families, the maps of Lima, Iquitos, and Cuzco. The only connection was the mirror. No one had a good idea. They had consumed too much coffee, cigarettes, and stale air. Adam stole a glance at Gonzalo—he was trying to stay awake. Adam realized they were involved in some kind of nationalistic rivalry to see which nation's police force would quit first. He put down his pen and said, "This gringo is brain dead. Shall we call it a night or morning?"

Roberto smiled at Gonzalo, thinking "Cuzco police one, FBI zero."

But Gonzalo had a more experienced cop's view and said, "I'd also rather our chief didn't see us up at this hour. He might get ideas."

Adam nodded and felt himself liking this veteran.

"Let's go, then."

The three men could hear the phone ringing in the detective's room as they were halfway down the stairs, but nobody wanted to trudge back up and answer it. It stopped ringing.

They continued down the steps when they heard a yell from the top balcony.

A uniformed officer shouted down: "It's Dr. Ramirez. She's called in an emergency."

The front door of the forensics lab was open. Adam and Sergio ran inside, Gonzalo and Roberto behind them.

"She said she was in the morgue."

Adam pointed to the left, and they followed him into the autopsy laboratory. Nina was sitting on the floor, leaning against a desk, her hair soaked with sweat and her lab coat stained with vomit. Gonzalo called in an ambulance. Nina's eyes were open, but she was groggy and weak.

Adam bent over her.

"Someone sprayed me. Mace, probably. My eyes hurt like hell."

"Don't rub them," said Sergio. "You'll make it worse."

Nina shook her head. "Too late. But water would be nice."

Gonzalo handed her a water bottle. She emptied it over her eyes. She pointed to the wall of cadaver lockers. "The one on the end."

Adam could see that the door of the locker was ajar. He looked at Nina.

"The boy was in this one."

"That's right. He was."

Adam looked at Sergio. "Is it the same group, but now they're taking dead children?"

"But why would someone steal a corpse?" asked Sergio.

Adam replied, "Maybe they wanted to put him back."

Nina and Sergio looked at Adam. Of course.

CHAPTER 30

CUZCO POLICE HEADQUARTERS

Luis Davila was polishing the marble banister of the staircase that led to the second floor detectives' offices. As he had done for the past forty years, he started at the top and worked his way down using a towel and a small bucket of soapy water. It was his job, had been his ever since his brother-in-law Aurelio had pocketed the 500-*neuvo-sol* bribe and pronounced that Luis was now officially part of the janitorial workforce. He had bought himself a civil service job, and it came with a salary, a pension, and paid vacations.

Aurelio had died ten years ago, which had given Luis the right to sell his job to a younger man, and move up and replace Aurelio as head janitor. Luis was now eligible for retirement, but the station house and the policemen in it were so much a part of Luis's life, he couldn't bear to leave work. His children were grown, and his wife wanted him out of the house. As head janitor, he could keep the lighter jobs for himself, including his favorite—polishing the marble banister. He enjoyed the feel of the cold stone and he knew every vein and bump under his moist rag. He liked to greet and sometimes extend a pleasantry with police officials on the stairs. He enjoyed drinking tea in the basement with his workers. Now that there were policewomen in the force, the conversations were spicier. The basement group was well informed from reading the waste papers they collected and emptied in the evenings when they cleaned out the offices of the detectives and city prosecutors. They also knew who was being held in the holding cells in the basement. One of the perks of the job was that they were allowed to sell the prisoners cigarettes, food, and brandy.

There was a lot of talk about the gringo cop who was spending so much time with Detective Varela on the kidnapped children case. Luis waited until he made sure that the American cop was *comprensivo* before he approached him. That he had heard him speaking to Varela in excellent Spanish was a good sign. Thus, when Adam entered the building after dropping Nina off at her apartment, Luis felt he could speak frankly, man to man and tell him something important.

"Señor?"

"Yes."

"Are you having any luck finding the children?"

"Not much."

Adam started up the stairs.

"Don't worry, señor. They will come back. Just like the last time."

He stopped and looked at the old man.

"The last time? There was a last time?"

Luis was happy to be in the detective room with the gringo cop and the rest of the team. They listened politely and one of the detectives even took notes. Luis told them as much as he could remember about the child kidnapping in Cuzco in 1962. He explained that the reason he recalled it so vividly was that the victim was María, the daughter of his neighbors Diego and Miriam Chávez. Luis's own wife, Adela, had practically moved into their house to be a support to Diego and Miriam after María disappeared. She watched Miriam's other children, cooked meals, did laundry, and kept the house clean while Miriam spent her days in church praying for the return of her daughter. One night, the door opened, and little María walked into the kitchen. Her first words to her mother were to ask why a place had not been set for her at the table.

"Where was she?" Adam asked.

"She couldn't remember. She had no memory of where she had been, how she was kidnapped, or who did it. It was, señor, as if three weeks were missing from her life."

"What happened to her?"

"Miriam wouldn't let her out of her sight from then on. But eventually, she married and moved to Lima. I don't know where she is now. Miriam and Diego are dead."

"Was anyone else kidnapped around that time?"

Luis thought for a moment. "Yes, I think so. Or maybe it was a rumor. It was a long time ago. But I do remember that people were watching their kids a lot more. There was a detective, Arnoldo Gutierrez, who worked on the case. He was convinced that María ran away with a boy and made up the whole kidnapping story."

He regretted telling them about Arnoldo. He never liked him, and he resented him for causing so much pain to Miriam's family.

"Is this Gutierrez still alive?"

"As far as I know. He's retired."

Sergio issued orders. "Roberto, find him and bring him here. I doubt our case files go back to the sixties, but if they don't, go to the library and bring back all the newspapers for that period. Gonzalo, contact the larger newspapers in Lima, Iquitos, and Arequipa, and see if they have articles relating to child kidnappings in 1962. They might have converted them digitally, and if they have, send them via email."

In a matter of hours, the desks of the crime room were laden with bound volumes of newspapers. The team divided the volumes among themselves and went to work. Adam asked Luis to stay in the room with them in case there was anything else he could remember about the events in 1962.

Detective Gonzalo was the first to find what they all had been looking for. It was in a yellowed edition of *El Commercio*, Cuzco's oldest newspaper.

Adam and the others crowded around him, peering over his shoulder, as he read the article out loud. "October 12, 1962. Another child abducted. Twelve-year-old Blanca Arroyo was dragged into a car on her way home from school. The kidnappers have made no ransom demands. The parents have pleaded with—"

"Then there were two in Cuzco," Gonzalo interrupted. "And here's one in Arequipa. October 15: A young alpaca shepherd in the Urubamba highlands disappeared while tending his father's herd."

"And here's another, from Lima," said Roberto. "It references two kidnappings, one in Lima, another in La Playa. October 13."

As the accounts of kidnapping for that year came in, Roberto put them up on the wall. He had attached another map of Peru next to the one they had been using and placed colored pins where the kidnappings had taken place.

"So if this is the same kidnapper, how old is he now?" Sergio said. "Eighty? Ninety. This is ridiculous."

Adam scrutinized the news articles on the wall. He counted nine children kidnapped over the fall of 1962. They were from different locations: Arequipa, Yupanca, Espiritu, Cuzco, Lima, Iquitos, Potosí, Urubamba, and La Playa. The children ranged between ten and sixteen years old: five boys, four girls. All classes were represented, rich and poor, and no ransom demands of any kind were made to any of the parents. He moved over to the second map, where the detectives had placed pins representing the recent kidnappings. Ronaldo in Iquitos, Gabrielle in Cuzco, and Jimmy in Lima. Next to the wall were pictures of the children and the accompanying newspaper articles. They, too, were in the same age range, foreign and native, and no ransom demands were made. He wondered what the children had in common with the childen from 1962 even though they were fifty years apart.

Adam looked around at the working detectives. Even Luis, the janitor, was engaged. His head was buried in a volume of newspaper articles, and he made vigorous little notes on a yellow legal pad as he turned the pages of the thick book. The others were tired, probably bored, certainly hungry, and, collectively, they resembled a bunch of high school kids desperately waiting for the dismissal bell to ring and put an end to their misery. Adam wanted to yell, shake them, kick their asses into a new burst of energy, but he knew that he was still a foreigner on their turf. He played it again in his mind. He heard the voice of his criminal procedure instructor at Quantico telling him if there were multiple victims to reduce them to one, describe that one and determine what stands out. It's not gender, money, location, or nationality. But there is something.

He turned to Luis, "The child who returned. María. Did she escape? Was she released? There doesn't seem to be anything in the papers about the circumstances of her return."

"*Niños inocentes*. Makes me crazy."

"What was that?" asked Adam.

"The children," replied Luis. "Innocent children are always the victims."

The door opened, and Roberto and an older man walked into the room. Adam guessed his age at more than seventy, but he looked strong and fit.

Roberto said. "My fellow officers, may I introduce Detective Arnoldo Gutierrez, retired, formerly of the Cuzco police department."

One by one, the people in the room introduced themselves to Arnoldo. The last was Adam who asked politely if he spoke English. Arnoldo nodded his head proudly and offered that he had spent a whole year at the School of the Americas in the seventies and had honed his English. Adam knew he had also honed his interrogation skills and the use of certain electrical devices that were outlawed under the Geneva Convention. The school was a notorious training academy for South and Latin American army officers and policemen whose governments were engaged in fighting left wing and popular revolutions. Arnoldo looked the part: squat, broad chest, thick neck, and cold eyes that didn't say anything comforting. Despite his age, his handshake was like a vise, and Adam saw pained looks as he shook hands with the cops in the room. To Sandra, the only woman, he gave a short, curt bow and moved on.

Sergio offered him a seat at the table and the others took their places.

"I assume Roberto explained to you what we are facing now," Sergio said.

"Children have been kidnapped from various parts of Peru, and there have been two here in Cuzco," said Arnoldo. "I understand one was not successful."

He spoke slowly, looking at Adam to see if he was following his Spanish. Adam nodded and Arnoldo continued.

"We had a similar situation here in 1962."

Adam pointed to the photos and articles from the earlier kidnappings.

"I see you have collected the accounts of the kidnappings in the rest of the country," said Arnaldo.

"Tell us about Cuzco," said Sergio.

"There were two. One was a girl named Blanca Arroyo. It wasn't my case. The detective who was assigned to it is dead. Maybe the parents paid a ransom. I don't know. But she returned home."

"And the one you investigated?" asked Adam.

"Maria something. I thought, at the time, she had run off with her boyfriend, he dropped her, and the kidnapping story was her way of explaining what happened—or not explaining."

"Do you still believe that?" asked Sergio.

"I'm not sure now," said Arnoldo. "You see, over the years, I talked to colleagues on other police forces: Lima, Yupanca, Arequipa, and La Playa. Those guys told me the same story. Kids kidnapped, no ransom asked, and then they just showed up with no memory of where they'd been. Except for one."

"One?" asked Adam.

"His name was Steiner," said Arnoldo. "He claimed to remember every detail of his abduction. But after hearing it, we decided it was just as absurd and fantastical as the others who claimed to remember nothing."

"Steiner. Is he still alive?"

"I don't know. He was in a private hospital in Puerto Maldonado."

"Señor, we are trying to determine if there is something all these children had in common," said Adam. "Do you have any idea what that might be?"

The old policeman smiled, took a sip of his coffee, and said, "Well, with the possible exception of María, I think they were all virgins."

CHAPTER 31

CUZCO AIRPORT, PERU

At the far end of the runway was an antique Beechcraft Baron. It was a botched job with uneven numbers on the plane's tail, ugly patches on its fuselage, and bald tires on the wheels. Fueling finished; a teenage boy wheeled the gas pump away. The pilot signaled to Adam, Sergio, and Roberto to board.

Sergio asked the pilot, "Is this thing going to get us there?"

"No worries, sir. The previous owner assured us that it seats five comfortably with up to three hundred kilos of cocaine in the luggage compartment. Since we aren't carrying any cocaine, we have plenty of weight to spare."

Reassured, Adam found a seat with cracked leather and settled in. He liked the element of danger—the flight southeast to Puerto Maldonado would take them over the Andes at twice the height of the Alps. He knew that the views would be stunning and, he hoped the kid knew what he was doing, or they would be bouncing off their faces all the way down.

About twenty minutes into the flight, Sergio tapped Adam on the shoulder.

"Ollantaytambo, below."

The pilot banked the plane for a better view of the ruins of a sprawling city/fortress. Its massive stone walls flowed down the flank of the mountain in a series of terraced buildings.

"It's where the emperor Manco Inca stopped with his army," said Sergio, "after they were driven out of Cuzco in 1536."

Adam knew it was the last stand for the Inca in their war against the Spanish. A brilliant strategist, Manco Inca fortified the steep terraces, created narrow passages to force the Spanish to advance in small numbers, and, most importantly, built dams and rerouted two rivers across his defensive plain, making any attack impossible for the Spanish cavalry.

"And it was here that he beat the Spanish," said Sergio. "Kicked their asses. Drove them back to Cuzco. But he knew that they would be back—with a larger army. They were arriving in boatloads, their diseases were killing his people—so Manco Inca decided to retreat into the Amazon forest, where the Spanish would never follow, and try to keep the Inca civilization alive."

The airplane gained altitude, and once again they were flying above the cloudbank. The pilot passed back a thermos of coffee and a basket of wrapped sandwiches. Two hours later, as they were circling the Iquitos airport, waiting for clearance from ground control to land, Adam's phone buzzed.

"Adam, it's Nina. Are you in Puerto Maldonado?"

"Just about ready to touch down. You okay?"

"Fine. Listen, I've got the two maps with the locations of where the kids were taken. We've been looking for a pattern. I found one."

"Hold on. I'll put you on speaker." He held up the phone and gestured for Sergio and Roberto to come closer.

"Okay, what is it?"

"We've been looking for a geographical pattern. Something that might mimic a journey, predict a next location where another kidnapping might take place, or even give us some kind of pattern. But there is no correlation except for the kidnappings in Cuzco and Lima, and that's too coincidental. But what if it's not geographical but astronomical? That is, the abduction locations of the nine in 1962 reflect an astronomical constellation, the condor.

"I didn't know there was a constellation like that."

"It's not in our star description. But it is in the Incas. They named the constellations out of their own experience. They don't have Aires or Orion, or Taurus. They have the river, the condor, the jaguar, and the anaconda."

"Okay, makes sense. What's the point?"

"The kidnapper is taking children according to their celestial location and leaving behind little mirrors as markers."

"So fifty years ago, nine children were kidnapped from locations that mirrored an Incan star constellation. Is there one for the present kidnappings?"

"Ironically, the problem is we don't have enough of the recent kidnappings to make a pattern."

"And if the kidnappers are dead, then there might not be anymore," said Adam.

"Exactly."

There was silence.

"But it does suggest that the 1962 kidnappings have a connection to Incan astronomy," said Nina. "And I bet these do, too."

The plane bounced on the runway at the Padre Aldamiz Airport in Puerto Maldonado.

"Nina, we've just landed. I'll call you after we see Steiner."

The plane taxied toward the terminal. Beyond the airport, Adam could make out the tall smokestacks of a logging mill. Puerto Maldonado, he recalled, was once the center of the region's rubber industry. Now its remaining economy was logging, boat building, and tourism. In addition to Amazon River trips, there were also eco-lodges catering to bird-watchers, botanists, and lepidopterists. And, Adam saw, they all advertised in the airport.

A Puerto Maldonado police officer in a white shirt waved to them next to his van. He was a tall and intelligent-looking young man with short red hair. He was obviously proud to be selected to liaison with the Cuzco police officers and the American FBI agent. He opened the sliding doors, and the men climbed in. He slipped into his seat and turned to his passengers.

"I'm Lieutenant Jaime César. I left the air-conditioning on. I assume you wish to go directly to the asylum."

The word *asylum* hung like a bad smell in the air. Seated behind Sergio, Adam could feel the Cuzco detective's skepticism. Adam realized he shared some of it—they were on their way to a mental hospital to interview a patient about his memories of an event that had occurred sixty years ago.

Sergio smiled at Adam and answered, "Yes. Directly to the asylum."

CHAPTER 32

PUERTO MALDONADO, PERU

The hospital sat in a tropical park compound enclosed by a crumbling stone wall. A guard opened the tall iron gates and Lieutenant César drove the van up a tree-lined driveway. The pair of llamas grazing on the lawn lifted their heads and stared as the van passed an empty swimming pool and a weed filled tennis court. Lieutenant César spoke over his shoulder. "The hospital was once the home to Robert Sullivan, an American rubber baron. He was one of the richest men in South America. It is an exact replica of Commodore Vanderbilt's house on the Hudson River. It was the most beautiful home in Puerto Maldonado."

Adam thought that it might have been at one time, but what was once beautiful, was now decaying—thick cracks in the walls, weary columns straining under the weight of their porticos, dead fountains, and rotting moss-covered statues. Ornate sculptured flowerpots with no flowers dotted the porch of the mansion. It was on the verge of a fire, a flood, or maybe, Adam thought, one of these days, it would all crumble. Lieutenant César was first out of the van. "Would you like me to wait, señor?"

"No need," said Sergio. "We'll call you."

Lieutenant César handed Sergio his card, saying, "My phone number is there." Then he took out his cell phone and showed it to Sergio and remarked, "It's a Nokia."

A middle-aged nurse in a crisp white uniform came out of the main building.

"Welcome to our hospital. I'm Julia Mora. You are the gentlemen who wish to visit Señor Steiner."

Adam introduced himself and the others.

"You are fortunate that Señor Steiner has recovered from his cold and is receiving visitors."

Her tone gave Adam the sense that Julia considered them fortunate to be in the presence of Señor Steiner. She led them around the side of the mansion to a grove of mangrove trees intersected by neat gravel paths that led to small brick cottages.

"Señor Steiner has been with us for many years. Some time ago, we converted old staff quarters into living spaces for those patients who do not require constant supervision. In fact, at one point, Señor Steiner was urged to leave and return to his home in Iquitos, but he refused, saying he wanted to spend the rest of his days here."

She stopped at one of the cottages. There was a paved patio at the side of the cottage with a dusty glass-topped table and threadbare wicker chairs. A hulking ginkgo tree provided some shade. Julia knocked gently.

She whispered, "Señor Steiner is a very talented painter."

She knocked again, timidly, and the door opened. Steiner was in his late sixties, rail-thin, wearing a paint-stained smock over a frayed three-piece suit. He held a palette in one hand and a brush in the other. He was European, with a thin nose and a neatly trimmed vandyke beard. He reminded Adam of an artist who taught the techniques of oil painting on television. He, too, wore a smock, and could produce a flock of flying geese with just a few flicks of his brush.

"Señor Steiner, these are the people who have come from Cuzco to talk to you."

Steiner lowered his palette, cocked his head, and put his hand on his chin. Adam realized the man was posing as someone who might have forgotten that people were flying from Cuzco to see him. He glanced at Sergio, who wasn't buying it, either.

"Ah, yes. Of course. Gentlemen, enter please." With a flourish, Steiner opened the door wider and ushered everyone into his sitting room. There was a writing desk, a teak table, and leather chairs. The walls were lined with eighteenth-century colonial portraits of minor Spanish civil servants and one large canvas from the Cuzco school. It portrayed Saint George as a conquistador in the act of thrusting his sword into the belly of a mortally wounded dragon. Above him, horn-blowing angels hailed his victory, while below, spiked monsters snapped at his stirrups. At the edge of the painting, a group of conquistadors were engaged in conversation, indifferent to his victory.

There was an artist's smell in the air—oil paint, brushes soaking in turpentine. Steiner put his brush and palette on the table.

"Welcome to my humble home. I am sorry that I don't have anything to offer in my cupboards at this moment, but my servant Julia will be happy to serve us coffee on the patio."

Sergio took out his wallet.

"Please, señor, allow me to provide for the refreshments, as you are so generous in your valuable time." He slipped the nurse some bills. Steiner led them through the cottage to the patio.

"I get few visitors. Puerto Maldonado has lost its attraction, it seems. Please sit down, gentlemen."

Adam, Sergio, and Roberto faced Steiner around the table. Adam knew he wasn't going to get answers immediately. The man was desperate for conversation, and whether his guests responded didn't make any difference. He had three people at his table, and he immediately began a monologue that quickly and deftly outlined the history of Puerto Maldonado, its glories and downfall, then moved into a condemnation of abstract art, his admiration for

Russian literature and, by the time Julia returned with a tray of cups and a pot of coffee, he had moved on to local politics.

"I have long given up on following the hypocrisies of our elected leaders. I think a better system existed in an Indian village in Guatemala. They elected their chief but had a unique inauguration ceremony. The new chief had to sit naked on a red-hot stone. Of course, he received a serious burn. The healing process lasted about a year, roughly coinciding with the moment in which he had to decide whether he wanted to be chief for another year. A good system, yes?" He laughed at his own story then said, "Now gentlemen, what do you want to talk to me about? I am all ears."

Sergio jumped in. "We would like to discuss an incident in the past."

"The past? Nothing to fear. My memory is excellent."

Sergio continued. "When you were eleven years old, you were abducted from your school, Saint Ignatius."

"No, no, no. I was not abducted."

"This was in the police report . . ." said Sergio.

"It is wrong. I was summoned."

"Summoned? By whom?"

"The Inca, Túpac Yupanqui."

"And where were you taken . . . sorry, summoned to?"

"Vilcabamba, of course."

Adam knew that Steiner's answer regarding Vilcabamba, the so-called Lost City of the Incas, only served to remind everyone that they were in a mental asylum and conversing politely with a madman.

"Vilcabamba, señor?" asked Sergio.

"Where the palace of the Inca is filled with baskets overflowing with precious gems, where common citizens eat on plates of silver, and the priests' vestments are sewn with gold threads and the Inca priestess and her maidens walk with heads bent from the weight of the gold chains that hang around their necks."

"You are talking about the Lost City?" asked Sergio.

"I can assure you," replied Steiner. "It is not lost."

"Do you know why you were summoned, señor?" asked Adam.

"For the *capacocha*."

Adam looked at Sergio for help.

"In Quechua, it is the Inca sacrifice of children."

"Was someone being sacrificed?" asked Adam.

"Yes. I was," Steiner replied as he stared defiantly at his visitors.

Sergio started to push back his chair. Adam leaned in quickly and grabbed the chair.

"Wait," said Adam.

Sergio sat back down.

"But you are here. Alive."

"I will tell you. I will tell you everything," said Steiner.

He's pronounced crazy because he remembers being kidnapped, but the others are sane because they don't.

"It was the Machiguenga who came for me one Sunday as I as was walking home from Mass. My parents were artists who had no use for the church. As they rebelled against their parents by refusing to worship, I rebelled against them by embracing Catholicism."

"Would you say you were kidnapped?" asked Sergio.

Here, Steiner paused. He cocked his head slightly to show how deeply he was considering the question. "I was, at first. I was taken to a place where there were other children who had also been chosen. We were put on a boat and traveled east on the Río Santa until we reached the foothills of the Diablo Mountains. The Machiguenga were our guides, our protectors."

"Were the children afraid?" asked Adam.

"Yes, at first," replied Steiner. "But when Puro, the leader, explained where we were going, one by one we came to see what an incredible adventure we were on and what wonderful stories we would have to tell when we returned. So it was at that point when we could say we weren't kidnapped. We were there willingly."

Adam recognized Steiner's reaction as Stockholm syndrome, in which hostages began to feel empathy, and eventually had positive feelings toward their captors. This was clearly the case with Steiner, if he had actually been kidnapped.

"Please go on, señor," said Adam.

"I had so much on my mind. I would sit up after the others had gone to sleep in their blankets and listen to Puro tell me how the Machiguenga were the descendants of the jaguar god, and when a boy came of age, he had whiskers tattooed on his cheeks. They were fierce warriors and because they could, like their jaguar god, move silently and invisibly in the jungle, the Incas were never able to conquer them. In the end, the Incas made an alliance with the tribe and used their warriors to lead them to secret places in the jungle when they were on the run from the Spanish."

"Do you think you could retrace your path through the jungle to the city?" asked Adam.

"Which path? In the Amazon of dreams, there are jungles within jungles. We were in the grove of trees that had their roots on the other side of the river and they crossed and trees grew. We approached the tree that doesn't change size no matter how close you get to it or how far it is from you. We watched as the chained dogs ate the leaves of the *ayahyasca* and the fierce one became calm and the calm one became fierce. We gathered the black rocks on the sand of the river that were hard and smooth and yet could be cut in half revealing a succulent fruit. And then, just before we came to the city, we stopped in the forest of trees that rained golden pollen that put the children to sleep so that when we woke we would have no memory of our journey."

"But why do you remember and the others don't?" asked Sergio.

"I have always had the visions of the city—ever since I was a little boy. I studied the ancient language while my friends were learning to kick a ball. I read the accounts of the Spanish. I knew about Vilcabamba. And I knew someday I would see it. My mother took me to the Museo Nacional de Antropología, Arqueología e Historía del Perú, and I saw a quipu. I felt deep inside that I could read it. It was not necessary to play tricks on me on the trail to the *capacocha*. I was prepared."

Steiner paused and sipped his coffee.

"Could you tell us more about the forest?" asked Adam. "The golden pollen?"

"There are no sounds and thin rays of light beam down through the treetops. Our guides ordered us to rest, and the children lay down on the floor of the grove. One of our guides went to a large tree and shook a branch and a delicate snowfall of golden pollen fell upon us. Within a few minutes, we were all asleep."

"Could you see the Vilcabamba from the grove, señor?" asked Sergio.

"No, but we could see a different shade of green in the jungle. I knew that's where it was. And I was right."

Steiner sat back in his chair, satisfied—like a lawyer who has just destroyed his opponent's case. He smiled victoriously at his guests and dared them to contradict anything he had said.

"The child sacrifice. Were you a witness, señor?" asked Adam.

"Of course. I saw everything."

"How many children were sacrificed?" asked Sergio.

"All nine."

Sergio held up his hand and said, "But not you. How did you escape?"

"I didn't. I was sacrificed, too. Along with my brothers and sisters."

There was a silence. Sergio sneaked a look at his phone, then at Adam. His look said *enough.*

Steiner noticed. "Frankly, gentlemen, your questions are starting to tire me."

"Sorry, señor," Adam said. "Just a few more. Could you tell us what happened after you left the grove?"

"Our hearts were happy. We knew something wonderful was going to happen to us. The guards released our bonds, and we sprang forward in anticipation of the miraculous events to come.

All along the way, people came out of their homes and villages to honor us. We were given fruit and cool drinks. Flowers were laid at our feet, and the path had been cleared of every sharp stone to make our progression smoother and more comfortable. There were priests and shamans to bless us as we passed through the jungle villages. When we stopped to rest, village women bathed us in aromatic waters, and we slept on feather quilts under soft alpaca blankets. For the final part of our journey, we were given white robes to wear."

"And no one tried to escape?"

"Why? We all knew we were on a divine journey. When we reached the city, we climbed the steps of the sacred pyramid willingly. The people lining the steps of the pyramid threw so many flower petals that our feet were buried in a thick carpet of red and white up to our ankles. Waiting for us at the summit were the priests in gold condor masks. I was not the first so I could see the child ahead of me, a delicate boy from Cajamarca. The priest held a silver bowl of red liquid. He took the brush and washed it over the boy's mouth. The taste of the liquid—I can still remember it to this day—was sweet and honeyed. And at the same time, the drums which had been beating slowly and softly now grew louder and faster. Then the flutes joined in. The priest removed the boy's white robe. In the square below the pyramid, the people were swaying and chanting. The priest blessed the boy and led him to lower his head to the great jade bowl. He blessed him again, and then the boy was sent to the gods. It was magnificent. And I was next. I ran up the stairs, so impatient for my journey that I tripped and lost my footing. Fortunately, one of the warriors caught me, or else I might have tumbled down the whole way and not be here to tell you my story of my miraculous journey."

"Where did you go on that journey, señor?" asked Adam.

Steiner closed his eyes and said, "To the sun. To see the creator, the god Viracocha, and Inti, who rules over fertility and crops, and Supai who rules over death. And Pachamama, and Mama Quilla. To plead with them to keep the light and warmth as a gift to the

Inca people. We asked them to forgive us for the paucity of our sacrifices and our lapses in devotion. We begged not to be punished."

"And were you successful?" asked Adam.

Steiner waved his hand dismissively. The answer was self-
evident.

"And yet you are here."

"Am I? How do you know? Because you see me?"

Steiner leaned in close to Adam and took his hands. Steiner's
eyes probed Adam's. "You see many things. Do you believe them
all?"

"Should I believe in this lost city? Vilcabamba?"

"It is not lost. You just haven't found it."

"Can you take us there?"

"Only if you can become an eagle and fly over the snows of
Salcantay. Only if you can become a jaguar and race through the
jungle in Manu."

Sergio reached for his phone. "I'll call our driver. It was a pleasure, Señor Steiner." Then he turned to Adam. "I'll meet you at the
van. Roberto?"

Adam could see that Roberto wanted to stay.

"I have a few more questions for the señor," said Adam. Then he
cocked his head and fake-smiled Roberto.

Sergio's expression read *Leave now, please.* Roberto nodded and
followed.

Now it was just Adam and Steiner.

"I appreciate your taking the time to speak with us, señor."

"The pleasure was mine. But I can see that unlike your police
colleagues, you are a victim of *la rata en calavera.*"

"And what is the rat that is gnawing at my brain?"

"You look at me and you see a man who tells you about an Inca
city in the jungle, plants that take your memory, human sacrifice, a
journey to the gods, and a safe return. You say to yourself, ah, clearly
the ravings of a madman. But at the same time it is there: The rat in
the skull eating away at your certainty. And because you are a ratio-

nal man, a man who suffered loss and a man who has learned that he was wrong about what he held to be right, a part of you wonders if I am telling the truth. Correct?"

"You are correct, señor. But can you convince me?"

"I will show you my art. If you open your eyes, you will see something that will disturb even you."

"I am always up for something disturbing," Adam said.

Adam figured that for Steiner "disturbing" was when his maté tea was served cold.

"Lead the way."

Adam followed Steiner into the cottage, through the curtain to his studio. Steiner switched on the lights.

The entire room was covered with a realistic and perfectly executed painting depicting the Inca and Spanish universe.

"I suggest you begin here," Steiner said, pointing to a spot near the door.

Steiner's mural was populated with figures from pre-Inca civilizations to the present: Inca emperors, Spanish conquistadors, colonial leaders, military men, writers, musicians, artists, and politicians. The colorful tableaus illustrated great moments in the history of Peru: the Spanish invasion, the revolt of the Incas against the Spanish, liberation by Bolivar and San Martín, war with Bolivia and Chile. Then the modern era: García, Fujimori, the Shining Path, natural disasters; earthquakes, floods. All of the people and events were woven into hundreds of tiny figures: men, women, children, animals, and warriors. Inca gods and goddesses bathed in gold soared across the ceiling. Floating among them, elbowing for space, were Jesus, the Virgin Mary, Moses, Mohammed, Buddha, and a parade of fantastical animals—dragons, centaurs, nymphs, harpies, sirens, phoenix, hippogriffs, minotaurs, and unicorns.

Adam followed the painting around the room, realizing he was also seeing a visual representation of Steiner's abduction: joining the other children, their march across the Andes peaks, descending into the jungle, and falling asleep under the golden trees. He looked further; there was the procession of the children in white robes into an Inca city.

Everything was depicted in painstaking detail. The work must have taken years. Adam remembered the museum in Lausanne, Switzerland; the Collection de l'Art Brut; paintings by artists who were amateurs, primitives, some certified insane. Artists who had created their art in various mental institutions—obsessive, intricate crazed visions of their own nightmares and memories. Or were they, as one critic argued, simply outsiders—artists without galleries? Was their work any crazier than the silent screams of Munch, the convoluted and strained watercolors of Ensor, or Dalí's melting clocks? Steiner's vision of the Inca world was in the same tradition of Brueghel, Grünewald, and the angels and saints that adorned the ceilings of the Sistine Chapel.

Adam glanced at Steiner—he assumed he would be watching him intently as he examined his work. Instead, the artist was standing in a corner dabbing a tiny paintbrush on the figure of an Inca flute player. Steiner, who had pleaded exhaustion, seemed revitalized. The act of painting fueled his energy. Adam could imagine Steiner working all hours, forgetting meals, probably collapsing into sleep on his bed when he could no longer hold the paintbrush.

"The damp climate keeps me constantly repairing my work. Do not let me interrupt your viewing."

Adam moved to a part of the wall that portrayed the battle of Cajamarca where Pizarro and his force of two hundred conquistadors defeated the twenty-thousand Inca army of Atahualpa.

Steiner painted the conquistadors' horses in precise detail, but he added his own touches: flaming nostrils, wings, knives embedded in their front hooves ready to slice anyone in their path. He showed little sympathy for the conquistadors; he portrayed them as grotesque; teeth filed to sharp edges, long sinewy fingers clutching huge Seville swords, their eyes red and blazing as they massacred the Inca army. Following on the heels of the Spanish warriors were fat Jesuit priests clutching Bibles and rosary beads, stepping over the bodies of the Incas, scooping up gold trinkets from the dead. Steiner painted the Spanish as a cruel, demonic force that brought down a superior Inca civilization.

Further along the wall, in a series of images, Steiner illustrated the events that followed the capture of Atahualpa: burly conquistadors dragging the emperor into a room and chaining his arms to the wall. A Jesuit priest entering, carrying a Bible and a staff. The priest presenting the Bible to Atahualpa. Next, the Inca emperor on the floor being whipped by the two conquistadors as the priest holds the Bible above him. Then, Jesus floating above the blood-streaked body of the Inca emperor, red tears dripping out of his eyes as he beholds the atrocity committed in his name.

Suddenly, Adam felt tired. Steiner's artwork demanded concentrated attention, and Adam had seen too much. Steiner wore him down. There was no place to rest the eye, no island of color like a swath of blue in a Sargent gown. Steiner's art was too detailed. It wasn't enough just to paint a conquistador's sword. A closer look revealed that he had also inscribed the blade. Adam returned to the scene of the Spanish attack at Cajamarca. Steiner's conquistadors' horses were nervous, baying, magnificent equine missiles ready to be launched. The Spanish had attached bells to the saddles, and Steiner drew them with a cartoonist's shiver of motion so that Adam almost heard them clanging.

The riders were ferocious men in armor astride their prancing, hyped-up mounts. Steiner had given some of them long Toledo swords; others were hunched over pointed steel lances. Bearded, sweating, wild-eyed, these fighting men on their horses looked like human tanks. In a moment of fancy or craziness, Steiner had painted some of them with steel helmets straight out of the 1940s Wehrmacht. They were waiting, deadly calm, for the order to attack.

Facing them was the Inca army; armed with clubs, battle-axes, and slings. Unlike the Spanish, it was a moving, disorderly mass of infantry—a swarm of bees surrounding their queen—in this case, the Emperor Atahualpa. Seated on a platform, surrounded by his palace guard, reclining on a pillowed couch, consulting with his generals, supremely confident and unconcerned by the small Spanish force of eighty that confronted his twenty-thousand-man army.

Steiner's voice broke in. "He is in the last moment of his arrogance, wouldn't you say?"

"It's hard to blame him," said Adam. "Twenty thousand against eighty. Anyone would like those odds."

"His priests told him that the Inca army would drive them back into the sea where they would be eaten by sharks. But first, he had to defeat Pizarro."

Steiner had placed the Spaniards on a hill overlooking the battleground; lighting fuses to canons placed strategically to support the Spanish horsemen. On another panel, four big yellow explosions burst among the Inca front ranks, throwing soldiers into the air and creating a gap in the Inca lines. As Steiner's work continued, the Spanish sliced through the Inca army to the platform throne of Atahualpa. Then his capture, his imprisonment, and Pizarro receiving a priest's blessing, while Christ, angels, and seraphim looked on.

Adam turned away from the painting. He had had enough. Why was the man in a mental hospital? Steiner was a talented artist. In his mural, he chronicled, in a compelling manner, the history of his country, from the Spanish invasion to modern times, and his nightmarish depictions of the horrors of war and the subterranean monsters of the mind and the flesh were as frightening as Hieronymus Bosch, or Goya. His evocations of the life of the Inca and the Peruvian peasants transcended folk art and were the work of a sophisticated and well-trained artist.

"Tell me, sir, what do you think of my portrait of the greatest conquistador?"

Francisco Pizarro. Adam scanned the portrait again. What could he say to this madman? That it takes a madman to paint a madman and get it right? Should he offer congratulations? Adam was drawn back to Pizarro standing in his stirrups, his sword high in the air.

His mouth was open in a silent scream that must have come from the depths of his savage soul.

"It is said that his cry of 'Santiago' was so loud that it silenced both armies." He pointed a thin finger at the painting. "Do you recognize him?"

Do I recognize him? It's my face.

"There aren't many photographs of me. Where did you find one?"

"I didn't. It seems to be an amazing coincidence. I may have missed the nose slightly."

Steiner advanced closer. Adam could smell his tobacco breath and the stale coffee. Beads of sweat appeared on Steiner's forehead, his cheeks reddened. He hissed at Adam.

"Tell me, Señor Pizarro, why do you wish to go to Vilcabamba? To finish what you couldn't do in Cuzco? To destroy the Inca once and for all?"

As Steiner jabbed his finger at Adam's chest, spittle crept out of the corners of his mouth. This was the real Steiner, Adam realized. Steiner the rational, urbane artist, living out his days in semi-retirement in a gentle mental hospital was gone. Steiner the madman had introduced himself.

"If you go there this time, we will kill you. I am telling you. If you go to the city, you will die. Do you understand? If you go to Vilcabamba, you will die."

CHAPTER 33

PUERTO MALDONADO, PERU

At a Thai restaurant near the airport, Sergio, Adam, Roberto, and Lieutenant César ate spicy red noodles, yellow curry, and sticky rice with mango, with bottles of ice-cold Singha beer. When the waiter had cleared the table and brought them cups of black coffee, Sergio began to sum up.

"We all agree the man is crazy, but we also know he was kidnapped in August of 1962 along with eight other children. He claims to have been taken to an Inca city, ritually sacrificed, and sent on a journey to the gods. None of that is worth our attention. We know the Inca did not sacrifice children as a blood offering to the gods like the Mayans. They sacrificed children as emissaries to plead for the Inca in times of famine, plague, or natural disaster. The children were messengers. I had a conversation with a professor of Inca history, and he said they are aware of the subsequent sacrifices starting in 1532."

"Which corresponds to the arrival of the Spanish and the capture of Atahualpa," said Adam.

"Correct."

"1536?"

"The battle of Cuzco. Manco Inca loses to the Spanish and is forced to flee to Vilcabamba."

"1962?"

"There were no Incas in 1962."

"Now. Today?"

"Again, there are no Incas today."

Adam persisted. "But let's look at the world. Suppose there are crazed imitators. What would be a disaster for them, in 1962?"

Sergio thought for a moment.

"The Cuban Missile Crisis?" said Adam. "The world was on the brink of nuclear war."

"How that would impact an imaginary, sorry, hypothetical people is a reach," said Sergio. "Unless, of course, they heard it on their Inca radio."

Adam said, "Okay. Today? What threatens our imaginary or hypothetical Incas?"

Sergio scoffed. "Now? You are saying that children are being kidnapped by these pseudo-Incas to sacrifice because there is a major threat to the world? Steiner's madness is contagious."

"But children have been kidnapped," said Adam. "And we have a sacrificial victim of two weeks. I know it sounds irrational, but this crime is irrational. Suppose someone is kidnapping children to sacrifice them in the Inca manner to send to the gods to plead for . . . what?"

Sergio sighed and said, "Adam, would you like me to list the problems in the world that need a god's intervention?"

"Just the ones close to home. Peru."

"Poverty, inflation, labor strife, earthquakes, floods, corruption . . ." Sergio said, laughing.

Lieutenant César interrupted. "What about the fires in the Amazon?" He took a sip of his beer. "You are lucky being in the city, gentlemen. On some days here you can hardly breathe, the air is so thick with the smoke from the fires. We are losing sixty thousand square miles of forest a year. If the present fires move south, the whole Amazon basin is at risk."

"It qualifies as a disaster," Adam said. "And when there is a disaster, the Inca sacrifice children."

"Only there are no Inca," said Sergio.

He was quiet for a moment, thinking. Adam realized he was considering this seriously for the first time.

"There is no Inca Empire," said Sergio. "The Inca civilization is gone. Ruins for tourists. But there are still Inca."

"There was a boy. He broke into Nina's lab. He may be the link."

CHAPTER 34

CUZCO, PERU

At breakfast, Adam figured the young couple with the Planet Earth Guidebook was his best choice. He found out that they were from Piedmont and, since Adam said he was from San Francisco, they chatted about restaurants and the difficulty of getting into The French Laundry. Done, he thought. We have trust.

"I wonder if I could borrow your phone—my battery died and I need to tell my wife I changed my flight back to Lima," Adam said.

Naturally, he offered to pay for the call. And, naturally, they graciously declined and even gave him some space while he called a man whose phone calls were monitored.

An hour later, he got out of a taxi in front of the Museo Inka on Cuesta del Almirante. Adam squeezed past a class of local schoolchildren listening to their teacher and found a group of Canadian tourists listening to their guide. He was standing in front of a large painting of colonial Spanish soldiers with drawn swords surrounding a bleeding, prostrate conquistador.

"The dead man on the ground is Francisco Pizarro. His assassin, on the right, is Diego de Almagro, whose father obtained financing from the Spanish king for Pizarro's first expedition. But despite his help, Pizarro was unwilling to share power and wealth with Almagro. The son was embittered and, with his followers, rose against Pizarro. He was killed on the eighth anniversary of the death of the Inca emperor Atahualpa. You will also see Friar Valverde, another member of the original party that sailed with Pizarro. He met his death at the hands of a band of Indians, was hacked to death. Some say the ghost of Atahualpa had come back to claim the lives of Pizarro, Almagro, and Valverde—the three men who were most responsible for the emperor's death."

The tour leader paused, took a swallow from a plastic water bottle.

"My friends, you may step into the museum shop for a few minutes and then we will meet at the bus, which is parked directly outside."

The Canadians drifted off, leaving Adam standing next to the tour guide.

"It's good to see you above ground and not in a smelly sewer. Have you found your children?" the tour leader asked Adam.

"I've lost one here in Cuzco. He only speaks Quechua. He's a very special child."

"There are many children who only speak Quechua."

Adam kept his voice low, never taking his eyes off the painting. "But this one has a fantastic story to tell. He may even know where the missing children are."

"Why do you think I can help you? Or why should I?"

"I saved your life, Victor."

"My life? I thought I had saved yours."

"Either way, we are bound together. I need you to find the boy. His name is Quiso."

"I will see what I can do," said Victor as he trundled toward the exit. "Enjoy the painting."

Adam sat on the padded bench facing the painting, pondering what there was to enjoy about it. Pizarro lay on his side, blood pouring from a dozen wounds. He reminded Adam of portraits of the martyr Saint Sebastian—always indifferent to the arrows in his body. This Pizarro was calm in death. Was death welcome? He was sixty-five and weary. The fruits of his labors were betrayal, murder, and revenge. He'd had enough.

The museum guard observing Victor and Adam was employed as a part-time informer for SIN, Servicio de Inteligencia Nacional, the National Intelligence Service. He recorded in his notebook that he had observed (but not heard) a conversation between a male American and Victor Garza, a suspected revolutionary whom he was assigned to watch whenever he entered the museum with foreigners. The museum guard called his handler at SIN and reported the meeting. His handler ordered his own aide to collect the surveillance tape for the day and bring it to him immediately.

The tape was sent to SIN headquarters in Lima where the American was identified as Adam Palma, an FBI agent. The colonel dictated a memo that was sent by courier to the minister of internal affairs, General Jaime Uriarte. The courier was forced to wait two hours as the general was in a conference with his mistress in the Miraflores Park Hotel. When General Uriarte returned to his office, he read the report and called US Ambassador Casey to ask if he would join him for coffee and cognac at his residence to discuss a sensitive issue—at the ambassador's convenience, of course.

Ambassador Casey knew protocol required Uriarte to first contact someone at his own level in the embassy—an undersecretary, who would arrange the appointment himself. Casey vaguely recalled meeting the minister when he presented his credentials upon arriving in Lima, and subsequently at diplomatic cocktail parties. He remembered a pudgy unathletic-looking man with a gaudy row of medals on his army uniform. He had wondered if Peru could have fought in so many wars. The Latin American generals wore medals like jewelry. But for Casey to be invited—summoned—at this hour, it must be important. So sometime after midnight, a phalanx of police motorcycles escorted an armored Jeep Cherokee through Lima to the tall iron gates of a mansion in the exclusive Malecón de la Reserva neighborhood. A soldier cradled his M16 as he examined the driver's credentials while another stood a few feet away. A few moments later, the gates opened and the convoy was allowed to enter. The minster of the interior waited at the door. He was wearing a brown alpaca turtleneck sweater under an embroidered smoking jacket. Casey realized the last time he had seen one of those was in a Fred Astaire film. He couldn't wait to tell his wife, Linda.

"Ambassador, you do me a great honor in coming to my home."

"Minister, I was prepped at State before coming to Peru. They told me you had the best cognac in South America."

"Amazing. American intelligence is nothing if not thorough."

A butler took Casey's coat and led them into a wood-paneled library. A fire blazed. Uriarte gestured for Casey to sit on a couch and he took a chair and faced him. The butler rolled an antique liquor cart and poured a luminous reddish-amber liquid into tulip glasses. He handed one to each man, bowed to the general, and left the room.

Casey held his glass up to a light and swirled the cognac.

"Shall I taste and comment, or are you going to intimidate me by telling me what it is first?"

"Please. Drink some and let me know what you think. But be brutally honest."

If Casey were brutally honest, he would tell this asshole that his wife was really pissed that they weren't watching *Dancing with the Stars* together. So whatever this tin soldier wanted to tell him better be good. Really good.

Casey took a sip of his cognac.

"General, before I say anything, I want you to promise to pour me a second glass."

"Yes, of course."

"Because this is the best cognac I have ever had in my life. I don't care who made it."

"Hennessy Ellipse. They only produced a hundred bottles a year."

At around four thousand dollars a bottle.

"Well, General, you must have some pretty bad news for me to preface it with this."

"I appreciate your honesty, Mr. Ambassador."

An hour later, the ambassador had seen enough. General Uriarte had shown him photographs from surveillance tapes of Adam talking to Victor in the museum. His name wasn't Victor, it was Ullmen Levia and he was a paroled former member of APRA, a revolutionary group linked to the Shining Path. The ambassador was shown the intelligence agency's file on Nina and an accompanying file on her brother, Arturo. Uriarte took pains to explain that their associations were not considered treasonous nor were they a present danger to the state, but they had both been active in student groups that were, as Uriarte put it, problematic. Although Special Agent Palma's purpose was the investigation of a kidnapping of an American citizen, his presence was becoming problematic also.

Blah, blah, blah. Casey didn't know exactly what Palma was doing in his attempts to find the boy, but he wouldn't admit it to this little blowhard. It was fine with him if the Peruvians wanted Palma out of the country. He wasn't going to go to war over an FBI agent. He nodded his agreement, but the minister kept going.

"And so, in the recognition that our two countries have common interests and have enjoyed a long tradition of cooperation and friendship, it pains me to request the transfer of Special Agent Palma, allowing our own police forces to find the American child and return him to his mother."

Casey told the general that he, too, had full faith and confidence in the ability of Peru's police forces. Why not, he reasoned. It had only taken those guys twelve years to catch Abimael Guzmán, a professor of philosophy who was the leader of the Shining Path. In that time, more than seventy thousand people lost their lives and the government of Peru was almost overthrown. Casey rose and shook hands with the general and promised that he would personally guarantee that Special Agent Palma would be on the next plane to Washington. Uriarte kept his hand in Casey's and said that this would come back to him in many ways, which Casey knew was diplomatic for "I owe you one." In the car on the way back to the embassy, he tried to think of something diplomatic to tell his wife.

CHAPTER 35

CUZCO, PERU

Adam knew if Victor was going to contact him regarding Quiso, it would be indirectly through a third party. When he stepped out into the hallway from his hotel room, a chambermaid pushing a linen cart pressed a note into his hand. In the elevator, he unfolded it.

Past Marti's, turn left, right, find an orange door, go inside and ask for Dr. Pastor.

Nina was waiting for him in the lobby. He handed her the napkin. "Marti's is just off the Plaza de Armas. It's a few blocks from here," she said.

The evening air was crisp and cold. Adam walked easily, his body having adjusted to the altitude. Tourists from all over the world were looking for their evening meal. The locals would be out later. Cuzco had a variety of restaurants, and a few were run by former trekkers who decided to stay: Jack's, owned by Australians; Fez, a falafel joint; Heidi's for Swiss food; and finally, Marti's, a bakery and coffee shop. In the window of the bakery there were trays of Peruvian desserts: *piononos*, rolled cakes stuffed with dulce de leche; *alfajores*, pastries layered with flavored creams; *queques de limón*, lemon cakes; rows of cookies; and a selection of bagels. Marti was previously Marty Klein from Bensonhurst.

The directions led them past the bakery and onto a cobblestone street. A narrow water channel bisected the pavement.

"In the time of the Incas," Nina told Adam, "this carried fresh water from the mountains. Fairly ingenious I'd say."

"But they didn't have bagels," said Adam.

"The wheel, a written language, and bagels. It's why the Spanish were able to conquer them."

She was wearing jeans and a soft leather jacket over a blue work shirt. She turned to him and smiled and that made him take her arm.

"What is it?" asked Nina.

Adam felt there was something he wanted to say at this moment and he realized he didn't have the words, so he maneuvered her into the recessed doorway of a shuttered shop and curved his arm around her lower back and drew her to him. It was a long kiss, a pirate's kiss, and in it, with it, he told her that it was something he wanted to be able to do whenever he felt like doing it.

"You will just have to get used to this."

"I will," said Nina. "I promise."

They stepped out into the street and continued to the orange door. The wood was weathered, the paint was faded, and there was no handle, just a doorbell.

Adam glanced up and detected a security camera. A moment later, the door was opened by a lanky young man in jeans, a Black Sabbath T-shirt, and a white jacket. He was young enough to be struggling to grow the beard that would make him look older.

"Come in. I'm Dr. Raúl Pastor. Ah, it's you, Nina. I thought I recognized you."

He led them inside and shut the door.

"We don't have a sign. We treat poor women's reproductive issues. It's wiser to keep a low profile. Word of mouth."

Nina introduced Adam.

"Our friend Victor speaks highly of you," Raúl said to Adam. Adam nodded.

"He must trust you. I am sending you to some very private people. That Nina's with you makes me feel better."

"You don't have to worry," said Nina.

"These people are very special to me."

Then he led Adam and Nina through a series of rooms and out into an alley behind the clinic. He handed them a piece of paper with a map drawn on it.

"Addresses don't exist in there. Just follow the map, and you'll find it."

The hard-packed dirt of the alley soon turned into muddy passageways, and the distance between the buildings became narrower and narrower. Adam and Nina ducked under electric wires and clotheslines while balancing on rickety planks bridging open sewers. Looking up, they could see the darkening sky. If they didn't find their destination within the next half hour, Adam knew they would be hopelessly lost in this labyrinth of shacks and possibly prey to whatever gangsters ruled this part of the slum.

"It's here. Look." Nina pointed to the ground near the door. There was a small pile of damp flowers and a lighted candle floating in a bowl.

She knocked and waited. She knocked again and then pushed the door open and stepped inside.

The room smelled of incense and kerosene. Light came from a small television. The walls were bare; the floor was a haphazard collection of wood, linoleum, and dirt. An Indian woman was seated on the floor in front of a camp stove stirring a pot of soup. She looked up at Nina and Adam and smiled.

"Go through that door, but mind your head," she said. "The ceiling is low."

The next room was as elaborate as the first was spare. There were candles everywhere, and the air was scented by pots of fresh flowers. Woven rugs covered the floor, brightly colored thick tapestries hung from the walls, silencing the sounds of the outside world. Miniature gold figurines of animals and Inca warriors were dangling from strings. At one end of the room, there was a table covered by a simple white cloth and on it surrounded by flowers and candles floating in ceramic bowls, lay the wrapped corpse of an Inca mummy. It looked as it must have before it was taken from the frigid earth of the mountaintop. As befitted a boy about to embark on a long journey, there was an extra pair of sandals tied to the bundle. He wore a necklace of thin red seashells. Tiny gold llama figurines were tied to the leather cover.

The curtains separated, and Quiso entered holding the hand of an old man. Two solidly built men followed them and took positions at the entrance. Quiso guided the old man into a chair facing Adam and Nina. Quiso looked at them and nodded.

The old man turned to them.

"Welcome, señora, señor. I am Titu." He said this in Spanish, then added, "I hear you both understand and speak Quechua."

Nina answered in Quecha. "Thank you. My name is Nina. I'm a doctor. My friend Adam and I are searching for missing children." She indicated Quiso. "I think he may be able to help us."

"Señor, you have a question for me?" asked Titu.

The Quecha words came out of him slowly trying to catch up to his thoughts but as Adam spoke, they accelerated, and he heard the old man say, "You speak our language well, my son."

"When I was younger," said Adam. "I worked here and tried to learn as much as I could. Can you tell me where the boy comes from?"

"He says he comes from his city," replied Titu. "It is far away."

"Does this city have a name?"

"Vilcabamba."

Then Nina asked Quiso, "What happened to your brother?"

Quiso stared at her for a moment. Then he got up and whispered into Titu's ears.

"The child was sent to the gods," Titu said. "To ask them to save the Inca."

"From what?"

"They say a great evil has returned."

"What evil?" asked Adam.

The old man reached for Quiso's hand. "You may tell them your story, my son."

Quiso straightened, took a deep breath and began.

"I was next," he said, then paused. "On the mountain. I was next. After . . ."

Nina leaned forward. "After Manco?"

The boy nodded. "The priests had helped me out of my warm clothes and into the thin white tunic. A maiden came to me carrying a bowl of the red *ayahuasca* and a brush. Her lips were blue from the cold and she shivered. I could see men standing at a shallow pit where my body would rest while my soul traveled to the gods. Earlier, I had seen her paint my brother Manco's mouth with the brush before he climbed the steps. I saw Manco sway back and forth from the *ayahuasca* as they led him up the steps. The high priest was waiting with his long knife on his belt. He was wearing the condor mask. I heard the music of the flute and the sound of the drums. Then they stopped, and I knew that Manco had reached the altar. The high priest and his men gathered around him, and I couldn't see him anymore. And then the high priest held up his arm to the heavens and in his hand he was holding my brother's heart. It was bleeding. I knew then what awaited me, and the fear was so big that I didn't feel the cold anymore—all I could see was my mother weeping as the priests and the maidens led me and Manco out of the city. I knew my duty, and I also knew of the miracle of my journey and how it would help save my people and how my family would be honored. But, even then, I was so afraid. A priest took my elbow and turned me around so that I faced the stone platform. The high priest held out his hands as if to welcome me.

It was also a signal to the maiden. She dipped the brush into the bowl and raised it to my mouth. And then she stopped. She heard it, I heard it, the high priest and his men heard it: hoofbeats—it was the sound of llamas walking up the trail. I knew the mountain played tricks with sound and the *clip-clops* of the llama's hooves and the voices of their owners could have been a half day away or just a few pole lengths below and out of sight. Everyone jumped off the platform. I did, too. The priests quickly wrapped the body of Manco and placed him in the pit. They shoveled dirt over him and threw rocks on top. Two soldiers wedged their spears under a supporting stone and pried it loose. The whole platform collapsed into a pile of rocks. Everyone was rushing this way and that way, the high priest yelling to leave the mountain before the Spanish army arrived—so when I ran away, no one noticed. I hid in the deep cave."

Titu gestured to the two men guarding the door, and they sat down on the floor clustered around the boy. They spoke softly in Quechua, occasionally turning their heads to look back at Nina and Adam.

Adam looked at Nina, who shook her head—Titu and the men were talking too softly for her to hear. The reflections of the burning candles flickered on the gold figurines tied to the mummy's wrapping. Adam was in a home where there was the body of a child, waiting for three men and a boy who claimed to be from a lost Inca city conversing in Quechua, and outside he could hear Michael Jackson singing and motor scooters. The conference was over. Titu got up and brought the boy forward to Nina and Adam.

"In my time," said Titu, "the children were not harmed. Only their spirits were sent. But the high priest has gone back to the old ways. He will kill the children."

"I want to stop him," said Adam.

"Then we will take you to the city."

CHAPTER 36

CUZCO, PERU

Adam picked out the two cops in the hotel lobby. They were wearing suits and smug expressions. One was tall and thin, the other short and squat. The tall one shifted a toothpick from one side of his mouth to the other, and the short one couldn't take his eyes off a tall blonde American woman leaning over the desk discussing her bill with the clerk. The short one continued to stare, content to let his tall partner deal with Adam.

"Señor Palma?"

"Yes."

"We're here to take you to the airport."

"I don't remember calling a taxi."

The tall one pulled his jacket back and revealed a badge in a leather pocket holder.

"Your bags are packed."

"Where am I supposed to be going?"

The American woman walked away clutching her bill, and the short one became interested in police work again.

"Lima, then Miami."

"You gentlemen are with . . . ?"

"The Servicio de Inteligencia Nacional, the National Intelligence Service."

Adam didn't doubt them, but a plan was forming in his mind, and he needed more time.

"Do you mind showing me something else? Like ID that isn't pinned to your shirt?"

The tall one spun the toothpick a few times while he considered kicking the gringo's ass out into the street. But since his orders were to treat Adam with respect, he took out his wallet and showed him his laminated ID with a picture of his face without the toothpick.

Adam examined it for a moment, then compared the picture with the face and nodded.

"I'll have to call my embassy," said Adam.

The two men looked at each other for a moment trying to decide, but Adam was already tapping out a number.

He got Señor Cortero on the first ring. He knew that ever since the kidnapping of Ronaldo, Cortero kept his special 4S iPhone with the red cover within reach. He slept with it on his pillow, carried it to the bathroom, hung it from a towel rack when he showered, and placed it next to his plate when he ate. Adam was the only one who had the number.

"*Hola.*"

"This is Special Agent Adam Palma. I need to speak to Ambassador Casey."

The cops eyed him skeptically, and Adam could hear Mrs. Cortero demanding the phone.

"I'm putting you on speaker."

Adam knew that was for Mrs. Cortero. He waited a moment.

"Mr. Ambassador? It's Adam Palma. I'm fine, sir."

"What's going on, Palma?"

"Thank you, sir, she's in good health. I'm standing here in my Cuzco hotel with two men from SIN who have orders to escort me out of the country. I'm close to getting these children back . . . Yes, I know where they are. I need some more time."

Adam turned to Tall and asked, "What time is my flight to Lima?"

"Ten fifteen."

"Did you hear that? Mr. Ambassador, the ten fifteen from Cuzco to Lima and then Lima to Miami. If I'm out of the country, I will not be able to find the children. No, I do not have confidence in the local police. You cannot let them put me on that plane."

Cortero said, "Don't worry."

"I don't agree with you," said Adam. "I need to be here."

He glanced at the cops, they were happy for his bad news.

"Sir, do you want me sitting in Miami or finding the children? Yes, I hear you. Yes, sir. Orders are orders."

The cops were smiling now.

Adam flipped his phone shut.

"Asshole. You guys pack my socks?"

Adam walked out of the hotel between the two men. A Jeep Cherokee was parked at the curb. Short opened the back door and motioned Adam inside. Tall started the engine and pulled out into the street. There was almost no traffic. They drove past parked army trucks on every tenth corner with groups of soldiers trying to keep warm around an oil-drum fire. Adam leaned forward and tapped Tall on the shoulder.

"I want to say good-bye to someone."

"Use the phone."

"It's on the way—a quick stop. You have my word."

"No."

Adam sighed and took out his phone.

"Nina, it's Adam."

"Where are you?"

"I'm on my way to the airport. They are ordering me out of the country. I fly to Lima and then Miami. It's not my decision."

"Does Sergio know?"

"I don't think so. Would you tell him good-bye for me?"

"Is this a joke?" asked Nina.

"Actually, it is. But you are one sexy woman and I'll miss you."

"Sexy woman?"

Adam and the two SIN cops left the city and turned on to the highway leading to the airport. Except for an occasional tanker truck, there was little traffic. Tall drove with the window down and his left arm hanging out the window. Short smoked a cheap cigar in the passenger seat. He turned around and blew a cloud of stinking tobacco in Adam's face.

"You must be a big deal if they want you out of the country so fast."

"Bigger than you know. In fact, this ride will be the most important thing that will ever happen to you in your brief and shitty career."

Tall laughed, but Short was clearly wounded.

"Fuck you, gringo."

"Right. Fuck me."

The Cobra helicopter with the bulldog insignia picked up the Jeep Cherokee about five miles outside of Cuzco. Adam heard it first. The cops did, too, but they paid no attention. These guys worked fast. But it would be a relatively simple task—he had noticed the Bulldog was pimped out with an ARC laser range-finder and tracker, and an infrared jammer mounted above the engine exhaust, all standard equipment. He knew its altitude system would keep it at a constant six hundred feet above the highway while its huge night vision spotlights illuminated the road below. It was easier than easy.

He heard the Cherokee kick up speed, and in a few seconds the helicopter was a half-mile ahead of the jeep. Now the cops were interested. The pilot lowered it to twenty feet above the road and rotated around so that when the Cherokee came over the hill it faced the helicopter. "Blinded by the Light" played in Adam's head. They were blinded by the light.

Tall hit the brakes hard and skidded the Cherokee to an awkward stop.

The Cobra eased to the left to get a better look inside. Adam gave the pilot a friendly wave as he lowered the helicopter to a few feet above the ground.

A man jumped out of the helicopter wearing body armor and holding a HK416 assault rifle.

A voice boomed out of the helicopter speakers. "Get out of the car with your hands where we can see them."

Tall, Short, and then Adam obeyed.

"Keys, phones, and weapons on the ground."

Tall and Short emptied their pockets. They recognized the emblem on the helicopter and decided silence was the best policy.

"Anyone else in the car?" the man in the body armor asked.

Adam said, "No."

The voice from the 'copter politely asked Short and Tall to step away from the vehicle. They moved a few feet, but apparently not far enough as the voice had a change of personality. "Further, assholes."

Sensing mayhem, Short and Tall ran away from the jeep. A moment later, there was a cannon blast from the nose of the helicopter that blew the Cherokee off the ground. It rolled over in flames, mortally wounded.

The man in body armor collected the phones and weapons. The two SIN cops looked at Adam.

"I told you it would be a big day for you guys."

Tall started to say something, but Short put his hand on his chest and stopped him.

"Go home, fellas," said Adam

Adam watched Short and Tall begin the walk back to Cuzco, then he climbed into the helicopter.

"I'm Reuven, I'll be your pilot tonight. And that's Samson."

Adam got the accent. "Tel Aviv?"

"No, Santa Monica," then he added with a grin. "Just kidding, yes, Tel Aviv."

They shook hands and Reuven handed Adam a pair of earphones.

"Where to?" the pilot asked.

"Back to Cuzco. You know the fortress at Sacsayhuamán?"

"Of course. You are a tourist now?"

Adam smiled and turned and counted seats.

"When we get there, one of you guys will have to hitch home."

"Samson goes," said Reuven. "I'm the driver."

Samson shrugged.

The flight back to Cuzco was fast. On the way, Adam explained that they would be picking up additional passengers, equipment, and supplies.

Reuven brought the helicopter to the ground. Adam called Nina, but there was no answer.

"How long do we have before somebody notices us and the police show up?"

"This thing is equipped with an infrared engine emission suppression system, so it's not going to show up on anyone's radar," said Reuven. "Where's your friend?"

Adam heard the noise, and then the headlights of Nina's Toyota bounced up and down the helicopter. She parked and turned off the engine. Titu and Quiso got out, followed by Nina.

"I picked up some extra equipment." She opened the hatch door. Adam and Nina transferred camping gear to the helicopter: a tent, sleeping bags, a Coleman propane stove with a fuel cylinder, some tin cooking pots, a carton of freeze-dried food packages, and a water purifier.

"It's pretty basic, but it'll keep us alive." Nina tossed a cloth sack to Adam. "And this."

Adam dumped the contents out on the ground: a pair of hiking boots, wool socks, gloves, and a down jacket. "Unless you want to hike the Andes in your suit."

Nina handed Samson the keys to the Toyota.

"You can leave it at the institute."

Quiso looked at the helicopter. Its rotor blades were whirring silently like long knives. He closed his eyes and muttered a prayer to *Pachamama* for the courage to enable him to go in the flying machine. Sensing the boy's fear, Nina put her hand on his shoulder.

"This will take us to the top of the mountain faster than any bird."

"My brother's soul is dying. Soon he will not be able to make his journey. I can feel it."

"Then we'll hurry."

She took his hand and they climbed up the steps into the belly of the helicopter.

Nina strapped seat belts on Quiso and Titu.

Titu took Quiso's hand. "Have you ever seen one of these machine birds flying over your city?"

"Not like this, Uncle. The ones we saw were silver and had big wings and smoke came out of them, and they shit long white lines across the sky."

"This machine doesn't fly that high, but it will land wherever we want."

Quiso nodded and looked out the window.

Reuven watched Samson drive away in the Toyota. "If those cops get to a phone, we're going to be chased by some very expensive jet fighters."

A Cuzco police motorcycle came to a stop, and Sergio jumped off. He carried a backpack and was dressed in a down jacket, corduroy pants, and hiking boots.

Sergio climbed into the helicopter.

"Why are you coming?" asked Nina.

"Because I insisted. You'll get to the bottom of this mystery, but not without me." He pointed to his backpack. "And I'm armed."

Reuven glanced over his shoulder to make sure Sergio was strapped in, then lifted the helicopter to fifteen hundred feet. Within moments, the lights of Cuzco were behind them.

"Directions, someone."

Nina handed a piece of paper to Reuven.

"These are the coordinates of the site where we need to go."

"Twelve thousand feet. That's high for me. You'll have to bail pretty quickly, or I'll lose my air and never take off."

The helicopter banked and headed for the mountains. Quiso stared out the window. He could see what the birds, the condor, and the gods saw. His heart pounded, and he clutched the edge of his chair so tightly that he forgot to breathe. He was in the belly of this noisy machine that carried him so fast across rivers and sailed over deep gorges to the tops of mountains in two heartbeats—mountains that he knew took days to climb. The Spaniard's metal bird roared and shook like . . . he realized that there was nothing in his life to compare it to. The noise was louder than the cave under the giant Gocta waterfalls where he and Manco could only make signs to each other. He was speeding faster than a freefalling condor. He knew he would never be the person he was before this journey. What would he do with the knowledge, the experiences that he had acquired, how could he explain this to anyone? The questions kept coming. And as they did, he became accustomed to the noise and the shaking.

Adam checked his watch. It was after five in the morning. The sun was peeking over the eastern side of the Andes. The helicopter slipped the flank of the mountain ridge at three hundred feet. He could see that Reuven wasn't taking any chances in being detected by radar. Adam looked at the group and tried to assess the advantages and liabilities of each. Nina was strong and experienced in trekking Peru in every environment. Her medical training would be extremely valuable in case of emergencies. Quiso was the one with the knowledge of the location of the city and could lead them there. He was, in a sense, the most valuable, and would have to be protected. Sergio was a tough cop and he would be fine. Adam realized that he was the wild card. As a North American, he would be the most vulnerable to the water and the altitude. And he had disarmed two members of the Peruvian secret service with a helicopter that belonged to a narco-trafficer and disappeared into the jungle without a word to any of his superiors. It would be enough to guarantee that he would be persona non grata in Peru and dead on arrival at the FBI. If he did survive this expedition, it would be a toss-up whether he could resign before he would be fired. And Nina? Would she come to New Mexico with him? He had asked her once, and she had refused. But that was a long time ago. And how would Katie react to another woman? At that moment, Nina reached over, took his hand, and pressed it. He looked at her, the noise of the helicopter was too loud for any casual conversation, so she smiled and then returned to studying her maps. A few moments later, Reuven turned and signaled Adam to look below.

On the crest of the mountain, the ruins of the Inca sacrificial site were visible. Quiso turned to Titu and spoke excitedly in Quechua. Reuven maneuvered the helicopter to one hundred and fifty feet. He pointed to his instrument panel and yelled back to Nina, "This is going to be tricky. I've got pretty bad winds."

The helicopter lurched and twisted in a sickening, stomach-emptying fall. Sergio, who had unbuckled his seat belt for sleeping comfort, flew out of his chair and crashed against the hull. Reuven pulled the stick back and planed the helicopter away from the summit and over the edge of the precipice. Sergio, who was more embarrassed than hurt, squeezed back into his seat.

"The winds are blowing straight across the crest of the mountain," Reuven said to his passengers. "If I get hit broadside on the ground, I might tip over. I'll try a different approach, but you will still have to exit quickly."

"Let's dump the supplies, then we'll jump," Adam yelled.

"Good idea. Let's do it."

Nina crawled out of her seat and into the rear of the helicopter. "Everything up front for quick unloading."

Knapsacks, tents, cooking supplies, all went into Nina's seat. Reuven swung out over the mountain, flew to the end of the narrow spine of the crest, and lowered the helicopter to fifteen feet.

"Careful."

He leaned over and opened Nina's door. The cold air burst into the cabin like an explosion. Nina, closest to the door, started pushing equipment out until her area was clear.

Adam took over, pushing more gear out.

"That's everything."

Reuven lowered the helicopter. "It's only two feet, but be careful. No broken ankles." Nina went first, then Adam. Sergio guided Titu into Adam's outstretched arms, and he gently lowered the old man to the ground. Clutching the bag that held the corpse of his brother, Quiso jumped next, followed by Sergio.

Reuven waved, shut the door, and lifted the helicopter away from the ridge until it disappeared into the clouds. Westward below them, the fertile coastal plain stretched to the Pacific; to the east were the lowland forests and then the Amazon jungle itself. The expedition site itself was unremarkable—a wind-swept ridge on a plateau with rock outcroppings, scattered boulders, and a path that led down on the western flank of the mountain. It was the path the archaeologists had taken, a moderate and gradual descent. But on the eastern side of the mountain facing the Amazon, the helicopter passengers would have to negotiate a morass of jagged rocks and cliffs. There was no visible path. If the boy was telling the truth, then he and the others had come up from the jungle to this place, and he had to know the way back down.

CHAPTER 37

NEVADO SALCANTAY, PERU

It was clear to Adam that reburying the Inca child was going to be a problem. The ground was frozen solid. Titu declared that the opened tombs were desecrated. They would have to dig a new one. Nina's small folding shovel and climber's ice pick could do the job, but to break through the frozen ground and dig a hole deep enough to bury the corpse could take hours. And time on the mountain was dangerous.

He remembered that Quiso had told them about a cave where he had hidden after Manco had been sacrificed. Quiso led them to a cluster of huge boulders and pointed to an opening. Nina aimed her flashlight into its depths and said, "Manco will be safe down there. No one will find him."

Quiso nodded. Adam wrapped a rope around the bundle containing the boy's body and handed it to Quiso. Titu chanted a prayer while Quiso lowered the bundle. When the rope played out to its end, he released it and Manco's body fell silently into the void.

Titu went to him, reached out, and drew his hand across the boy's forehead and spoke softly. The boy nodded. Adam sensed that Tito was telling Quiso that he had completed his mission and his brother was in a safe place and would remain undisturbed forever. Clouds parted and sunlight shined on the cave opening. Titu turned his blind eyes to the sun, extended his arms, and lifted them to the ray of sunlight. Adam knew it was the path Manco's soul would follow on its journey to the gods—he wasn't sure how he knew it, but there was the feeling and it all made sense. On the distant peaks, sharp lightning strikes exploded in a quick succession. A moment later, the thunder rolled in and the sky darkened.

A harsh wind swept across the mountain peak and slapped their bare cheeks with painful cold. Snowflakes began to fall. Nina turned to Titu and said, "This is dangerous weather. We could be in a blizzard in minutes and we're not prepared for a night on this mountain."

Titu nodded and spoke to Quiso. The boy pointed north along the mountain crest. "He says we have to go higher first."

"Higher?" asked Nina.

"Then we will go down," replied Titu.

The time Adam had spent in Cuzco's altitude had acclimated him to the thin air. But they were starting at twelve thousand feet. Walking was difficult. At Nina's suggestion, they began with a schedule of fifty beats of walking followed by twenty beats of rest. Gradually, they increased the walking time and reduced the time between the rests. Quiso and Titu were at the front of the column. Sergio caught up with Adam during a rest.

"We are passing paths that look like they go down the mountain."

Nina heard him and said, "I asked the boy. He said they are dead ends that will leave us trapped on the mountain face. We have to trust him."

Ahead of them, Quiso and the old man kept up a steady pace, but the winds were increasing. Quiso stopped and examined the ground.

Titu shouted to Nina, Adam, and Sergio, "He's found the trail."

The boy took a few steps down. Loose rocks slid away under his feet and bounced down off the side of the mountain. He turned and waved for the others to follow him.

Sergio wasn't convinced. He turned to Nina and said, "We are putting a lot of faith in the boy."

"I don't see us having much of a choice. We have to get off the mountain."

"He says there's a cave further down the trail where we can take shelter," said Titu.

His words were followed by a sudden gust of wind followed by a flurry of snowflakes. If there was a trail down the mountain, it was a mystery to Adam. There was no defined route; they were merely following Quiso down the slope of the mountain, trying to maintain balance on the increasingly slippery rocks. Then, gradually, the stones disappeared, and the ground under their feet was smooth and solid. As they descended to steeper intervals, stones were firmly embedded in the ground, making clear steps. The trail clung to the side of the mountain, a solid rock wall. Where it narrowed dangerously, there were ropes attached to iron rings that were embedded in the cliff wall for safety. Three hundred feet down from the ridge, Quiso stopped. There was an opening in the mountain wall. One by one, they squeezed through the narrow passageway into a small cave. Its ceiling angled down and met the floor ten feet inside. There was barely room for them and their equipment. It wasn't much, but it would be shelter for the night. Titu spoke to Nina, "The boy says this isn't the cave. It's above us."

Quiso pointed to the ceiling.

Sergio shined his flashlight. "I don't see anything."

Quiso jumped up, barely touching the ceiling with his outstretched fingers.

Adam reached up and felt a slab of wood. "There's a cover." He pushed up with both hands and shoved the wood aside.

Sergio aimed his flashlight into the hole.

"Give me a foothold and I'll climb up," Adam told him.

Sergio made a stirrup of his hands and hoisted Adam up.

Sensing a much larger space, Adam thrust his arm down and said, "I need some light."

Sergio handed him his flashlight.

Adam stood up and swept the flashlight. He was in a large cave with a high ceiling and a hard-packed dirt floor. At the far end, disjointed shafts of light broke through a vine-covered opening in the wall. It would never be noticed from the path below it.

"Everyone come up," said Adam. "There's plenty of room, and we'll be a hell of a lot warmer here."

One by one, they squeezed through the hole. First Sergio lifted Nina, then Quiso and Titu. Adam lowered a rope and pulled Sergio up.

They found a pile of firewood, built a small fire, warmed themselves, and rested. Nina passed out some energy bars. Adam opened one for Quiso and watched as he bit off a small piece, tasted it, and smiled. The boy unwrapped another and put it in Titu's palm. The blind man sniffed it and took a bite.

"Pastel! Delicioso!"

Adam watched them devour the rest of their energy bars. Then the old man began to question Quiso. They whispered back and forth rapidly. Suddenly, the boy shook his head. Titu's whispers grew louder, and he pointed his finger at Quiso who kept shaking his head back and forth. A moment later, Quiso helped Titu to his feet, and they walked over to Nina and Adam. Sergio edged closer.

"The boy knows another way down the mountain."

"What's wrong with this path?" asked Sergio.

"The other way is shorter," replied Titu. "This trail we are on now will take a whole day, perhaps two. And if the snow comes in, we will be walking blindly. Too dangerous."

Sergio was skeptical. "Down is down, señor. The distance is the same to the jungle floor. Am I right?"

"There is another way."

Sergio shrugged, then said, "Let's hear it."

"He says that you must promise never to reveal what he shows to you."

Adam, Nina, and Sergio all nodded.

Quiso spoke to Nina, "If you are ready, we can leave now."

Sergio gestured to the mouth of the cave. "Nina, there's a violent storm outside, and if we don't freeze to death, the wind will blow us off the side of the mountain."

"The way down is in the mountain," said Titu. "The boy says he will need your lights."

Adam handed Quiso a flashlight and showed him how to turn it on and off.

Quiso took the old man's arm and walked toward the rear of the cave. He shined the light ahead of them.

Sergio looked at Adam. "I guess we follow the leader."

They shouldered their packs and followed. What had started as a walk to the end of the large gallery turned into a descent into a labyrinth as large tunnels parted and branched off into smaller ones. Quiso led the way, barely pausing at the junctions, hesitating just long enough to look up at the walls that were covered with pictographs of animals, serpents, and mythical figures. Adam realized that the boy was reading the walls for directions. It was obvious that the Incas had constructed the tunnels. At junctures, intricate stonework and arches supported the ceiling. Wooden beams buttressed walls. A few of the tunnels had neat stacks of logs and bricks for repairs when needed.

Quiso paused for a moment and handed Titu a bottle of water. The old man spoke to Nina who translated. "These tunnels were connected to silver and gold mines in the mountains. The Inca mines were always dug into the mountain, as they were careful not to desecrate the exterior of the mountains. After the Inca defeat, the tunnels were used for hiding."

Adam could see traces of past campfires around clear underground streams and sparkling pools of water. The Incas were masters of the art of preserving and storing food. If they had water, an entire population or retreating army could survive in the mountain for a very long time.

Adam noticed that the group looked tired. They were travers-
ing the heart of the mountain but not descending. As a result, the
altitude was the same, the air was thin, and breathing was difficult.
Adam said to Quiso, "When do we begin to go down?"

"Soon."

"Then we should stop for a few hours," said Adam. "We can
camp easily here. I don't know what's ahead, but we'd better be
rested."

Sergio found some pieces of old timbers that were once used to
shore up the tunnel walls and built a fire. Nina brought out packets
of freeze-dried meals she had stuffed in her backpack and tossed
them in a pot of boiled water. Quiso watched, fascinated as Nina
served them out on tin plates. Quiso smelled, tasted, and then
devoured his chicken pasta primavera.

"How does he like it?" Adam asked Nina.

"Apparently, very much," she replied as the boy held out his tin
plate for more.

Quiso and Titu wrapped themselves in their serapes. Adam,
Nina, and Sergio unrolled sleeping bags, and they were all asleep
long before the embers of the fire had died.

*Adam dreams of a city. It is in the jungle. Tall trees and giant ferns provide
a canopy over the city so that it is invisible from the sky. A gentle breeze
keeps the leaves and fronds moving in a lattice effect that allows streams of
light to shine down in crazy patterns. The buildings are constructed of brick
and thatched roofs. The cobblestone streets are narrow and bisected by flow-
ing rivulets of spring water. There is a high wall surrounding the city, but
entanglements of thick vines hide it and allow no entrance. There are people
and they move in one direction. They pay no attention to Adam, who is carried along with the crowd. Now he is in a small plaza facing a stone pyramid
with steps leading to the top. Standing in a line at the foot of the pyramid are
ten children, boys and girls, dressed in diaphanous white robes. The youngest
girl turns to Adam and waves. His daughter. His daughter, Katie.*

"Katie."

"Daddy."

"I'm here to take you home, sweetie. Come with me."

"I can't, Daddy. It's my turn."

He tries to force himself through the crowd to the children, but the people are standing too close together and they won't give way. He pushes and shoves and manages to reach the front, but he faces a ring of sturdy soldiers with their arms interlocked. They form an impenetrable wall.

Katie takes tentative steps to the pyramid. She looks up to the summit. Adam's eyes follow hers. He sees what she sees—a tall figure in a white robe, his face covered by a jaguar mask, and at his side two men, also in white robes. Priests. One holds a bowl, the other a small brush. The man in the jaguar mask, the jaguar priest, opens his arms to Katie—in one hand he clasps a circular mirror, reflecting the sun into her eyes. On his waist belt, there is a long silver blade.

Adam pushes harder against the soldiers.

He screams, "Katie!"

He sees himself, from the top of the pyramid, a white face in the crowd of Indians, straining against the line of soldiers, unable to move.

He dreams the music—a trio of screaming discordant flutes, fierce drum poundings.

Now Katie is a few steps from the top of the pyramid. The jaguar man pulls her to him. He towers above her. One hand slides down to his waist and withdraws a silver blade from his belt.

Nina was shaking him. He raised his hands. If he had been screaming in the dream, it was because the jaguar priest had raised his silver knife and was holding it to his daughter's throat.

He unzipped his sleeping bag. "We have to go. Now."

Nina nodded, then roused Quiso and Titu while Adam woke Sergio.

In a few minutes, they were following Quiso along another tunnel.

By then, Adam had lost all sense of direction. His compass spun wildly, useless in the presence of the mineral deposits.

The boy stopped.

Titu said, "Our way down."

Two wooden doors faced them. Quiso took hold of the carved door handles and swung them open.

Inside the mountain was an elevator.

They all stared at it until Nina burst out laughing. "I don't believe it." She entered the cage. "Going down. Next stop, the Amazon."

It was ludicrous. Here they were, sixteen thousand feet high in the Andes and staring at an elevator.

Nina looked up above the elevator cage.

"There's got to be a relay system. We will probably have to go down in stages. There's no way they could build one that could sustain fifteen thousand feet of rope weights and pulleys." She looked at the engineering and said, "I don't understand something. How could they know about the pulley and not the wheel?"

There was an oil lamp in a corner with a rock and a flint to light it. Adam turned on his flashlight and said, "This thing is scary enough without a fire in it."

Quiso shut the door and turned to a perfectly coiled rope in a pile on the floor. It traveled upward through the roof of the cave, passing through a wooden winch. Quiso yanked on the rope and released the lock on the winch. Slowly, he let the rope out and the elevator began to descend.

The boy held the rope lightly as it flowed through his hands. There didn't seem to be any weight or pressure. Adam knew this meant a sophisticated system of pulleys, weights, and counterweights for the elevator to descend so smoothly; a sophisticated solution of a problem of mechanical engineering. How many other wondrous accomplishments of the Inca civilization were either hidden or destroyed by the Spanish in their effort to "civilize" the population. The Spanish considered the Incas rich because they had silver and gold. They didn't know that was the least of their treasure. They never learned about the medicines that could have cured their diseases or the genius of their agricultural science. They never studied their irrigation. And, although they prized the gold and silver in their mines, they didn't care about the Inca technology of the actual extraction of the metals.

Nina was right. They switched elevators four times. The air temperature and humidity rose as they neared the jungle floor. The last elevator deposited them in a large room. Quiso found a slab on the floor. Sergio and Adam pushed it back, and they lowered themselves to the interior of a shallow cave, a replica of the one they had entered at the top of the mountain.

Symmetry—the Incas worked it out so you couldn't find your way in. And if you did, you couldn't find your way out.

They emerged from the cave into bright sunshine. They were still high enough to see to the horizon. In front of them, a pine forest gave way to the green braided canopy of the Amazon rain forest. And then, further on, a hint of the Amazon River itself. And somewhere between Adam and the river was the lost city of the Incas—Vilcabamba.

Quiso knew exactly where he was going. According to Adam's compass, as much as the boy led them around fallen trees, over jungle streams, and once, taking them on a long detour around a fifteen-foot boa constrictor, he never deviated from a strict southeastern course.

Titu walked at the boy's side keeping a firm grip on Quiso's tunic. Sergio and Nina followed. The trek settled into a routine; they stopped every two hours for a fifteen-minute rest, drank water, ate an energy bar, and then moved on. Late in the afternoon, they crossed a shallow stream. A few yards from the stream was dry ground. There was a shallow pit with a circle of fire-blackened stones and nearby a neat pile of logs and kindling.

"Nina, we're in the middle of the Amazon rain forest and there's a camp ground," said Adam, "and it looks like it's still being used."

"There is something else that is strange about this place."

"I can see the sky," replied Adam.

Sergio looked up and said, "You're right. We're in a clearing."

"And the trees that surround us. They're a species I've never seen before. Look at this leaf," said Nina as she handed the leaf to Adam. But a gust of wind seized it, and it floated away light as a feather. Nina bent down and picked up another.

It looked like a maple leaf, but smaller. There was a yellow light dust on its surface that came off on Adam's fingers.

"It's like gold," said Adam.

Another breeze rustled through the trees, this one stronger. It loosened the dust on the leaves so that it rained down on the clearing, permeating the air and settling on their skin and clothes.

"It has an amazing odor," said Nina. "If gold had a smell, this would be what it smelled like."

Sergio lowered himself to the ground. "Sorry. I am suddenly very tired."

Adam felt it, too. The energy leaked out of his body; all he wanted to do was sleep. Quiso and Titu were seated on their blankets. Nina slowly sat down, looked questioningly at Adam, and then fell backward on the ground. Adam couldn't keep anyone in focus. He felt his legs buckle under him. "I am drugged."

The last thing Adam heard was Quiso laughing.

The dream returns.

Adam is on a jungle path holding his daughter's hand. They are running fast and he has her hand in his and, when he takes giant strides, she flies off the ground with him. In his hand, his daughter trails like a silk scarf in the wind. And then he and Katie fall gently to the earth in a clearing surrounded by trees with gold leaves.

"You're safe now, Katie," he says.

But he realizes he isn't holding her hand anymore and the same sick feeling comes back to him that he had in the bathroom of the federal building.

• • •

When he awoke, Adam wasn't facing a deranged murderer, he was staring at two men holding short swords, a third with a spear, and another standing behind a sixteenth-century Spanish harquebus on a tripod. The warriors' faces were painted, and tattoos covered their muscled arms.

Adam realized he was staring at men dressed as Inca warriors almost six hundred years after their civilization had come to an end. One of the warriors rapped the soles of his feet with the blunt end of his spear. Cops did it with billy clubs, and apparently these warriors did it with spears. Adam knew the drill. He got up slowly and moved next to Nina and Sergio.

The warrior who rousted him came closer and sniffed at Adam. "You have the stink of the conquistador."

"He is a friend of the Inca," Quiso said to the warrior.

Sergio looked at Nina and whispered, "These men are from the so-called Inca city?"

"It's starting to look less so-called," replied Nina.

The warrior came forward and faced Adam.

"Capac." He repeated it. "Capac."

Adam pointed to himself. "Adam." And then indicating the others, "Sergio, Nina."

"Who are these men?" Adam asked. "And what about the children?"

Nina nodded and turned back to Capac. They spoke briefly, then she returned to Adam and Sergio.

"This is the situation. These men are part of a rebel group that has left the city—yes, it exists, and I'll tell you more about that later. He says the children are being held in the royal palace. There is a high priest who will decide when it is time for the gods to receive them."

"And 'receiving' is a euphemism for sacrifice," Sergio said.

"Yes."

Capac spoke again, "The city is ruled by this priest and the people are unhappy. He has armed men on his side, and they protect him. If we help them depose this priest, then the children can be released."

"What do you propose?" asked Adam.

"We will meet you inside the walls tonight," replied Capac. "Quiso will guide you to us."

"That's not a plan," said Adam. "So far it's those two, you, me and Sergio."

Sergio opened his backpack. He unzipping it, he revealed a folded Uzi and two handguns: a Colt .45 and a Smith and Wesson Bodyguard. It was a midget weapon—five inches long from hammer to muzzle. An ugly little stunted killer.

"We can do a lot of damage," said Sergio.

"Replay of the battle of Cajamarca?" said Nina. "Our superior technology defeats the Incas once again?"

"Exactly," Sergio said.

Adam wasn't convinced. "It's not enough. Nina, get them to draw a map of the city. Where the children are, how many men in arms they have, what kinds of weapons, and what kind of popular support we can count on." He turned to Sergio. "The purpose of this mission is to rescue the children. Bring them all back, and safely."

Sergio ignored the implied criticism and agreed. "No question. The weapons are a last option."

Later, before they started for the city, Sergio found Adam alone.

"It's time to settle our affairs, my friend."

"As in debts, letters to next of kin, what do you want on your tombstone, or on mine?"

"No. We're going to make it out of here. We're too smart, too modern, and too well armed. And I don't think you owe me any money."

"Then you must be talking about love," said Adam. "And maybe Nina."

"I suppose I am. How do you say it, in English? You are the man."

"That's what we say. You are the man."

"Okay. You are the man."

"Only if she says so," said Adam.

"She said so."

"Nice of you to let me know."

Sergio smiled and walked back to the camp.

CHAPTER 38

AMAZON JUNGLE, PERU

Adam insisted on a strategy. He wanted the rebel soldiers in on the planning. They were the most familiar with the city. They decided that it would be best for Quiso and Titu to get Adam, Sergio, and Nina into the city. Once inside the walls, they would rendezvous with the Inca rebels who would lead them to the house where the children were being held. The rebels said it was lightly guarded, and once the children were freed, two of the Inca rebels would escort them out of the city as quickly as possible. Adam and Sergio would stay behind and support the other Inca rebels in deposing the high priest. They would catch up with Nina and the children and make their way back to the closest village where they could be met by the police and returned home. It all made sense. The rebel soldiers slipped away.

Adam walked to the edge of the clearing and looked out at the expanse of the Amazon rain forest. Green from left to right, to the far horizon and in spots, black smoke rose from the fires. He went over the plan in his mind. They had firepower and strong men on their side. And they shouldn't meet any serious resistance if the people in the city truly disliked the rule of the high priest.

But he also knew there were other problems. Would they be allowed to leave with the knowledge of the city? He and Nina could remain silent, but what about Sergio? Adam knew these were problems that would arise only if they were successful.

And then he saw the anomaly—a patch of green that was darker than the forest around it, the size of a small lake. At first, he thought it was a cloud shadow on the forest, but he glanced up and the sky was clear.

"Nina."

She walked over to him. He pointed and said to her, "Look over there."

"It must be the city," said Nina.

The trek through the last part of the forest was relatively easy—Quiso led them to a well-traveled path on a gentle descent from the glade until they arrived at a wide gorge with a turbulent river at the bottom. Adam estimated that it was at least a hundred feet to the water. Waves splattered crazily against jagged boulders. Even if they could find a way down the walls of the gorge, there was no way across the river. Quiso pointed downstream—there was a rope bridge that sagged so heavily that it was hidden by an outcropping of the cliff. They followed Quiso along the edge of the gorge to the bridge.

Nina said, "It's the real thing—an Inca bridge—a *keshwa chaca*, made of woven grass and reeds. Every year, the people in the surrounding villages have to tear it down and weave new cables. It was part of their public service obligation to the Inca Empire."

There was no other way across the gorge. Going up or downstream in an effort to cross the river was a task that could be measured in days. The thick rope cables were anchored to rectangular stones that were buried in the ground. Sergio examined the cables and asked Nina, "And how old is this one?"

"I don't know. But it looks pretty fresh. Or . . ."

"Or it's five hundred years old," said Sergio. "No way am I stepping on that."

Adam took off his backpack. "I'll go first."

Sergio smiled grimly. "Be my guest."

The slats of wood braided into the floor of the bridge and the thick rope of the sides of the bridge felt sturdy to Adam. He took a few steps forward and at once the bridge dipped and swayed. He knew if the bridge failed it would likely come loose from one of the anchors and not from some weakness of the construction. He took a few more steps and turned around.

"It feels fine. Just wait for me to get to the other side."

He wasn't sure it felt fine. *He* surely didn't. It wasn't that he was afraid of heights, he had just made a point of avoiding them all his life. Another step and the floor of the bridge twisted crazily under him. He grabbed the cable rail and threw his weight to the other side. This wasn't a bridge; it was a ride. He'd only make it worse by looking down. He just needed to keep going, show no fear, make it to the other side, and bring everybody across.

A few more feet and he reached the opposite bank and solid ground.

"Go one at a time. And don't look down. Always straight ahead."

Nina was next and she quickly crossed the bridge.

Adam held out his hand to her. "Here's another bit of intelligent defense." He pointed to the two massive stones that flanked the end of the bridge.

"You can defend the bridge with one man," added Nina.

"One very skillful man."

Titu and Quiso crossed, and then Sergio.

Sergio looked pale. "That wasn't so bad. But I have to confess to a fear of heights."

"You don't have to confess," said Adam. "It's written all over your face. And remember, we have to do it one more time on our way back."

One by one, they squeezed through the narrow passageway between the boulders.

The trail past the boulders was well defined and solid beneath their feet. Quiso led the way and they progressed easily. Then he motioned them to stop.

Titu told Nina, "He says we are very close to the city wall. We must get off the trail and wait until it is dark before we go any further."

Quiso led them a few yards further along the trail. He stopped and pointed to a mass of fallen tree trunks that would give them a natural hiding place. They settled in under the decaying branches. Nina handed out power bars, and Sergio opened his backpack and laid out his weapons: the two pistols and the folded Uzi.

"Help yourself," he said to Adam.

Adam picked out the Uzi. Quiso pointed to the Bodyguard pistol and held out his hand. Adam shook his head to say no. Quiso made a grab for it, but Adam parried his hand.

Darkness came quickly. The thin crescent moon was feeble and couldn't penetrate the thick jungle canopy. Adam took out his flashlight, wrapped a kerchief around the lens, and shined the dimmed light on Quiso.

The boy nodded and took Titu's hand. Guided by Adam's muted flashlight, they found the trail and continued.

Night sound in the jungle was different from day sound. At night, the bats took over and filled the air with their fluttering wings. The monkeys were sleeping, but warily as the jaguars patrolled the trees, too. An animal or a bird fell from a tree; there was a grinding screaming struggle on the ground, followed by the silence of death.

A few minutes later, Capac and his three warriors met them. Even in the muffled light of the flashlight, Adam could see the nervousness on their faces. Titu placed his hands on Capac's shoulders, leaned forward, and touched his forehead against his. The other three warriors stepped forward and, in turn, received the same blessing.

The city began to make its presence known by smell—wood fires, food cooking, animal manure—and then by sounds—a melody on a wood flute, a baby's cry, a dog bark, a gruff male voice followed by laughter. People were doing what they do at night. That the city they were about to enter was frozen in time for five hundred years made no difference.

Capac raised a hand to stop. A few feet ahead of them was a wall. Adam pointed his flashlight. It was covered with vegetation: vines, flowers, strange plants with thick pointed leaves. Whatever species they were, they looked sharp and dangerous. The wall was a living defense system and at the same disguised as a part of the jungle flora.

"How the hell do we get in?" Sergio whispered.

Capac gestured to them to follow him on a narrow path that circled the wall. He stopped and pulled back a section of the vegetation revealing a short, narrow door. He drew it open and motioned them to wait, then crawled through the hole.

A moment later, he poked out and motioned them to follow. One by one, they squeezed through the narrow portal.

They were inside the city. Nina saw thatched cottages, some dark, some slightly illuminated by what must have been small oil lamps or candles. There were few people about, two children playing and a few old people sitting on overturned thick logs, talking quietly.

Gradually, as her eyes grew accustomed to the dark, she began to see the larger areas of the city. Straight narrow paths of hardened dirt seemed to go on into the void, intersected by other narrow ones. They passed tiny parks, squares with water troughs and fountains. There were fruit trees everywhere; oranges, bananas, limes, lemons, and avocados were the ones she recognized, and an equal number of trees bulging with fruits she did not.

Her eyes were wide, darting back and forth trying to take it all in.

Nina looked at Adam. She wanted to tell him what she was feeling, but they had agreed not to talk. She would have told him that she was experiencing the antithesis of what she had spent her whole life preparing for. Instead of examining the relics of the Incas, their corpses, jewelry, fabrics, art, language, and DNA, she was seeing everything alive. She was the opposite of Quiso. He had experienced the future, and she was experiencing the past. Someday they might compare notes.

Adam saw the pyramid. It rose out of an empty plaza. Square around its base, and flat on the top, Adam estimated its height about twenty feet because it had to fit under the canopy above the city. Its sloping sides were speckled with tufts of moss. On one side, there was a narrow row of steps the sacrificial victims would climb to a flat summit and a stone altar. The pyramid had no grandeur or beauty, it was a simply a civic monument constructed for the purpose of ritual murder. A covey of macaws screeched hell in anticipation for the blood that would be spilled.

The light exploded in his face, and Adam felt his arms pinned behind his back. Someone behind him thrust a foot into the back of his knee, and he went down. There was more light coming from men holding torches, all wearing the same clothes. They must be soldiers. A blade against his throat and spears aimed at his chest. Adam saw Sergio and the others on their knees in the same position. The Inca soldiers quickly stripped them of their backpacks. A soldier with measured ropes approached and tied Sergio's wrists. Adam looked at Quiso. The boy nodded. The rope-bearing Inca soldier approached Adam. There was a moment when the soldier holding the knife had to step aside so the other soldier could secure Adam's wrists. Adam struck the man hard in the wrist. The knife fell, Adam rose to his feet, but four soldiers leaped on him and wrestled him to the ground. No one noticed Quiso running off into the dark.

Adam's hands were tied behind his back, and they were separated into two groups: the rebel Incas who led them into the city in one, and Adam, Nina, and Sergio in the other. There seemed to be an argument among the soldiers as to which group Titu belonged, and in the end, he was taken away with the Inca rebels.

The light of the torches illuminated the city as they were led off. It was not as deserted as Adam thought. Clusters of people stared at them, Inca children held on to their parent's hands, awed by this strange procession of light skinned and exotically dressed prisoners.

Adam, Nina, and Sergio emerged into an open plaza via a narrow alleyway. Sconces held unlit torches stuffed with straw, ready to be lit on a moment's notice.

As Adam was being led forward, he tested the binding on his wrists. He could loosen them. It was just a question of when. He looked over at Sergio. The detective smiled. Adam liked that. He was a tough guy and, like Adam, he knew it was too early to panic.

The procession of guards and prisoners stopped in front of a row of squat one-story buildings. Two guards opened a door and pushed Nina and Adam inside.

He saw Sergio being led away. Smart. They were weaker if separated.

In a small cell, his wrists were untied while another guard used the end of his spear to jab and prod at his clothes until he understood that they wanted him to strip. Once Adam did, they pushed his clothes into a corner. A guard emptied a jug of liquid over his clothes and ignited it with a flint. The clothes burst into flames. The guards motioned him into another room where there was a wooden circular bath. A metal tub of water was being heated by charcoal fire. Two guards lifted the tub and poured boiling water into the bath. They motioned for Adam to get in the water. Adam lowered himself into the bath. It was blistering hot, and he sprang up, but a powerful hand pushed him under. He was lifted up—he took a deep breath and was pushed down again. Of course, the Incas were making sure he was cleansed of what had killed more of them than the conquistadors: germs. The guards lifted him out of the water, and an older man stepped forward. He placed himself a few feet from Adam and quietly stared at him.

"Your hands, please."

Adam held out his hands. The man looked at them, studied his fingernails, then removed a short polished stick with a blunt end from his shoulder pouch. He prodded and poked Adam, ran the stick over his stomach, felt the lymph nodes under his arms, his groin. Adam realized he was being examined and concluded that this man was some kind of doctor. The man placed the stick over his heart and held it lightly, like a tuning fork. He nodded, then went behind him and ran the stick over his back. Adam wondered if the man could find the piece of shrapnel the Army surgeon didn't want to remove from his back. The man moved the stick over Adam's back, stopped, and then tapped on a spot close to his spine. He pressed hard, and Adam knew he had found it. He saw the man reach into his bag, remove something, felt a sharp pinch, then a cooling sensation. The man came around him and held up a jagged piece of metal the size of a dime.

"Not bad, Doc. Got any more magic for me?"

The man shrugged, smiled, and brought out a polished flat stone from his pouch. He held it up to Adam's mouth then spit to the side to demonstrate what he wanted Adam to do.

"You understand?"

Adam asked, "You want me to spit on the stone?"

The doctor nodded. Adam obeyed, and the man reached in his bag, took out a little gold vial, and poured out a few drops of a colorless liquid on top of Adam's saliva. He shook the stone, waited a few seconds, and examined the mixture. Adam wondered if the doctor was satisfied. Was he clean? The man dipped the stick and the stone in the hot water, shook it off, and nodded to the guards who handed Adam a towel. He dried himself and was given a stack of linen clothes: a pullover shirt, a skirt that wrapped around his waist, and a pair of sandals. He reached around and felt his back where the doctor had removed the shrapnel. There was something attached to his skin covering the wound. Adam now knew the Incas could diagnose with a wand and do painless surgery. They could test saliva. And he figured they weren't going to kill him yet if they had an interest in making sure he was healthy.

Adam was in a square room with a dirt floor and bare mud-brick walls. The door was made of thick wood with iron hinges. Through a narrow window in the door, he could see three Inca soldiers outside. They had a view of Adam and enough light from the wall torches to keep him under observation. They would hear any noise he made.

Adam continued his investigation. There was one window with bars, but it was high on the wall. It may be out of reach for the shorter Incas, but not for him. He tested the strength of the bars, and they were solidly implanted in the thick walls.

Peering out the window, he saw two armed and alert Inca soldiers staring back at him. His prison bed was a thick fiber pad with a blanket. He had a clay pitcher of water and a large pot for his waste. He stretched out on the bed.

He closed his eyes. He wasn't going anywhere.

CHAPTER 39

THE CITY

The sound of the door opening woke Nina. A guard placed a bowl of food on the floor and shut the door. A banana, an orange, a guava, and two round flat breads. She downed the meal; a few minutes later the man returned, retied her wrists, and led her outside.

In daylight, the city was bathed in a soft green tint. She looked up and saw why—overhead was a translucent canopy of intricately woven green fabric. The green color served as camouflage—from thirty-five thousand feet up in the air, it would just be another patch of Amazon jungle. She remembered Adam pointing it out to her from the plateau, seeing it as a slightly darker green on the Amazon carpet. But what held it up? It seemed to float above the city; there were no masts, trees, or poles supporting it. Like a green haze, it floated above the city letting in light and yet protecting it from observation. Another mystery.

It was early morning, and the city was vibrant and busy. There were people in motion doing everything that one would imagine in a sixteenth-century Inca city. Only, for the first time, Nina realized, what she was seeing was not imagined, but real. This was something not even the conquistadors had witnessed. As a conquering army, they experienced the Inca civilization as both the enemy and also the repository of wealth. They viewed Inca accomplishments from the other end of a spear. The Spanish saw the cities just before they set them on fire, or looted them, or dug up the streets and temples for the stones to construct their cathedrals. There were the chroniclers, like Guamán Poma, who tried to record everything he could about the Inca civilization even as the Spanish were destroying it. His book was a letter to the Spanish king protesting the treatment of the native peoples by his own conquerors. He illustrated it with more than three hundred drawings, the only contemporary account of sixteenth-century Inca civilization.

Nina realized she was seeing normal Inca life. The irony was that she had nothing to preserve her observations except her memory. Poma, at least, had pen and paper. At the same time, if she ever returned to Cuzco, would she really disclose the location of the city? It would surely lead to its destruction. She knew of a protected Amazon tribe that was invaded by an English reality show. The tribal leaders told the producers that they wanted no part of the enterprise. They did not want money, fame, or a new generator, which they had no use for as they didnt have electricity. What they wanted to be was left alone. The TV show's producers bribed a local official, and they were granted permission over the protests of the tribe. One of the TV crew had the flu and infected the tribe. Twelve people died. Whatever knowledge she absorbed about the Inca civilization, if she was able to return, she would have to keep the city a secret. Still, if there were one thing she could take away, it would be the code that would enable her to read quipus.

As she was led through the city, she tried to observe as much as possible and, at the same time, check it against what she already knew about Inca culture and life. The people she passed looked healthy, well fed, and strong. Obviously, the society was working.

The men wore sleeveless tunics, made from a single piece of cloth. Some had linen cloaks wrapped around their shoulders and fastened by a silver or gold pin. The heads of the pins were discs large enough to be decorated with images of animal and human figures, and the edges were sharp enough to function as knives. All of the tunics were colored, but some were brighter and the patterns more detailed. She assumed that the wearers were of a higher station in life. Some men, probably military officers, wore bright feathers and seashells sewn to their tunics, in rows like medals. Everyone, men and women, wore simple leather sandals, probably made from llama hides.

The women wore a one-piece dress that combined skirt and blouse, reaching to the ankles and bound at the waist by an ornamental sash. It seemed to be shopping day, and the women carried large woven bags for their purchases. Clearly, they were on the main street of the city.

Women crowded around food stalls filled with fruits and vegetables, baskets of hulled grains, and corn—dried, in husks, and ground to a rough meal. There were pots of spices, rows of bright and shiny peppers, and yellowish dried fish placed on banana leaves. Nina didn't see any meat—she assumed the Inca never acquired a taste for monkey, tapir, or snake. If the people in this city were the descendants of sixteenth-century Inca, then they most likely brought their own eating habits with them and never changed. She wondered how and where they grew their vegetables. Corn, potatoes, and some of the other grains wouldn't do well in a rain forest. Nina didn't see any exchange of money in the market. People just helped themselves to the food and moved on.

In between the food stalls, open-air workshops were busy. In one, an old man was pouring melted gold into molds. He looked up at Nina and pointed to some of his work cooling on a flat rock. They were little renderings of Andean animals and birds—exactly like the ones that were attached to the wrappings of the Inca mummies in Nina's laboratory. In another stall, a man was sharpening knives; in another, a woman was laying out balls of wool dyed in bright yellow, red, and blue. They passed three women who worked at large looms weaving cloth. Some women carried infants in slings across their chests. The older children sat in open-air classrooms in circles around their teachers. Some were learning how to assemble and tie quipus; young girls were being instructed in sewing and weaving. Older boys were practicing martial arts. The youngest ones were singing songs.

The teacher looked up and smiled—behind him, his children stared at the invader. In another stall, what must have been a medical clinic, an old man was applying a poultice to a baby's chest. A few other women with their children waited their turns. The whole scene seemed to depict a well-ordered, peaceful society—until Nina heard the anguished cry of a man being dragged by the arms by two Inca soldiers. Behind him, a third soldier prodded him with his long spear. Everything stopped. The people in the vicinity stared silently at the soldiers. A few teenage boys followed the soldiers. One threw a rock. It bounced off the back of a soldier. The soldiers stopped and turned, but the teens continued to stare. The soldier holding the spear raised it threateningly. The boys backed away.

A few paces further, Nina entered a more heavily guarded area. The path was no longer dirt, but polished marble. Magnificent conch shells lined the path. The grounds were planted with magnificent orchids, exotic fruit trees, and flowers. Rising out of the earth were tall reed cages filled with hundreds of chirping birds—some flying around the cage, others perched on branches—a blur of color and noise. Ahead stood a one-story building constructed of polished mahogany. The roof was thatched with green palm leaves tied together in sturdy neat knots. Four Inca warriors stood at attention along the path, unsheathed swords at their sides. At the door, two more men holding lances guarded the entrance. She entered a lush garden, a courtyard that was surrounded by the walls of the building.

Fountains bubbled; fruit trees and orchids lined pebble paths. Small birds and butterflies darted among the flowers that grew out of elegant clay pots. Graceful young women in thin cotton robes cut flowers and placed them in baskets. Nina recognized them as *mama-cona*, the young women selected to serve in the households of the

Inca nobility or the temples of the priests. The most beautiful ones would be selected as wives. The building's tall thatched roof brushed the green fabric of the canopy. Nina noticed that the guards had left her, and she was free to wander the garden. The women ignored her, eyes downcast as they went about their work. The air was suffused with the scent of the flowers. It was almost intoxicating, or maybe Nina was just suffering from some kind of sensory overload. She felt like she had been dropped into another world. She realized she was feeling what Quiso had experienced, only she was in the past and he was in the future. It was mind-bending. Under the eaves of the roof, the walls of the building were painted with murals depicting battles against the conquistadors, ferocious animals spitting fire against invading monsters, and Spanish priests suffering the same tortures as they imparted to their Inca brothers in Christ: One was seated in a baptismal chair lowered into a mountain lake, another tied to a stake surrounded by flames while impotent angels floated overhead blowing puffs of air in an attempt to put out the flames consuming the burning bodies. She realized that history wasn't the only propaganda of the victorious; art was, too. On one wall, silver-white streaks were painted in the blue sky. Perhaps they were the exhaust of jet planes crossing the Amazon. Though the world was unaware of the Inca city, Nina guessed that the Incas must have a sense that the world had changed. They saw jet planes fly overhead and they had contracted with an obscure Amazon tribe to kidnap children and bring them to their city.

At the far end of the garden a door opened and a man in a robe motioned her to come forward.

The hard bench was uncomfortable, and Adam's wrists hurt. The guards on each side of him looked tough and alert. He was facing a little stage for someone who must be really important.

The room was bathed in the soft light of the scented oil lamps that were placed on tables and hung from the ceiling. Adam realized he was in a palace that would stand up to anything of the same era in Europe. The walls were covered from ceiling to floor with thin sheets of gold over what must have been carved wood underneath. The three-dimensional images depicted the history, religion, and culture of the Inca world. Adam realized he had seen parts of it before in Steiner's cottage. Steiner's was a European painter's version of this seamless bas-relief. Steiner had been here. Intricately woven tapestries hung from the ceiling like medieval flags. The tapestries were composed of colored concentric circles, others of interlocking diamonds, and mazes of floating geometric forms. It spoke of a sophisticated taste. Time may have stood still in this Inca city, but not in the development of art.

A door opened. Nina was led forward and sat down next to Adam. She lowered her shoulder and nuzzled her cheek against his neck. He turned his head and kissed her.

"You okay?" asked Adam.

"I'm fine," responded Nina. "Sergio?"

"I don't know. We were separated."

"Adam, this is beyond anything I could have imagined. We are either in a demented theme park called Inca-land, or we've gone back in time five hundred years."

"You tell me. You're the expert."

"It all looks real," said Nina. "It's a living time capsule."

Beside them, the guards came to attention. Two more guards entered and stood on either side of the platform.

A towering figure walked into the room through parted curtains. A long robe made of blue and black bird feathers covered his body, and as he moved, the feathers shimmed and rippled. He looked like he was wearing the sea. On his head was a gold mask—a snarling jaguar. Blood red rubies blazed from the eye sockets; its mouth was open in a threatening snarl, exposing long silver fangs. In his hand, he held a long wooden staff entwined with ribbons of gold.

You must be the high priest. I hallucinated you or your brother, in a tunnel in the American Embassy. You tried to kill me, bastard. Are you real now?

Nina leaned closer to him. He could feel her body. She was real.

Adam stood up. "Where are the children?"

The guards pinned Adam's arms behind his back and forced him down.

Nina added, "Give us the children and we'll leave."

Jaguar man, the high priest, came down from the platform and stood over Adam. He could feel the guards' grip on his arms tighten.

"You have returned." The jaguar man's voice was high-pitched, singsong, and he banged his staff on the floor for emphasis.

Returned? Oh, Christ, another one who thinks I'm Pizarro. He wanted to tell Nina the high priest was familiar to him, but he knew it would sound mad. She needed him to be sane now—saner than this child murderer.

"You have returned to steal gold and bring death to the Inca," said the high priest as he banged his staff again.

"You have me confused with someone else," said Adam. "I don't want your gold, or your death. I want the children. There will be others following us if we don't return. You can keep me as a hostage. If you like, a ransom . . ."

"Another ransom? We believed you once when you promised one for the release of Atahualpa—we won't make the same mistake again. The word of the conquistador is poison. You promised gifts before. Instead you brought death from your diseases. You have brought slavery."

"They wanted treasure."

"And we would have given it," said the high priest, "not the gold you came to steal. But what our civilization had that was really valuable—a way to live in the world in harmony with nature. Our citizens live one hundred and fifty years. That is our gold. That is the gold you didn't see."

"You kill innocent children," said Nina.

"And Pizarro? The bodies of Incas are buried by the thousands in the silver mines of Potosí. You worry about three children? You only worry about the lives of children because they are yours."

"Why don't you sacrifice the children as you did in the past?" Nina asked calmly. "Without killing them."

The man in the mask sighed. "Our dangers are closer. The half measures of the past are not good enough. Even here, we have lost touch with some of our customs. They must be restored. You will both be permitted to witness the sacrifice. Then your own death will follow."

He said to his guards, "Take them away. If they resist, kill them."

CHAPTER 40

THE CITY

dam paced in his cell. A narrow moonbeam shot a dim light into the room. The guards outside had stepped out of the hallway for the cooler air of the portico, the iron band around his ankle that chained him to the wall made their presence unnecessary. He heard a shuffling noise outside. A panel under the door opened and hands pushed in a bowl of corn mush and beans. A floppy corn cake covered the mush. As he ate his food, Adam considered their situation. He, Nina and Sergio were prisoners. Quiso had disappeared, and Titu wouldn't be much help anyway. There was an insurrection brewing in the city; he could see it in the faces of the people. But at the moment, the odds seemed to be with the forces under the control of the high priest. But what about those soldiers? What were they thinking? They must all have family in the city, and their loyalties would be divided. Adam hoped it wouldn't take much to turn them against the high priest. But he couldn't do anything as long as he was in this jail.

The whistle was so soft that he almost didn't hear it. Then he heard it again and moved to the window. The room went dark. Someone at the window was blocking out the moonlight by pressing his body against the outside window. It was Quiso. He was holding on to the bars with one hand, and with the other he tossed something into the room. He let go of the bars and fell away, and the room was flooded again with moonlight. On the floor lay a small cloth bag tied together with a thin rope. Adam tore the package open and took out a knife blade, its handle wrapped in strands of twisted twine, a short steel baton with a chiseled edge, and one of their flashlights.

Adam took the chisel and attacked the iron band around his ankle. He jammed the sharp edge into the space where the lock was attached to the band. The quality of the metal was poor, and it was old and rusted. One strong push and it separated. Now he was free to move about. He tested the bars in the window, but realized they were embedded too deeply in the wall. His only chance was the door. It was hung on hinges on the inside. They could be loosened and removed. But there were guards outside. He would have to work quietly. If necessary, the gun held seven rounds, but there were more than enough soldiers to defeat him.

It took him a half hour of steady work quietly prying the bolts out of the hinges. He managed to keep the hinges aligned without the bolts so the door now rested on the shelves of the joints. With his knife, he tore the blanket into long thin strips and put them aside. Adam pounded his fists on the door until he heard the guards approach. They unlocked the door and swung it open. The door came off the hinges and fell forward. The two guards were thrown off balance. Adam grabbed the first by the neck and hit him with the baton. The second guard leaped into the room, drawing his sword. He knew what to expect. Adam parried the attack with the baton and followed it with a sudden elbow to the man's throat, and the guard went down. Adam quickly tied both guards' hands and gagged them with the blanket strips. It wouldn't last long, he knew, but it would give him some time.

In the hallway, Adam stopped at the next door.

"Nina?"

Her door was secured with a simple iron bar. He lifted it and opened the door.

"Lets get out of here," Nina whispered.

There was a rear door that was close to the city wall. The vines and trees gave them cover while they got their bearings. The streets were deserted; people were asleep. A guard passed by. He stopped for a moment, and then resumed his patrol.

There was a whistle, a high-pitched shriek, and a guard rushed out of the building. His cries brought other guards holding lit torches—all of them were armed.

"I think they just noticed we're missing," said Nina.

"If we can find Sergio, we would be stronger."

In the square, an officer was barking orders to a squad of guards. Adam said, "I stick out like a sore thumb."

Nina removed her shawl and bit quickly into the material and then tore the shawl in half. She tied the cloth around his head covering his eyes.

"Perfect." Adam said. "I can't even see through this thing."

Nina said, "Hold my arm." They stepped out of the bushes and merged into the crowds of people who had come out of their houses to witness the commotion.

The city was alive with soldiers and guards carrying blazing torches. In groups of two and three, they swept through the streets, emptying residents out of their homes. There seemed to be no method, they entered buildings at random. Sometimes different teams searched the same buildings.

"Where do we begin?" Nina whispered.

"Wherever they aren't looking."

Ahead there was a simple building with a thatched roof.

"That one?" Nina suggested.

A guard stood at the doorway, but his attention was focused on the activity of his fellow soldiers rushing about.

"Get me closer to the side of the building," said Adam.

The guard at the doorway started toward Adam and Nina. Adam

felt in his bag for the knife. The guard was just a boy about Quiso's size. Adam wasn't sure what to do with him. Someone shouted, and the boy stopped. An officer was calling him. The boy turned and ran off toward the man, and Adam and Nina dashed into the unguarded building.

Inside there was a large room in the middle of the floor. Adam took out the flashlight and flicked it on.

They descended the steps into the floor below and found themselves in a circular room. Two oil lamps revealed a bench with a folded blanket on it. A water bucket and a ladle sat on the floor. Adam could see that whoever was guarding the place also lived there.

"Adam, someone's coming," warned Nina.

They backed into the shadows. A moment later, a guard entered carrying a tray of food. He was slight of build, an older man. He placed the tray on the bench and sat down. Adam nudged Nina forward.

The guard stood up slowly, not sure what to do.

Adam came forward. The man drew his sword slowly. It looked to Adam as if the man didn't really want to fight. Adam raised his hands as if to say he wouldn't hurt him. Nina smiled. The man handed Adam the sword and asked, "Did you come for the gold?"

Nina looked at Adam. He nodded.

The old man took one of the oil lamps and handed it to Adam.

"*Pizarro.* They said you would come. How many llamas did you bring with you?"

Another one. Another one who thinks I'm Pizarro. He decided he would do or say whatever it took.

"We have forty llamas," Adam said.

The guard went to a door, took out a key, and unlocked it.

"And you will have to take enough men to carry the emperor's chair," the man told them as he opened the door.

Adam and Nina entered. Adam held up the lamp. A firestorm of yellow lit up the room. Gold covered every inch of the floor, rose halfway to the ceiling, and flowed right up to the door where they were standing. They were facing solid gold ingots, gold statues—both human and animal. Trunks overflowing with gold necklaces, bracelets, rings, and chains. One trunk was filled with *tumis*, the ceremonial knives, their handles adorned with gems. There were stacks of plates, bowls, goblets, pots, and cups. All gold. Pots overflowing with small figurines of birds, animals, fish, and reptiles. The presence of the gold was so overwhelming that Adam thought he could smell it.

Nina bent down and picked up a foot long statue. "Look familiar?"

"Familiar? On a trip to Easter Island, I saw the real ones. They're ten feet tall sculptures of ancestors, buried in the soil, backs to the sea. They're called *moai*, right?"

"Yes," said Nina. "This is just a smaller gold version, like something a rich tourist would buy."

"How about an Inca emperor?" asked Adam.

"Why not?" said Nina. "Although it does screw up some time lines."

Nina put the statue down. She looked around the room and realized everything in it was invaluable—not because it was gold or gems—but for what each artifact could teach, confirm, or dispel. The objects in this room could change histories.

There were large thin sheets of gold in a neat stack. She picked one up. Attached to it was a quipu.

"There are markings on this. What if it corresponds to the knots on this quipu? My God, Adam, we may have just found out that the Incas did have a written language." And then it hit her.

"This is the second ransom. The one that was never delivered to Pizarro. The old man thinks we're here to collect the ransom. We're in Vilcabamba."

And if they were in Rome watching Michelangelo paint his ceiling or Julius Caesar was about to bump into Brutus and Marc Anthony and there were three kids in danger, Adam would have said the same thing, "Nina, we have to keep moving."

"Sorry. It's the archaeologist in me."

"Pizarro," said the old man.

"He's calling you." Nina said. They went into the anteroom.

The old man said, "When will you return our Emperor Atahualpa?"

Atahualpa had died five hundred years ago. Adam crossed his arms, put his hands on his biceps, and said, "I don't want your gold. I want something else."

"What do you want *Pizarro?*"

"The children."

The man thought for a moment. "I would give them up happily. But the high priest won't. He needs them for the sacrifice tomorrow."

"Then you will not get Atahualpa," said Adam. "I will order my soldiers to kill him."

The man tilted his head and screwed up his face to show Adam how hard he was thinking about this before saying, "You can't get the children out. They are very well guarded."

"What about a boy named Quiso?"

"The high priest says he is a traitor. He betrayed our city. When they find him, they will kill him."

"Can you find him?"

The old man cupped his chin. "Yes. I will try."

"We will wait for him here."

When the old man started to leave, Adam said to him, "And tell him I want something he has."

Adam thought they had been waiting for at least an hour. Was Quiso captured? Was he even in the city? The rebel soldiers weren't the only ones who were opposed to the sacrifice. How to mobilize them? Could he get Sergio out and where were the weapons? He had the beginnings of a plan, but it depended on Quiso.

Nina had returned to the gold room. Periodically, she shrieked in joy at another amazing discovery and said, "Adam, you have to see this."

But the only discoverey that Adam wanted was Quiso. He entered the room. Nina was holding up a yellowed manuscript. "It's a letter that was included in the ransom—from one of his generals," said Nina. "They must have had a prisoner write it. Listen:

To the Spaniard Marques Don Francisco Pizarro and those who have accompanied him. I, Chalcuchima, do hereby send you as much gold as our engineers have measured to fill the room in which our beloved Emperor Atahualpa now waits in cold and darkness. This gold will be in exchange for his life as you will deliver him to his chair and he will return to his people. We do not wish to wage war against those who come to our kingdom, except we ask them to find a way to live peacefully with the Inca, respecting our laws, our religion, and becoming people of the Inca empire. We will not ask you to give up your language, or to give up your religion, or your ways of organizing your society as long as it does not disrespect or violate the laws of the Inca. We do not hold slaves, and we will not be slaves to others. We donate a portion of labor to the common good and, as we understand that there are labors that are harder than others, no one will be forced to spend more than sixty days a year in mines. In return, we assure our subjects that they will have the benefit of our warehouses of grain in times of famine, our protection from enemies in times of war, and access to our medicine and healers, and our academies for your youth so that they may be trained in the Inca language and customs. Those who live under Inca rule can advance in many areas, and even in their own civic or tribal jurisdictions, but know that people in high positions who commit crimes are punished more severely than lesser people. I understand that these are not the terms of one who is offering treasure for the return of our beloved emperor, but we have only lost one battle. We do not wish to wage war, but if you do, we will promise you years of strife, as the Inca will never give up. Let us begin a council of peace, rather than a council of war.

She rolled up the manuscript. "It's very sad, isn't it?"

He wanted to tell her that it was just diplomatic bullshit—a self-serving adulatory and romantic description of a totalitarian state that was in reality devastated by civil war and smallpox, and facing a dozen rebellions of conquered people who were tired of seeing their children sacrificed. He knew, and Nina knew also, that the reason the empire fell apart was that there were too many people who welcomed the Spanish as liberators, not conquerors. He also didn't have to remind her that Chalcuchima, the author of the letter, was later burned alive by Pizarro.

Then Adam saw what was really important in the room—a row of ceremonial masks on a shelf. Their value was evident—they were constructed of gold and silver, and they were studded with precious gems. Animals, gods, demons, devils. Masks.

A plan began to take shape in his head.

"Adam?"

Quiso and the old man stood in the doorway. The boy held out his hand to Adam. In it was the Bodyguard pistol.

Adam said to Nina, "I know how to do this."

CHAPTER 41

THE CITY

At dawn, the drums started beating. Mercifully, the high shrieking Andean flutes were silent. The city was shut down: the food stalls were empty; in the crafts stations, no one was weaving, sharpening swords, or making pots. There was a sense that something was about to happen. People came out of their homes and stood silently as if waiting for a parade to pass. Their mood was sullen.

The drums stopped, and the city was absolutely quiet. Even the parrots and macaws were silent, and the monkeys that usually shrieked at the tops of the trees had disappeared.

A horn blasted three times, and a troop of soldiers came out of the palace building. They split into two units and began herding people away from their homes and toward the pyramid plaza.

The people went obediently; the soldiers escorted them politely, but it was clear that attendance in the plaza was mandatory.

The drums grew louder. Soldiers divided the spectators into two groups and created an empty path between them that led to the base of the pyramid.

The first cadre entering the plaza was the high priest's palace guard. Wearing gold breastplate armor and plumed helmets, they marched in time to the beating drums. Behind them came the high priest, wearing a tunic of bird feathers woven into a pattern of red, yellow, and blue squares. He wore the jaguar mask, but instead of silver, his teeth were painted red. The other priests also wore animal masks—macaws, condors, and a caiman. Soldiers pushed the four Inca rebels forward, their hands bound in front of them. At the edge of the pyramid stairs, there was a stub of a tree trunk with iron rings embedded in it. The soldiers tied their prisoners' wrists to the rings and pushed them down to the ground.

The entire population of the city was now jammed into the plaza. At the back of the crowd, soldiers pushed people forward, giving them little space to move. Armed soldiers were stationed in front of the crowd and along the narrow path leading to the pyramid steps.

The horns sounded again. The children—Jimmy, Ronaldo, and Gabrielle—were escorted into the plaza. They were dressed in white alpaca robes, and they each held on to a thick gold rope. Their hair was wet, slicked down, and their mouths were painted red with the *ayahuasca*, the drug that would keep them docile.

The summit of the pyramid was surrounded by a foot-high stone wall. There was an altar with a shallow basin and an alabaster sluice that ran down the face of the pyramid into a bowl at the base. A round mirror was attached to a tripod easel behind the altar. Its circumference was decorated with seashells. In the center of the mirror was a small square opening. The reflection of the sun was a dot on the concave mirror. As it rose, the dot moved steadily toward the hole. It was the Inca clock. When the sun's rays reached the opening, it would be the moment for the ritual to begin.

The stage was set for the *capacocha*: The children were seated on a woven rug with their backs to the steps of the pyramid so they would not be able to see what happened at the summit. The young women ladled out servings of the maize beer laced with the *ayahuasca*. The children drank thirstily; the sweet liquid was almost addictive. It made their heads heavy, their eyes dead, and soon they drooped into fits of sleep, only to wake up a moment later in a panic, as if they had a sense of what was about to happen. Then the drug hit again, and the panic was replaced by euphoria.

The priests climbed the pyramid steps. At the summit, the high priest measured the position of the sun on the mirror. It was time. One of the *mamaconas* carried a tray to the top. On it was a hammer—a blunt oval stone tied to a wood handle. The high priest picked up the hammer and lifted it to the sky. The drums began again, and the young woman who delivered the hammer walked slowly down the stairs and placed her hand on Jimmy's forehead. Two soldiers helped Jimmy stand. They shifted him around so that they faced the pyramid, took his arms, and guided him up the stairs.

The priests backed the boy, helpless under the influence of the *ayahuasca*, against the altar and moved aside as the high priest lowered Jimmy backward over the altar bowl and raised the stone hammer.

And that was the moment when Adam removed the condor mask he was wearing, took out the little Bodyguard pistol, and fired two shots that tore off the high priest's hand from the wrist. The force rocked him backward. He tripped on the short wall and tumbled down the side of the pyramid. His bloody hand lay in the alabaster bowl.

The other three priests were frozen in their places. This was how Adam wanted them—in a state of shock. He grabbed one by his tunic, lifted him off his feet, and swept him around into the other two, sending them all down the side of the pyramid.

A pair of soldiers drew their swords and charged up the steps. Adam raised the pistol and hit the first one in the thigh above the knee. He fell sideways into the second, and they both fell down the stairs. The other soldiers inched toward the pyramid. He aimed the pistol. They froze.

Adam scooped Jimmy into his arms. The boy was breathing heavily, his eyes opened and he looked at Adam.

"You're okay, kid. I'm taking you home."

Jimmy nodded, and Adam swung him over his shoulder. He kept the gun in front of him and carefully descended the steps of the pyramid. The soldiers on the ground looked up at him but were too afraid or, Adam figured, too smart to come up the stairs. Their hesitation was a signal for the people in the crowd to advance and surround them. The soldiers were outnumbered and overwhelmed. As in the battle of Cajamarca, the loss of their leader—the high priest—was a signal to the Inca soldiers that further resistance was pointless. They dropped their spears. But Adam could see that the priests weren't giving up. They were backing away from the crowd looking for an escape. The people in the crowd began to advance on the priests. One of the village men picked up a spear and hurled it at them. The priests waved their sacrificial knives at the crowd and for a moment there was a standstill. Then the priests backed away and disappeared into the jungle.

Adam lowered Jimmy to his feet. He was unsteady.

"Who are you?"

"I'm the guy your mother sent to bring you back."

"She okay?"

"She will be when she sees you. It won't be long."

Ronaldo and Gabrielle, still drowsy, heard some of their conversation. Jimmy said, "Hey, guys. I guess we're going home."

Quiso and Sergio broke out of the crowd. Sergio had the backpack with the weapons. Quiso had a dog. It was a solid, friendly-looking mutt.

"I guess I missed all the fun," Sergio said.

"It's not over. The high priest and some of his men got away."

Nina said, "I think Capac and his men can handle him."

Sergio passed the weapons pack to Adam. "If he can't, we can."

Nina and the women attended to the children. They were given cold water to drink. Capac took a few steps up the side of the pyramid and faced the people in the plaza. They moved closer.

"Our city has been ruled by the high priest," said Capac. "But now that he is defeated, there will be no more deaths of our children; and no longer will we steal other people's children. The high priest will be seized and punished for his crimes against the people of the city. Until a new priest is chosen, the administration of the city will be taken over by a council of the elders."

He looked down at Adam, Sergio, and Nina.

"The Spanish people who have come from the outside world to save their own children have also helped us rid ourselves of the evil in our city. We are grateful."

As Capac descended the steps, Adam said to Nina, "Let's get the kids ready to go."

"Not yet. There's still one more thing."

CHAPTER 42

THE CITY

Nina watched the children line up at the base of the pyramid. Capac had explained to her and Adam that the children would be sacrificed in the new way—only their souls would be sent to the gods. They would plead for the Inca who were in immediate danger from the fires. And they would plead for the rest of the peoples in the world beyond the jungle. The jungle forest of the Amazon was the lungs of the planet, and if it were consumed by fire, the rest of the world would burn, too.

Nina could see the skepticism in Adam's face. She knew he wanted to leave the city as quickly as possible and get the kids returned home. Nina told Adam that part of her wanted to stay in the city forever and learn everything it could tell her about Inca culture and life. And then she realized that the knowledge was useless if she couldn't tell anyone. "I'll have to go back to figuring out the Inca the hard way," she said, "digging them out of the ground. Shit, do I really want to do that anymore?"

He took her hand and pulled her close to him, "There's always New Mexico."

"I think that might be a good idea."

• • •

One by one, they climbed the stairs. Again, Jimmy was the first. When he reached the summit, Titu reached out and quickly traced his face with his fingers. The drums beat steadily, and the haunting notes of the flutes carried over the rhythm.

"Close your eyes, my son, and let your soul fly to the heavens and meet the gods. You must ask the gods to put out the fires in the Amazon jungle."

Jimmy nodded. Titu lifted him a few inches off the floor and shifted his position so that the boy faced the sun. Then he lowered him. "Now you may open your eyes."

Gabrielle was next. Titu repeated the ritual. Lastly, Ronaldo climbed the steps and received the benediction from Titu.

At the base of the pyramid, the women had spread out woven blankets. The three children walked down the steps.

Nina pointed to the blankets. "They are there for you to sleep."

Jimmy, Gabrielle, and Ronaldo collapsed onto the blankets.

Later, and enough years later, when anyone asked Jimmy Del Vecchio about his time in Peru, he would say that he remembered being kidnapped by a man on a motorcycle when he was just ten years old and living in Lima. He counted it as one of the most amazing things that had ever happened to him in the otherwise ordinary life he lived with his wife and twin sons in Portland, Maine. The strange thing for Jimmy was that he remembered some parts really well and some parts, not at all. And then there were some parts he didn't like to talk about because he only remembered them in his dreams. He took an extension course at the University of Maine's Westbrook Campus called "Interpreting Dreams," and when it was his turn to get up and tell about a dream, he didn't want to talk about the Peru dreams, so he offered another one where he and his wife were sailing and they went too far out and were surrounded by a school of dolphins. Looking back, he might have made some of it up, but since it came out of his imagination, he figured it was just as good as a dream. In his discussion that followed, Roxanne Hurdle said that the dream was about how he really wanted to avoid being honest about his dreams but, even so, it was still valid. After the class, he had coffee with Roxanne and told her she was right—he made up the dream because he didn't want to talk about the one where he was led to the top of a pyramid in the jungle and fell asleep and the next thing he knew, he was having a frank conversation with a really nice man who had clawed feet and wings. In the dream he asked the man to send rain to the Amazon to put out the fires. How weird was that? And Roxanne said his dream must have worked because there weren't any more fires in the Amazon.

She wanted to hear more about the dream, but Jimmy had a feeling that she had a thing for him and he knew that exchanging dreams one-on-one was a fairly intimate activity and he didn't want it to go anywhere.

That night, he had the dream again.

He watched himself float out of his body and and fly up into the sky as his old body got smaller and smaller below him until he was above the clouds and he couldn't see anything. He had learned in "Interpreting Dreams" that people take images from the real world and repeat them in their dream, like using words in making up a sentence. So flying up into the air sounded like it came from *The Wizard of Oz*, his mom's favorite movie. And he had that feeling when he was in the dream that he was borrowing those images. But then, it took a different turn and he wasn't in Oz. He was on the sun and it wasn't even hot.

Ronaldo Contrero wouldn't talk to his parents for two weeks when he returned. His mother consulted a psychiatrist who told her that kidnapping victims often withdrew out of a sense of shame. Or, if they were children, may be angry that their parents didn't protect them. When Ronaldo finally emerged from his room, he was articulate about the reasons for his silence, and it had nothing to do with shame or anger. When he told them that he was too busy writing an account of his experience, they were relieved. But when he showed them what he had written, they were more disturbed than ever. It was a fantastical tale that had some elements of truth and a great deal of fantasy. Yes, he had been kidnapped and taken deep into the jungle. That was the first half. After that, Pachamama, the mother of the earth, escorted him to the golden throne where Inti, the sun god, sat and greeted him. Since it was too dangerous for Ronaldo to venture into Lima, his father arranged for the psychiatrist to be brought (under protest) to the heavily guarded Contrero fortress, where he spent a whole week dispensing therapy to Ronaldo. The irony of a kidnapped psychiatrist treating a kidnapped child was not lost on doctor and patient and, in some sense, it actually sped up the therapy. Ronaldo was advised and agreed to keep the later events of his kidnapping to himself, as Dr. Mendoza planned to do regarding his own abduction.

Gabrielle Le Tan had no memory of anything. The last thing she remembered was fainting in the fortress of Sacsayhuamán on the outskirts of Cuzco. Since it was where a Chinese tour guide found her, Gabrielle assumed that she had fainted, and Vincent went to get her help and hadn't yet returned. When her parents told her that she had been gone for two weeks, she shook her head and repeated her claim that she remembered nothing in between.

And once, when Adam fell asleep on a blanket under the piñon tree in Taos, he dreamed that he flew past the moon, the planets, and the stars, into the garden of the gods where the trees were silver, the earth soft and green—a place where the jaguar, the puma, the python, and the tiger lived among the llamas and alpacas. The borrowed souls of the children—Jimmy, Ronaldo, and Gabrielle were there. He couldn't see them but he heard them as they took turns speaking to the gods. He could sense them floating above the ground, lighter than the thin leaves of the mangrove tree, and then he looked down and saw that his feet weren't touching anything, either. He was a spirit; and no one could see him. Yet everyone was aware of his presence, and everything he experienced was true.

And, with the children, was his wife. She came to him invisibly. He knew it was Lynn because she took his hand and he felt it, and from there it was just a matter of floating into her embrace and letting her guide him in and out of the trees. He thought he would remember this when he awakened under the piñon tree in Taos, no matter what. But he didn't.

CHAPTER 43

THE CITY

The children stirred on their blankets, trying to get a sense of where they were. Women brought moist cloths and wiped the red dye from their mouths. Others brought jugs of cold water and maize cakes and distributed them to the children and adults.

Capac gathered Adam, Nina, and Sergio around him on a woven rug outside the royal palace. Bowls of fruit and platters of food were placed in the center of the rug. Quiso had brought his dog, Yarak, and the boy was all smiles. He squeezed in between Adam and Nina.

Capac recounted the history of the city, how after the last battles against the Spanish, it was decided to escape into the Amazon. It was more important to maintain Inca society where the gods and traditions would be respected than to wage perpetual war against the conquistadors.

Nina asked him about the sacrifices.

"We sacrificed when there were events that threatened the Inca people," said Capac. "We would send children to the gods to plead with them or beg forgiveness for our mistaken ways. But the retreat into the jungle was hard. We lost many people on the way. Our most precious possession was our children. We could not afford to lose any more. The priests devised an ingenious way to sacrifice the children, that is, to send their souls to the gods without killing them. But they also had to be in locations that reflected the constellation at the time. We had to go outside the city to find these children, bring them to the sacrificial site, and then return them. We used the Machiguenga for that and other tasks."

"What kinds of tasks?" asked Adam.

"They were used to capture and return a villager who tried to escape to the outside world. Or, they would come upon explorers who had strayed into our territory and were getting close to the city. At first, they would try to frighten them into retreating, but if that didn't work, there are many ways to disappear in the Amazon jungle." He paused, searching for the words. "But there is another matter. If these events come back to you, will you keep our city a secret?"

"Of course we will," said Adam.

"The world is a lot smaller now," said Sergio as he pointed to the sky. "One of these days."

"We have always known that," said Titu. "We are preparing for that day."

"What will you do?" asked Nina.

"We will do what our ancestors did," answered Capac. "We will abandon our city and move our people to another place. But this time, it will not be in the Amazon. We will not hide under a canopy of green, or be protected by a grove of golden trees whose pollen erases memory. We'll hide where no one will ever think of looking for us—Cuzco. We will take our knowledge, our wealth, our society, and live under your noses." He laughed and added, "Vilcabamba will live. The Inca will prosper and, who knows, we might even give you some cures for your diseases."

Women gave each of the children a neat pile of their original clothes; Jimmy, his Little League uniform; Ronaldo, his Nikes and jeans; and Gabrielle, her "Tourism Sucks" T-shirt. On top of each was a gift of a little gold animal. For Ronaldo and Jimmy, jaguars, and Gabrielle got an owl with pearl eyes.

Capac untied the strap around his waist that held his sword and handed it to Adam. "I would like you to have this. It once belonged to a conquistador. Perhaps a relative." Adam took the sword. It was about a foot and a half long, suited for combat at close quarters. He withdrew the blade from the scabbard and tested its sharpness against his thumb. It was lethal.

CHAPTER 44

THE RIVER

Quiso escorted Sergio, Nina, Adam, and the three children past the city wall to the bridge. As they followed him, Adam thought about the Inca boy's courage in stealing into Cuzco and rescuing the body of his brother, a sixteenth-century boy in the present—it must have been as alien as another planet. And here he was leading them back into the jungle. He was the reason they had all come out alive.

Adam scanned both sides of the path into the jungle as they walked. There were still dangers ahead before they reached the river and the bridge over the gorge. He figured the high priest was still alive and he had escaped with some soldiers—he would have to count them as a threat. Sergio carried the Uzi, and kept a wary eye on the jungle. But the trek was uneventful. The children were still groggy from the effects of the *ayuascua* and moved slowly. They squeezed through the narrow passageway between the two boulders and stepped out onto the platform facing the bridge. Quiso shook hands with each of the children.

He turned to Adam and Sergio and said, "Thank you for helping me return my brother to his grave. I don't like the Spanish for what they did to our people, but you are different, and I will always have a good memory of you." He stepped on the bridge, grabbed the side ropes, and jumped up and down twice to test its strength. The bridge swayed as he walked back to the platform.

"I think you are a brave warrior," said Adam, "and that you will grow up and be a leader of your city. And you, too, will always be in my memory."

Quiso nodded, and he and his dog walked back through the twin boulders and into the jungle.

Adam said to the children, "Go slowly across the bridge. I think one at a time would be best. Sergio, you first, so you can cover them from the other side and when I get to the other side, I'll cut the ropes."

Sergio took small steps, but he made it safely. He readied the Uzi and waited. Gabrielle was next, and she crossed quickly. Ronaldo followed, then Jimmy, and then Nina. There was a roar of distant thunder and neck-twisting lightning. The skies opened and the rain fell—Amazon rain, warm, and heavy enough to turn the ground to mud and the ropes of the bridge slippery.

Across the chasm, Adam heard Sergio's warning as an Inca soldier slammed into him, taking both of them to the floor of the bridge. The man had Adam on his back, his knees grinding into Adam's chest. Each of them reached for a weapon. Adam just wanted a free hand for his Bodyguard and then it would be over. But even as he reached for the pistol, the Inca was faster and he smacked the gun out of Adam's hand, and it disappeared into the river below. Now the Inca got *his* weapon—a jagged steel-bladed knife, good for slicing his opponent across the neck like one of his lizards. Adam blocked the sweep with his forearm and jammed his fist into the soldier's throat. His head snapped back, and Adam shot his legs up and wrapped them around the man's neck. He brought them down and the soldier's spine snapped. Adam pushed the dead soldier away and stood up.

He unsheathed the sword Capac had given him. One swipe

severed the thick rope that connected the bridge to the main supports. The second rope now held the weight of the bridge and when Adam sliced through it the bridge plunged like a spring to the other side of the bank, where it flopped like a twisted ribbon against the wall of the gorge.

He had no escape.

Adam shouted to Nina, and the rain drowned out his words, but Nina knew what he was saying. He would follow the river downstream until he found a place to cross.

Adam moved to the edge of the platform and waited.

That was when he saw the high priest and three of his soldiers emerge from the jungle. They were armed. One soldier carried a spear, the second, a war club—a polished stone tied to a short wooden club—and a shield, and the third, an archer with a short bow and pronged arrowhead. The high priest held his sword at his side.

Their ceremonial uniforms were soaked, lessening the cascading bird feathers on the high priest's cloak and making gaping holes in the fabric. Despite his ferocious jaguar mask, he looked like a miserable half-plucked bird. His soldiers were in no better shape. Their clothes were in tatters, and thin rivulets of blood streamed down any exposed skin. They had run wildly into the jungle after the aborted ritual, and the thorns and sharp leaves had done their damage. Still, it was four against one, and Adam was armed with only the short Toledo sword.

He stood squarely in the middle of the passageway. There was no way around Adam, and there was no place for him to go. The Incas would have to attack in single file. *What was his name?* Their most effective soldier would be the spear-carrier. He stepped forward and faced Adam. The man was short and powerfully built. *The guy on the bridge. What was his name?* The spear was a conquistador's, and it had to be at least four hundred years old. *I don't want to die on the wrong end of an antique.* The soldier might only have had rudimentary training—aside from chasing down wild jungle pigs—

there would have been no use for the weapon in this man's life. He was poised to charge at Adam, the spear slightly tilted, aimed at his chest, which was exactly where Adam wanted it. The Inca didn't jab or feint, which would have been a better tactic, but instead, sprang forward and charged. Adam sidestepped the shaft and caught it under his arm, allowing the man's momentum to carry him close enough for Adam to jam his elbow into his throat and bend him to his knees. Then Adam grabbed his tunic and pushed the soldier off the cliff into the river below. Now Adam had the spear. *The guy on the bridge. Greek?*

The next Inca carried a war club and a shield. He advanced purposely aiming to move Adam back toward the edge of the cliff. Adam jabbed the spear at him, but the soldier was fast and deflected the jabs with his shield. Behind him was the archer with a short bow and a pronged arrowhead. *Forget him. Concentrate on the man in front of you.* The soldier with the club took two steps further and swung the club in a wide arc. *Mistake.* Adam leaped forward and struck the man's club arm with a knife-hand strike just under his upper arm. He hit the nerve perfectly and the Inca dropped the club but, at the same time, swung his shield across his body and hit Adam in the ribs. The pain strengthened him and kept him alive. Adam swung the spear across the soldier's knees. As he went down, Adam grabbed the shield just as an arrow thudded into it with enough force to break through the steel and stop a half inch from Adam's chest. The archer carried his arrows attached to a woven cord around his waist. That meant he needed to lower the bow to load the arrow. *He wasn't Greek.*

Adam heaved the spear, and it struck the last soldier as he was raising the bow to fire. He flopped backward into the mud. Adam wrenched the spear out of the man's chest, and the artery gushed red into the air.

The high priest rose out of the mist of blood. In one hand, he held a Toledo sword. It was twice the size of Adam's. His other hand was a bloody stump. The fine colors of his jaguar mask had run together in the rain. The details of the face were blunted, and the skin bubbled and cracked like the sores and boils of smallpox. He was alone, and he had no more soldiers. He faced Adam, the man who desecrated his ceremony, snatched his sacrificial children, and killed his soldiers. "Pizarro."

Adam leaned on his spear. Breathing only meant more pain—he knew one lung was punctured. He wouldn't have a lot of time left on his feet.

The high priest spoke again. "Pizarro. You are Pizarro."

Adam glanced quickly at the opposite bank. Nina, Sergio, and the children must be far away by now. The high priest lifted his sword and advanced on Adam. He held the sword high in one hand ready to bring it downward in a slicing arc. It would be hard to parry at that angle and the momentum of the long blade would give it extra force. *If it hits me I will be sliced in half.*

Adam exhaled and shifted backward. He could feel the air move. The sword missed by an inch. The high priest raised it and measured carefully. At the same time, Adam brought his spear up. The high priest had only one or two more attacks before the sword became too heavy for his one-handed swing.

The sword slashed through Adam's shirt and engraved a straight line from the top of his breastbone to his opposite hip. It made a thin line—drawn by a fine pencil—and then, a moment later, the line began to bleed. The high priest came forward for the kill. *Come closer—just a few more inches. No. He was Roman.*

Adam swept the spear and upended the man at the ankles. The high priest sank into the wet ground and rolled to his side. He planted the sword in the mud and attempted to raise himself. Before he could get up, Adam jabbed him in the knee with the spear. The high priest screamed and dropped his sword. Adam leaped on him. The jaguar mask protected his head so Adam punched low around the kidneys. The high priest reeled but managed to wrap his arms around Adam in a headlock. He was powerful, and Adam's body blows weren't slowing him down or weakening him.

The high priest was moving to the sword. A few more inches and he would have it. *Go with him and match his strength. Don't fight him.* He arched his back and flipped out of the hold. He kicked the high priest in the head and dived for the sword. The high priest did the same, and their hands reached the grip at the same time. Adam jammed his knee into the man's stomach, and the high priest released his grip. Adam stood up and drove the sword into the man's chest.

Suddenly, Adam slipped in the mud. His feet went out from under him and he fell forward on top of the high priest. *Horatius. That was his name. Horatius at the bridge.* He ripped the mask off the priest's face to reveal a man dying in pain without the peace that comes with death—eyes open, bloodshot, a thin black line of spittle sneaking out of the corner of his mouth. Pleading eyes, defiant eyes. It didn't matter. He was just a man, a dying man.

Adam didn't feel the sword enter his body as the priest, in his last moment of life , pushed him off the cliff.

He heard a bell ring. A doorbell. Piercing the silence of the desert. The desert? Wasn't he in the jungle?

He was falling fast and the river was below him. He could hear the slap of the waves breaking over the great boulders that were waiting to meet him. . . .

But first, he had to answer the door. Something brushed against his legs. A brown dog raced past him to the door.

"Out of the way, Roxy."

The dog ignored him and barked excitedly. Adam opened the door. Outside he saw a piñon tree on a yellow lawn framed against the ridges of the San Cristobal Mountains. Katie was holding a bag of groceries and at her feet were six more.

"We cleaned out Trader Joe's," Nina said, getting out of the Cherokee. "And there's more coming."

"Who're we feeding?"

"Mostly you. . . ."

His shoulder grazed the boulder. It was smooth and wet and it eased him gently into the water like a greased slide . . .

"Need some help?"

"There's a case of melons in the trunk."

The water was ice cold. It froze his blood, froze ice over the holes in his body, and washed him up on a grassy sandbar to let him be discovered by trekkers on their way to Machu Picchu.

If he could see Nina and Katie and feel the weight of a case of melons, then that would be a sufficient explanation for being alive and he was seeing the future. . . .

The currents lifted him, and he broke through the surface of the river. He could see the sky, the green of the jungle riverbanks, and he could breathe. The current slowed, he drifted into an eddy, and spun around in a little circle of waves. The water was shallow and his feet danced on the bottom of the riverbed. Quiso's dog had Adam's wrist in his mouth and was pulling him toward the shore.

It kept raining in the Amazon. It was the kind of rain that turned dry riverbeds into deadly flashfloods, rain that opened dormant flowers, soaked towering trees and kept them alive for another millennium. In the Amazon, the rain would extinguish fires and replenish rivers. It was a rain delivered by the gods, and Adam knew that the children who had been sent on a journey for the Inca were successful.

He knew Titu had led the children to the grove where the golden trees shed their pollen. There he put them to sleep. Their memories were transformed into dreams that would come to them over the years as disjointed pieces of a puzzle. The pieces would appear and disappear before they could put them into place and make sense of their journeys.

Adam put the melons on the kitchen table.

EPILOGUE

As Adam did every night before and since he returned from Peru, he went into Katie's bedroom to say good night. He hipped Roxy off the bed to give himself some sitting room, and they had one last conversation for the day.

"I did my homework."

"I wasn't going to ask."

"But you were thinking it, I could tell."

"Show me?"

"It's on my desk."

On the way out, after he kissed her and Roxy jumped back on the bed and snuggled next to her, he picked up the spiral notebook and turned back to her.

"A history of Peru? You managed to get it all in here?"

"Should I change it to a brief history of Peru?"

"Can I read it?"

"Sure."

He turned off the light and closed the door, but not all the way, keeping it open a little, the way she liked.

Nina was in bed, reading. He showed her Katie's notebook.

"It's her seventh-grade history project."

"I know," said Nina. "I helped her."

Adam opened it and looked at the illustrations scotch-taped to the first page. There were two portraits side by side. The first was of Atahualpa. He saw the face of the high priest. The second portrait was of Pizarro, and he saw his own.

ACKNOWLEDGMENTS

In the construction of this fiction, I have been helped greatly by the truth found in *Pizarro Conqueror of the Inca* by Stuart Stirling, *Conquistadors* by Michael Wood, *The Highest Altar* by Patrick Tierney, *A Culture of Stone* by Carolyn Dean, and *Daily Life in the Inca Empire* by Michael A. Malpass. Essays by Garcilasco de la Vagea, John Murra, and Pedro de Cieza de Leon in *The Peru Reader* were most useful, as was *The Conquest of the Inca* by John Hemming.

I owe real and deep appreciation to my friend and agent Ed Victor, whose enthusiasm never flagged even when mine did. David Freeman, Dale Herd, Dennis Roberts, and Laurenz Frenzen, who read early drafts and offered invaluable help and encouragement. Bianca Roberts was a loving and tough critic, and gave me more of her time than she should have. I am grateful to my editor across the river, Kevin Smith, whose contribution towers over his title.

I was fortunate to have Tina Pohlman at Open Road Media. Tina, along with Lauren Chomiuk, was meticulous and gentle in steering a first time novelist into the light.

I doubt if he remembers me, but I would like to thank Gonzalo Pizarro of Mountain Travel for introducing me to Cuzco and the Valley of the Incas many years ago. I left with a love of Peru and its people, and a lifelong fascination with its history.

Open Road Integrated Media is a digital publisher and multimedia content company. Open Road creates connections between authors and their audiences by marketing its ebooks through a new proprietary online platform, which uses premium video content and social media.

Videos, Archival Documents, and New Releases

Sign up for the Open Road Media newsletter and get news delivered straight to your inbox.

Sign up now at
www.openroadmedia.com/newsletters

FIND OUT MORE AT
WWW.OPENROADMEDIA.COM

FOLLOW US:
@openroadmedia and
Facebook.com/OpenRoadMedia

CPSIA information can be obtained at www.ICGtesting.com
Printed in the USA
BVOW080650240513

321534BV00002B/4/P

9 781480 400030